PINK CORAL ISLAND

JOSIE RIVIERA

This book is dedicated to all my wonderful readers who have supported me every inch of the way.
THANK YOU!

CHAPTER 1

The Harbor Jewel Ferry glided through the Atlantic Ocean, carrying Jenny Ormani closer to her birthplace, Pink Coral Island. As she stood near the open area, the sea breeze tousled her hair and stirred up a mix of bittersweet emotions. The deck beneath her feet felt sticky, coated with a thin layer of oil, a reminder of her long journey.

Blue-green waters lapped against the boat's side, the gentle rhythm calling out, inviting her to the island of memories.

Pink Coral Island was more than just a place. It was a part of her, a tapestry woven with centuries-old superstitions and the vibrant African American Gullah culture.

She yearned to reconnect. This was where she had grown up, where she had experienced the world through the lens of folklore and tradition. It was a homecoming that carried both enthusiasm and a hint of uncertainty.

A sudden burst of excitement rippled through the passengers as a pod of dolphins appeared, leaping and dancing in the waves. In folklore, the Gullah revered dolphins as protectors and wise guides—a positive sign, a confirmation she was on the right path.

The ferry's engine skipped and stuttered, and gray, soupy clouds formed in the distance. She knew from experience that visibility could suddenly drop to only a few feet, leaving even the most experienced crewmen disoriented.

"Come on, Harbor Jewel, you can do it," she murmured. "You've done this dozens of times."

Her best friend, Maria, came to stand beside her. The faint smell of alcohol swirled as she munched on a peppermint sweet.

"Are you talking to someone?" Maria questioned.

"I'm talking to the boat."

"Right. Doesn't everyone? This island is making you irrational, and we haven't even arrived yet."

As Jenny reached into her tote bag, her fingers brushed against a crumpled note from her ex-boyfriend, Dominick. Memories of their complicated relationship flooded her mind.

"I must be seeing things." Maria peered over Jenny's shoulder and cast her an accusatory glance. "You're still holding on to Dominick's note?"

Jenny shook her head. "I wouldn't call it holding on." The weight of her past clung to her, making it difficult to move forward. The fear of choosing incorrectly always lingered, casting a shadow over her decisions.

Dominick had said that returning to America was proof of her commitment issues. He had a special knack for sending her into a tailspin of self-doubt.

"He's a jerk." Maria snapped Jenny back to reality.

"He doesn't understand the American mindset, where work is more important than play."

Maria scoffed. "Yeah, and it's more beneficial for him to sit around and do nothing rather than work."

This recent position on Pink Coral Island came at the right time. If she didn't try, she would never find out if she could succeed in the hotel industry.

"Goodbye, Dominick." With a sigh, she flung his note into the sea.

That was it, the end of their relationship. Leaving him was far better than him leaving her.

The dreaded fog descended without warning; a dense white mist that made visibility nearly impossible. The ferry rocked from side to side, sending water droplets down her arms.

Nearby, a passenger grumbled, his words barely audible.

The deafening blare of the foghorn left Jenny's ears ringing and her nerves on edge. Maria's sudden yelp and grip on her arm only added to her jitters.

"You promised this ride would be smooth sailing," Maria said.

Jenny flashed a wry grin in response. "It takes about an hour from Hilton Head and it usually is."

Maybe half the time. You never knew about the other half.

She swayed along with the ferry's motion, her body struggling to adapt to the constant pitching and rolling.

As the fog lifted, the few passengers on board erupted into a round of applause, their relief unmistakable.

Within minutes, the ferry gradually decelerated and readied itself to berth at the island's marina. A foamy surf hissed through the sand at the shoreline, and the navy-blue water reflected for miles.

Jenny's throat welled with emotion as she scanned the recognizable landscape, absorbing every detail. Every inch of this island held a piece of her past—the people she had loved and the experiences she had lived. Even with poignant recollections, she flashed a smile, reminding herself to stay present in the moment and enjoy the adventure.

Maria draped her shoulders with a cotton scarf. "How on earth … did you talk me into this?"

"The Grand Michelangelo Hotel might be a once-in-a-lifetime opportunity for us."

"You're forgetting that no one lives here."

"The Gullah people have lived here for centuries." Jenny inhaled the scents of seaweed and cedar as the familiar atmospheric vibe embraced her.

The boat swayed, and Jenny struggled to keep her balance.

Pink Coral Island was the Carolina's southernmost island, and summers were sizzling and steamy.

She still remembered the trails she had roamed as a girl. The same winding roads led to secluded beaches, where the sea met the sky. She imagined the rows of boats once bobbing in their wake. She remembered jogging with Christopher, their feet touching in the surf.

No. She refused to let her thoughts wander down that hard path.

Jenny glanced at Maria. "Remember that the Gullah beliefs differ from ours."

"Uh-huh, right. Different, how?"

"You'll see. Their stories are powerful." Jenny shivered as an unexpected gust of wind blew past, tangling her hair into a frenzy. She tied it back with a silk hairband from her tote.

Perhaps modern-day society has no business here.

"Just as I predicted." Maria took in the entire five-mile-long island. Her bangs flew into her eyes, and she pushed them under her straw boater hat. "No signs of anyone living or breathing."

Not a soul disturbed the wild and untamed beach. Sand dunes, flanked by tufts of hearty grass, rolled like waves in the wind, ever outward. The sand was light and fluffy, and Jenny remembered sinking her toes into it as she climbed to the top of the dune. A sweeping view of the island and ocean rewarded her effort.

"A slower lifestyle is a break from our chaotic, everyday lives," Jenny said. "A connection with nature is beneficial for the soul."

"You sound like an ad campaign."

"I'm an expert—I lived here a long time." Jenny bit her lip, and her breath quickened. Uncertainties about the new job had kept her up at night. Worry was a definite stimulant for insomnia.

Would her position offer enough challenges to keep her engaged? Would she click with her colleagues and superiors? Could she resist the urge to wander, even if it meant staying put in her hometown for an extended period?

She craned her neck to get a better view of the shore. She'd committed so much of this island to memory.

"The locals are friendly and look out for each other," she said. "Their lifestyle is more distinct than what we're accustomed to."

Maria would soon encounter the island's drawbacks—limited resources and the challenges of communication with the outside world.

But wasn't that part of life? Taking the bad with the good?

When the wind carried her hat off her head, Maria laughed. She flattened her bohemian skirt, which tended to fly up and give her a Marilyn Monroe pose. Her petite, curvaceous figure was in stark contrast to Jenny's tall and lean one.

Jenny had chosen a slim linen pencil skirt and sleeveless cotton blouse, tailored and professional, though both showed stains of wet sand.

Maria took another swig from her thermos.

Jenny hoped it was water; now she wasn't so sure.

"Did you enjoy living here?" Maria inquired.

"Absolutely. Who wouldn't?"

Well, Jenny's mother, for one.

She had never adjusted to the rural lifestyle and resented her husband for not being of a higher social status. She had even called the Gullah unintelligent, giving Jenny her first taste of intolerance.

What was worse than narrow-minded bigotry?

Jenny believed in fairness for all people, but she knew better than to argue. Her mother had a strong desire to always be right, creating a toxic and emotionally repressive environment in their household. Jenny had often felt unheard and unsupported.

"Didn't Christopher live here, too?" Maria asked.

Yes. Yes, he did.

Jenny kept her gaze downcast. "During the summer."

Christopher Drake. He was tall, with high cheekbones. His healthy glow spoke of the hours he spent outdoors, working on boat motors at his father's garage. His beaming smile drew attention to the dimples on his cheeks and his piercing blue eyes.

Maria chuckled. "Summered makes it sound like he's some sort of wealthy person who spent winters skiing in Colorado."

"He was my closest friend and dirt poor. I doubt he ever went skiing anywhere." They were more than best friends, but some things were meant for safe places in the heart—to take out and treasure in private. "He and his father were even poorer than my family."

"Men and women can't be best friends." Maria offered a bemused laugh. "Unless you're living in a romantic comedy. Then anything is possible."

Maria, the matchmaker, steered the conversation back to matters of the heart, and Jenny smiled.

"Of course, they can." Jenny pinched the last piece of

chocolate candy from her tote and popped it into her mouth. "Christopher and I hung out for years while my father worked for the wealthy, pruning hedges, mowing lawns, and watering flower beds."

"Years, huh?"

"Purely as *friends*. Christopher was skinny and unwell."

He had asthma and always carried his inhaler. She constantly worried about him.

But he was gentle and kind, quiet and charming. A Southern gentleman with a strong jawline and straight nose. He had an unpretentious yet disarmingly confident way of carrying himself. She vividly recalled his easy-going personality and approachable smile.

"My father put an end to everything," Jenny murmured.

"Why?" Maria nudged Jenny in the ribs. "Did he think you two had become too close and—"

"My father worked for a landscape company. The company's closure forced my family to leave the island." Jenny's voice cracked. She groped for a tissue in her tote because tears were inevitable. "When I told Christopher I had to move away, he just said ... goodbye."

He had plenty more to say, though Jenny refused to elaborate.

She dabbed her eyes dry. After all these years, the memories still hurt.

"Hey now." Maria squeezed Jenny's hand. "Guys are stupid sometimes."

"It's okay. It was for the best."

Yet, that didn't mean their love hadn't been real, though they were immature teens, and Jenny had expected too much. In her weak moments, she overly romanticized their relationship.

She retreated when an alligator swam near the boat. She knew enough to give it space.

Maria took a few hesitant steps back and collided with a man. He was lean, with a typical runner's build.

"Oops. My bad," Maria apologized with a winning smile, and touched his arm.

The man returned her smile, revealing a dazzling set of white teeth against his dark complexion. "No worries at all, miss," he replied genially, his accent laced with a hint of island charm.

Maria's eyes lit up. She was never one to let an opportunity to flirt with a handsome guy go to waste.

"So, you come to this island often?" she inquired.

The man chuckled. "I live here, but I'm always happy to meet new people. Especially a woman as pretty as you."

A few minutes later, a beaming Maria tapped Jenny on the shoulder to introduce Salifu.

"He works at our hotel." Maria gestured to Salifu. "The big boss hired him."

"The big boss?" Jenny wondered if this "boss" was Oliver Robinson, the elusive Welsh billionaire owner of the hotel, or the even more elusive silent partner.

After brief pleasantries, Maria reverted to beguiling smiles at Salifu, and Jenny tucked her questions away for later.

A gigantic crab flashed in the water, then disappeared beneath the murky surface, which triggered a thought about someone else who had vanished.

Christopher.

She had never found him anywhere on social media.

He'd promised to keep in touch.

He never had.

As she looked up at the Carolina blue sky, her mind spun with issues impossible to resolve. Since she'd decided to return home, she'd become an expert at reflecting on her past.

8

Through discreet inquiries, she'd learned that his father's garage had closed. Rumors swirled, Christopher had joined the army, while others insisted he'd married a woman from Kentucky in a quick ceremony, then moved to Alaska. A piece of her heart splintered when she heard he might have a child.

Christopher. The guy who didn't want kids.

Correction. He didn't want kids with *her*.

"Salifu said the island is haunted." Maria tapped Jenny on the shoulder and made an exaggerated eerie noise, like a banshee wailing in the night. "Which ghost do you think we'll meet? Casper?"

"Well, if it's a ghost, I hope it's a friendly one. It can teach us some cool ghost tricks."

"Like what? Floating through walls?"

Jenny couldn't help but laugh. "We'll wait and see."

Skipper Andy, the captain, an older gentleman dressed in a white shirt and pants, cut Jenny and the fellow passengers a sharp salute. The ferry lurched to a halt, prompting him to stop the engine, loop a line around the boat cleat, and fasten the ferry to the slip.

"Welcome to Pink Coral Island," he announced.

Jenny took a breath, taken aback by the grandiose building in the distance.

The Grand Michelangelo Hotel.

The hotel had once hosted millionaires and movie stars, but poor management, a horrific fire, and overspending resulted in its downfall. An entire seaside resort sat on the pristine Carolina coastline, eaten away by the salt, wind, water, and humidity.

"It looks a lot better than the photos from a few months ago," Jenny commented.

Oliver had sent them weekly updates.

A shadow of doubt crept over Maria's face. "I still don't

see anyone. How will we find out who is walking the red carpet in Hollywood if we're in the middle of nowhere?"

"We can always ask the staff. They probably know all the hotspots in town."

"Did you forget? We *are* the staff."

"Or we might just look for the paparazzi," Jenny suggested, grinning. "They'll be swarming around any famous celebrity."

"Not here, they won't."

"I'm joking with you." Jenny squeezed Maria in a reassuring embrace. "Don't worry, we'll get everything we need from the mainland. Look, I realize this is intimidating for both of us, but trust me, the view from the front windows of the hotel is worth it. It's like something straight out of a movie. Just imagine the Hotel Danieli in Italy."

Maria snorted. "Or the Hotel Transylvania."

Jenny chuckled and turned to pick up her suitcase and travel bag. They were all she owned, but she didn't mind. The thought of starting fresh was exciting.

"May I assist you with your bags, miss?" asked Thomas, a seasoned porter with a distinguished gray mustache.

Charmed by his old-world manners, she grinned and shouldered her bag. "Much appreciated, but I can manage."

Thomas focused on Maria. "And you, miss? Do you need any assistance?"

"I travel light." Maria displayed her nylon backpack. "Once we're settled, I'll wander through the boutiques in town." Her mischievous grin assured she was joking. "I sent my clothes ahead. Hopefully, they've arrived."

Hopefully.

Thomas studied them. "Are you both staying at the Michelangelo?"

Jenny paused before replying. "Is there a reason you're curious?"

He indicated a food stand near the marina selling crab cakes. There were zero customers. "Why else would anyone come to this island in the middle of April?"

"We're here to work at the Grand Michelangelo Hotel," Jenny replied.

"A rich guy and his unnamed partner bought it," Thomas said. "They're both from Canada."

"The rich guy is from Wales," Jenny corrected.

"He's never so much as stepped foot on this island. Wealthy folk with their seemingly endless bank accounts and hours to burn—hah!"

Suitcase in tow, Jenny accompanied the porter along the shaky ramp, then extended her hand. "I'm Jenny Ormani, the manager. The hotel will officially open at the end of June."

Maria waved from the shore. "I'm the kitchen and media expert."

"Is there decent Internet here?" Jenny pulled out her phone and scanned for networks.

"It's fairly reliable, but intermittent." With each stride, Thomas left imprints in the soft sand, and the women trailed behind. "Although I doubt if a lot of the folks on the island tap into social media."

"How many people live here?" Maria inquired.

"Around two hundred, or three hundred, or six hundred. The answer varies depending on the person you ask." Thomas said. "Most of the roads remain unpaved, and much of the land is untouched. We walk or use bicycles and golf carts to get around."

"Then nothing has changed." Jenny inhaled the refreshing ocean air. The sun warmed her cheeks. She almost heard the distant drumming of Gullah rituals and the whispers of ancient superstitions.

Maria gave a slight shudder. "Does the number of people increase during the summer tourist season?"

"A fair amount come to the Drifting Sands restaurant. It's owned by a local who lives on the island, unlike the owner of your hotel." Thomas leveled an accusing look at Jenny, and she bit back a retort. He was blaming her because Oliver lived in Wales.

"Make that owners. Plural," Jenny corrected.

The Drifting Sands was the only eatery that had ever flourished, though it wasn't high class by any means. The décor was simple—sturdy tables and chairs with rough-hewn edges, and plain wooden floors and walls. Mugs of cold, foamy beer and greasy hamburgers were standard fare.

The porter tapped his foot. "We hope that he, they, or whoever, has deep pockets. Every other investor has failed. Why should they be any different?"

Because Oliver and his unnamed partner had deeper pockets than anyone else. They had spared no money once renovations had begun.

Thomas squinted, scrutinizing the hotel with far too much deliberation. "This island is trouble-free and peaceful."

As if any sign of life was a negative thing?

"Hey, I'm all for quiet," Jenny replied. "It's a pleasant change after the hustle and bustle of city living."

"Have you lived here long?" Maria asked. "How did you come to be a porter?"

"Family ties on the island. Though job opportunities are limited, I found work as a porter to make a living."

Jenny's anxiousness about the future only got worse in the face of his remarks.

She peeked through the windows of an abandoned store-front, a stark reminder of how quickly businesses came and went.

"There are no medical facilities or physicians here, either," came Thomas's pithy statement.

"What if something happens to one of us?" Maria's thin eyebrows arched. "We're in the middle of nowhere."

"All of us are trained in CPR and basic first aid," Thomas replied. "One can never be too prepared."

"Don't worry. We're all healthy, and we'll be careful." Jenny put a comforting hand on Maria's shoulder. "We have a first-aid kit and medical supplies at the hotel. In case of an actual emergency, we'll contact the Coast Guard or arrange for a health-related evacuation."

When she was young, she constantly feared that Christopher might have a severe asthma attack. How would a doctor help when the ferry to the mainland took at least an hour? Should she borrow a boat?

Thankfully, the scenario had never occurred.

Pride in the island's peculiarities demanded she assure Maria that the lack of medical care was not a problem. Reason cautioned that the more they discussed the subject, the more likely Maria would jump on the next ferry back to civilization. While they were in Italy, Maria mentioned living with her unmarried sisters in Connecticut. Perhaps she would head back there.

"We're a sleepy little community, which is exactly how we islanders prefer it," Thomas went on, impervious to Jenny's warning glare. "We didn't get electricity until the 1950s. By the way, do you like sand?"

"On a beach?" Jenny forced a smile. "Sure. Who doesn't?"

"Good, because we have acres of sand beaches here." He stood back and eyed the women. "Are you two related?"

"No. While we worked in Italy, we ended up rooming together." Jenny swept an arm toward Maria, who over-inflated a curtsey. "Maria's degree is in media."

Jenny didn't mention her lack of a college education and was grateful the porter didn't pry. When she was a senior, the guidance counselor advised her to use her attractive appearance and friendly demeanor to succeed in life, as her grades were too low for much else.

Her cheeks burned. Their exchange was a repeating circuit in her brain, though in retrospect, she wondered what planet the counselor was from.

Jenny had stayed silent, disagreeing with the counselor's statement. She wanted to be appreciated for her intellect, skills, and contributions to society.

Jenny dragged her luggage down a dirt path, while Thomas ran to the dock to get a golf cart, promising a ride if he found one. Hot, moist air clung to Jenny's skin, and sweat pooled on her forehead.

Among the hum of passengers dispersing, only Jenny and Maria started toward the hotel. Salifu had vanished.

As low clouds gathered, blocking the sun, more doubts and apprehension crept into her mind. Was she making a mistake? Maybe the counselor had been dead-on, and she had nothing to offer the world except her looks.

"I'm assuming it couldn't possibly..." Maria gazed skyward as the palmetto trees swayed. Thunder rumbled in the distance. "Don't tell me it's going to—"

"Often, a storm comes without warning." Jenny followed the path of a sudden flash of lightning illuminating the shadowy clouds. Rain began to fall in a torrential, fierce downpour.

The women scrambled to a gnarled tree, with hefty branches that hung low to the ground. Underneath its canopy, they huddled together, shivering from the icy droplets that still reached them.

Jenny stuffed her sunglasses and hat into her tote bag and peered out from beneath the leaves to a curtain of water.

Maria glared at Jenny through wet eyelashes. "I am going to kill you."

"I don't control the weather. These storms usually start in the afternoon."

"This is a storm? The island summoned up a monsoon to welcome us." Maria abandoned the tree and jumped into the rain. She spun around, arms wide.

"Exactly what are you doing?" Jenny asked.

"I'm dancing. It's like a free spa day."

Jenny chuckled. "You are a wild and outrageous woman."

"I'm spontaneous and adventurous, but wild works, too. Come on. Join me." Maria swiped her drenched bangs from her forehead, her sopping hair framing her pretty face. "We should celebrate our safe arrival."

"I don't want to end up with pneumonia." Jenny shook her head and declined. "I'll wait for a steaming, hot bubble bath when we reach the hotel."

As Thomas arrived in the golf cart, the rain subsided.

"Care for a ride, ladies?" he grinned.

Jenny and Maria gratefully accepted and used the beach towels he offered to dry off.

He weaved the cart along the gummy path, pocked with puddles and furrows. The ruins of slave cabins stood visible through the trees—roofless and walls caving in—a heart-breaking reminder of the island's past.

He slowed as they entered the world of towering oaks draped in Spanish moss. Thomas braked for a lone raccoon scampering across the road. The unkempt grass rustled in the wind, dominating the landscape, as if revealing secrets that had been kept quiet for centuries.

Jenny glanced at Maria. Judging by the anxiety etched on her face, the barrenness of their surroundings didn't go unnoticed.

"My parents and I lived in a gardener's cottage near the Gullah community." Jenny gave a concise history of the island as they drove. "Look, there's an oyster house." She indicated a tiny residence, constructed using crushed oyster shells mixed with sand, water, and ashes as mortar, then pointed to another home. "Over there is the lighthouse."

Maria peered out from under her hand, squinting in the sunlight. "I don't see a lighthouse."

"It's not a typical lighthouse. Can you see the large white house with dormers?"

Maria nodded.

"The second story holds the light to illuminate the ocean."

"There's plenty more here," Thomas said. "We have a sizable population of loggerhead turtles. It's quite a sight when they hatch and make their way to the ocean. During nesting season, you might be lucky enough to witness a mother turtle laying her eggs on the beach. There are strict regulations in place to protect them, so don't leave any trash around."

Maria saluted. "I'll do my part."

"I'll ensure you pick up after yourself." Jenny chuckled. "We certainly don't want to upset the sea turtles."

By the time they neared the hotel, their skin and clothes had dried off.

"Suppose we opt to head back to the mainland?" At Maria's question, a Jenny's forearms prickled.

"The boat leaves from the dock twice daily." Thomas raised an index finger. "In the morning and early evening, provided you book a reservation."

"Please tell me this island has a fire department," Maria said.

"Most of the able men and women are volunteers, including me," Thomas replied. "The fire board is on call twenty-four hours a day."

"Nothing is worse than fire," Jenny murmured.

"Nothing worse," Thomas and Maria agreed.

Jenny used positive thoughts to erase her frightening

memories of the horrific fire on the island she'd witnessed all those years ago.

Thomas steered the golf cart to the front of the hotel. "The police ferry sails over at noon, so I suppose you could get a ride to the mainland with them, too." He held out a fist, gently shaking it. "However, any travel back and forth is weather permitting."

"What does that mean?" Maria swerved toward Jenny, then Thomas.

"Skipper Andy isn't willing to risk stormy seas," Thomas responded. "Whenever fog rolls in, it comes without warning. Legend has it that when the ferry crew gathers to discuss fog or mysterious currents, it means the island holds a hidden treasure."

Jenny smiled. "The secret of the mysterious waters. Who is ready to dive into the sea?"

"Not me." Maria's voice lowered. "It looks like we'll be spending our lives avoiding monsoons, searching for hidden treasures, or becoming unwilling castaways."

CHAPTER 2

a s they struggled to keep their footing on the slippery mud, Jenny collected her luggage, and the women thanked Thomas for his help.

Within a few seconds, Jenny's balance wavered, and she grasped onto Maria's arm for support.

"I think the island is telling us something." Maria's eyes darted around the grounds.

"Islands don't communicate," Jenny quipped back.

"Neither do ferry boats, but that didn't stop you."

The women stepped into the hotel lobby, and Jenny stood spellbound.

She marveled at the tasteful layout and the majestic ebony-black grand piano in one corner. Its presence radiated a touch of elegance and sophistication.

"I told you the view was worth it," she said, gesturing toward the ocean.

"You didn't tell me it was like stepping into a palace." Maria set her backpack on the hand-planked wooden floor, fell back on a chair, and kicked up her feet. "Wow!" She looked up at the lavish chandelier, larger than a compact car, hanging from the center of the ceiling. The spectacular size and unique design, shaped from sea glass and driftwood, created an impressive focal point.

Wow was the word, all right. The lobby was extraordinary, boasting an old-fashioned ambiance. Velvet and silk pillows accented plush comfortable chairs in neutral tones of beiges and creams. The integrating of crown moldings and wood wainscoting composed a cozy, classical style.

Nautical-themed, yet understated, the hotel boasted twelve rooms. Oliver envisioned a "boutique, beachfront resort," and had enlisted a top architect plus an up-and-coming designer. Two sweeping staircases flanked the customer service desk on either side.

Everything was iconic, inviting, and welcoming.

And then there was the other side of the lobby.

Jenny's smiling expression vanished, and she looked at the construction tools scattered everywhere. The scent of sawdust and wet paint hovered in the air. Interior hallway doors and a few windows waited to be installed, and an adjacent wall lacked a coat of paint.

"That lamp is shabby compared to all this glamour." Maria motioned to a seagrass lamp set on an end table. The artisan crafted the lamp from dried sea grass and bits of driftwood.

"A decorator redid the furnishings," Jenny said. "Bravo for incorporating the island's traditions into the décor."

Oliver had contracted for renovations to begin in January. From his emails, he'd expected things to advance regularly and weekly. He didn't anticipate island time, which ran a lot slower.

A recent report from him indicated the hotel was livable, at least for the staff, even though the final touches were a work in progress.

Irritable and overwhelmed, Jenny sighed in frustration,

dismayed at the amount of effort and planning left to be done.

She rolled her stiff shoulders to calm the kinks after her exhausting voyage. The women had flown from Italy to Charleston, South Carolina. They'd continued by Uber to Hilton Head and then boarded the ferry to Pink Coral Island.

She set her tote bag aside and collapsed like a sack of heavy groceries into a lavish armchair, taking in the picturesque view from the two-tiered window. Teak chairs draped with turquoise pads surrounded the in-ground pool, though there was no water yet in the pool. The tables sported orange and cream-striped umbrellas.

Pure luxury.

"I'm heading outside." A suddenly boisterous Maria kicked off her sandals. "I'm checking out the gorgeous beach for the rest of the afternoon."

"Bring me a seashell!" Jenny grinned at her friend's enthusiasm.

She wanted to highlight Gullah culture and make the hotel unique.

Each room's mini bar would be complimentary and stocked with bottled water, beers, island produce, and baked goods.

Fresh-from-the-oven cuisine would include fried fish and red rice, plates of Carolina blue crab, and in-season sweet peas.

The local bakery, Sun-Kissed Treats, was the perfect solution for the hotel's dessert options. Perhaps she'd even try her hand at Gullah baking again, and the idea caused a twinge of excitement in her chest.

Jenny vaguely noted a door opening from somewhere down the corridor. She spun at the sound of footsteps as a tall man carrying a miniature potted palm came toward her.

"Just arriving?" he inquired.

She assumed he was the bellboy assigned to the lobby, another of Oliver's army buddies.

She stood to offer a brief, businesslike smile, and her heart stopped when their gazes locked. He conveyed strength and authority.

His sun-streaked, wavy brown hair and sparkling blue eyes were all too familiar.

Her breathing stilled.

Christopher Drake. What on earth was he doing here?

Once, he lived here. Keyword. *Lived,* as in past tense. Now he lived in … where was it … Alaska?

Ten years had passed since she'd last seen him.

He had bulked up his lanky shoulders, and his forearms had become muscled and tanned. The bold white letters on his sleeveless gray T-shirt read: *Army Strong: United in Service, Unstoppable in Action.*

"Jenny? Jenny … Ormani?" He placed the plant in the corner and gaped.

She gaped back.

As gracefully as possible, she brushed the sand from the hem of her skirt. Her hands were sweaty. How could the mere sight of him still affect her so much?

"I can't believe it." He covered the distance between them in several lengthy strides. "Is it really you?"

"I feel like I'm in the middle of a dream." She blurted out the words before she could stop herself.

His smile widened. "If I'm in the dream too, then that's a good thing."

She collected herself and noticed the glimmer of heat in his gaze. "The better question is, what are you doing here?"

His dark eyebrows rose. "I work here."

"At the Michelangelo?" Not possible. Him … flitting in

and out of the hotel? She couldn't believe it. Her mind raced as she tried to think of something to say. "It's been so long since we've seen each other. You're a ... a bellboy?"

He grinned and didn't offer a reply.

She peered up at him. "What happened to your nose?"

Okay, Jenny, stop crying out questions, especially impolite ones, without considering them first.

He touched his nose with his forefinger. "Why?"

"Your nose looks a little crooked."

"It's a reminder of our argument on the beach the day before you left."

"Don't be silly." Heat surged to the tips of her ears, and she fumbled for an explanation. "I didn't hit you that hard."

"Uh, you hit me hard enough. For a girl who worried about my health, you showed no concern for me."

"You didn't have an asthma attack afterward, did you?"

"Nope. A mere bloody nose."

"Do you ... do you still have asthma?"

"I have no symptoms anymore, and the doctor said that I've outgrown it." He patted the pocket of his shorts. "However, I carry my inhaler, just in case."

"I'm truly sorry."

"Don't be. I'm a big boy. Then you moved off the island and deserted me."

Hardly. It had happened the other way around.

She blinked, attempting to process the situation. No, this couldn't be Christopher. Not standing in front of her. Not now. She needed this job. She didn't want any complications or interruptions. The hotel promised an exciting future and a chance to prove herself.

"You are as beautiful as when you were sixteen, Jenny." He gave her an approving once-over from head to toe. "Your hair is as blond as ever, and I like it long. You used to wear it in a thick braid down your back."

Her hair was a wind-blown mess, her makeup was gone, and she rarely wore lipstick.

She didn't believe his compliment for one minute.

She debated sitting again. No, it was better to stand. By standing, she was taller, at the height of his shoulders and nearer eye level, primed for any verbal volleyball he might initiate.

Of course, he had never done any of those things.

Still, she raised her chin. "Are you complimenting me?"

"Always." He studied her. "Where are your glasses?"

A confusing mix of emotions flowed through her. Christopher habitually helped others. He was trustworthy, and there wasn't a mean bone in his body.

"I wear contact lenses now." She looked better than when she was a teen, all gangly limbs and crooked teeth desperately screaming for a straightening. "Time has been generous to you as well."

To be fair, there was no justification for her ill temper. After all, their history dated back many years.

He'd certainly grown into a rugged, impressive man, exuding raw masculinity. Fit and athletic, his light-tan cargo shorts and black leather sandals lent a nonchalant island charm to his appearance. He could've come directly off a Ralph Lauren photo shoot for *Men's Outdoor* magazine, complete with a five o'clock shadow on his chin.

"Maybe the years haven't been as kind to me as you might imagine." He tensed, but only for a moment. "Much more interesting, how are you?"

"Fine." Whatever that meant. "Honestly, Christopher, I never expected to see you again."

This day brimmed with understatements. Being around him was surely inviting trouble.

Her head assured her that this was simply a job. A job she

could ditch if things went south. But then, this was a position she'd traveled thousands of miles to get.

He shifted and shoved his hands in his pockets, exactly like he'd done when he was a little boy. He'd offered her a shy hello when she'd first met him. He'd been scuffing at seashells on the beach in his bare feet. She was eight. He was ten.

"I heard you stayed in Italy for a while."

Really? He'd kept tabs on her.

"Yes." Jenny focused on the outdoors. Picturesque and exquisite, with palm trees swaying in the breeze, the distant lighthouse enhanced the tranquil sight.

Meanwhile, Maria soaked up the sunshine near the pool.

"I lived in Italy with my friend, Maria." Jenny gestured toward her. "The country is beautiful."

Brilliant, Jenny, just brilliant. Everyone knew Italy was beautiful.

He studied her face, his expression inscrutable, before exhaling a soft, "Absolutely gorgeous."

He was a master at disguising his emotions, leaving her to question if he had any inkling of the turmoil simmering within her.

"And you?" She feigned indifference. "Where have you lived these last few years?"

He thumped his chest. "I always knew I belonged right here."

She surveyed the opulent lobby while the late afternoon sun poured through the windows. The floor shone with polished marble, so shiny that it offered a mirror-like reflection. Exquisite Persian rugs adorned select areas, adding an elegant touch. The brass stair railings gleamed in the light.

Despite the luxury, she searched for some excuse to escape from him. The days they'd spent together had etched themselves into her memory, causing her heart to stutter at his presence. If only she could flee before humiliating herself over someone who had never reciprocated her feelings.

She managed a smile. "Are you the new bellboy?"

A crease formed between his eyebrows. "Several staff members live in the beach huts. I stayed in one for a while."

A vague memory stirred. In the past, she and Christopher often sat inside a favorite wooden hut, more isolated than the others, to escape the midday humidity and suffocating heat. Cobwebs hung from the thatched roof, the air weighted with the tang of the sea and the musty odor of abandonment.

Dimly lit and constructed of plain logs, the hut screeched and moaned under the weight of rainfall. On the uneven grass floor, Christopher had written poems in his notepad or sketched room layouts while she rested beside him. She'd teased him about being a Renaissance man. He was not only creative, but a jack of all trades.

She chatted about her baking plans, describing muffin and pastry ingredients.

"Are the huts still lacking basic amenities, like plumbing?" she inquired.

"We have renovated and modernized many."

"Money from Oliver, I assume. Have you had the pleasure of meeting him?"

Christopher's chin lifted slightly. "I have."

"So, you've lived here since—"

"January."

Great. She was once again on her beloved island. With Christopher.

Seeing him revived all the emotions she'd tried to avoid.

In times past, this encounter would've seemed surreal and all she'd ever wanted. How had they traveled so far to end up in the same place?

Sadly, the years in between had changed everything.

She fiddled with her skirt. "You moved back here from where?"

He regarded her with an annoying grin. She was too inquisitive.

She granted an apologetic smile. "Sorry. Old friend's interest."

"I lived out of the country, here and there. Some might call me a world traveler."

Somehow, he'd successfully deflected her question with a joke.

"Doing what?" she pressed.

No more cajoling. The guy hardly warrants a formal investigation because you were once best friends.

"I was in the army." His deep voice interrupted her thoughts. "In case you ever wondered, I didn't receive the scholarship to attend Carnegie Mellon University. I couldn't afford the tuition payments, so that was that."

He'd spoken of little else when he started high school, checking local libraries and speaking with librarians and various guidance counselors. He'd been obsessed with attending college, which sometimes overshadowed their relationship.

"Oh. That must've been tough." Where should she look? Down? Up? She settled on meeting his unbreakable stare. "I'm sorry. I realize how much that dream meant to you."

"Not every dream ..." He hesitated, studying the potted palm in the corner as if the answer was written there. None of the usual banter tinged his tone. "Not every dream comes true."

Her thoughts screamed. Some dreams could have come true if he had genuinely cared about her.

There was no use in ignoring the unspoken truth. "If you *had* attended Carnegie, you were going without me, anyway."

"You're forgetting that I asked you to accompany me."

But he hadn't suggested marriage.

"You would've resented me. Your entire career lay ahead of you, Christopher. I was your summer girlfriend. Besides, higher education was in your future, not mine."

"The single biggest regret of my life happened when I realized you were really and truly gone, Jenny." His deep-blue eyes drew her in. They always had. She attempted to avert her gaze, but he mesmerized her. "I should've never let you go."

The sincerity in his voice was unmistakable, and she gave in to a muffled sob. "You had visions, and drive, and brains, Christopher. It wasn't fair for you to choose between a teenage romance and your promising future."

"I hoped for a chance to prove myself. But I also wanted you, Jenny." He took a step closer. His hand reached out tentatively. "Even when we lost touch, I always wondered what could have been if we had stayed together."

"What happened between us was a thousand lifetimes ago. We can't change the past." Who did she try to convince? Him or her?

"I know, but I just wanted to say it. To tell you how I feel."

"My mother often said that the only way a high school romance lasted was if the girl got pregnant." She looked away, trying to compose herself.

He sucked in a breath. "News to me. That's a terrible thing to hear from a parent, but you realize it's not true, right? Look at us, we're still here, even if it didn't work out the first time."

"It's hard to shake off old beliefs, especially if they're coming from your own mother. She always had a way of making me feel like showing any sort of emotion was a weakness."

Christopher gently placed a hand on her shoulder. "It's

okay, Jenny. Emotion doesn't make you weak, it makes you human."

She looked up at him. "I was content to live on the island. My views aren't the same as many modern women, but I wanted a life providing a happy home for my husband and children. I longed for simplicity."

"You're the one who went away," he reminded her.

"A teenager dependent on her parents has no control over the circumstances."

"You never married, Jenny."

A statement or a question. She wasn't certain.

"Correct?" he inquired.

"Correct."

She couldn't read his expression. He'd spoken as if he'd memorized the dictionary rather than posing such a weighty query.

The realization caused her sadness. She'd lost that all-important connection with him. Once, she'd recognized every nuance, the significance of each subtle shift in his stance.

"When college at Carnegie didn't pan out, I joined the army," he replied.

"Did you like it?"

"The military provided me with the structure I never found at home with my dad."

"I was a little afraid of your father. He was a gruff man who never minced words."

"He came up with one hare-brained idea after another, and we moved constantly," Christopher said. "After a while, I couldn't keep track of all the schools I attended."

Folks on the island had whispered that the Drake household had spelled nothing but disaster. Two males living alone, without a wife or mother. Neither father nor son had ever gotten into any trouble that Jenny was aware of. She often defended Christopher, citing his exceptional grades and commitment to helping others.

She kept the emphasis on him. "How long were you in the military?"

"Several years." His words came slowly. "I was deployed overseas for a while and then stationed in Alaska."

So, the rumors proved true.

She didn't press him for details. A few of her high school classmates who joined the armed forces were wounded. A number never recovered, either physically, or emotionally, or both.

"And now?" She scanned his face, searching for clues.

"Now I'm the architect, and often contractor for the Grand Michelangelo Hotel."

"All that? You?"

"Yes, me." His mouth twisted into that memorable, wry grin. "I'm obliged to the US Army's support. I earned a graduate degree in architecture, which allowed me to pursue a fulfilling career."

"You've done an admirable job here." She gestured toward the little touches of elegance, from the fresh flowers arranged on tables to the carefully curated artwork. "This empty building had seen no activity in ages."

"I well recall." A hint of nostalgia shone in his eyes.

And now they were both invested in making this same hotel shine again.

"I'm proud of you, Christopher." She consciously avoided touching his forearm, though she wanted to. "Anyika once said you were destined for greatness."

"Ah, yes, our extraordinary friend who levels me with her intense scrutiny. The island's resident fortune-teller who never forgave me."

"Anyika is a person who would want to be recognized as someone diligent and intuitive, and I can't wait to see her again. We're in touch, and she lives in the same house near the historic Baptist church. Her grandson is with her."

Christopher inclined his head. "She's my friend, too, hopefully."

Jenny contacted Anyika before accepting the job offer and was overjoyed to learn she still lived on the island.

"Nothin' on this sea island ever changes, honey," Anyika had announced, noting that her daughter was a single parent of an eight-year-old son.

A million years ago, Anyika and Jenny had often baked. Jenny's mother had remarked that whenever Jenny was anxious, she soothed herself by baking desserts. This was also an insinuation that Jenny might gain too much weight, and her mother regularly reminded her to maintain her figure. An idle woman, she placed high regard on physical appearance, asserting that thinness was of utmost importance.

Jenny took in the view before her. With the progression of spring, dusk fell later in the Carolinas, and the sun cast languid, stretched silhouettes of the palm trees upon the sand.

She glanced at her watch. She and Maria needed to locate their rooms, unpack, and shower. Then she had piles of tasks to attend to.

Christopher, however, didn't seem to take the hint. He stayed where he was. "I've missed you, Jenny."

She attempted to ignore his low, husky tone and wiped her clammy hands along her blouse. Breathe, Jenny, breathe.

"How did you get this job?" Uncertainly, she tripped over her words. "Did you apply to the online ad?"

He shifted his weight from side to side. "We've put a lot of effort into this project."

We? As in, Christopher and the ever-discreet Oliver?

As she pondered, a young boy, his features surprisingly

familiar, burst through a side door and barreled down the corridor. His brown hair bounced up and down with each of his energetic steps.

"Hey, buddy!" Christopher ruffled the boy's hair affectionately when he reached them. "Did you finish your reading assignment?"

"I'm done," the boy declared, as he leaped into Christopher's outstretched arms. "I read a whole chapter book."

"That's amazing. Which one?"

"It's called *The Magic Tree House*. I loved it. Can we go to the bookstore and get the next book in the series?"

"There's no bookstore on the island, but I'll have it shipped from the mainland."

The boy clapped his hands. "Yay! Thank you!"

"Spell *island* for me," Christopher prompted.

The boy's mischievous smile lit his entire face. "I-S-L-A-N-D." His eyes shone, and his dimpled cheeks were adorable.

"What a darling child." Jenny gave Christopher a questioning glance. "Is he related to anyone here?"

Christopher hugged the boy closer before he wiggled out of his arms. "This is Sebastian, my son. I named him after my father."

She took in both father and son, connecting the dots. The similarities—dark hair, blue eyes, and the peppering of freckles—were readily apparent.

She swallowed tightly to keep her composure. "His resemblance to you is remarkable."

"Lots of people say that."

"How old is he?"

"Seven!" Sebastian grinned. He had the cutest button nose.

During the strained pause, she assessed her reaction. This wasn't how a woman with Christian beliefs should behave or

31

think, and there was no justification for resenting Sebastian. She loved children.

"You're quite the clever young man." She reached for a large, fluffy white towel from a stack on the counter and lowered herself to Sebastian's height. "Are you interested in seeing a nifty trick I picked up during my stint in Italy?"

Sebastian's grin widened. "Yes, please!"

She sunk into a deep leather armchair arranged by a low coffee table, and Sebastian sat beside her.

Drawing on her experience, she expertly twisted the towel into a shape resembling a wriggling serpent. She had mastered the skill when she wasn't cleaning showers and toilets as a chambermaid.

"First, I fold the towel lengthwise." She creased the pointy ends over and began rolling, then constructed the head. When she finished, she placed her sunglasses on top.

Christopher chuckled and encouraged her with a thumbs up. "Excellent."

"Cool!" The boy beamed. "Can I keep the snake?"

"All except for my sunglasses." She rose and smoothed her skirt. "When I have time, Sebastian, I'll make you some other animals, like a rabbit and a turtle."

"Can you teach me how to do it?"

She winked. "Happily."

"It's more difficult than it seems," Christopher cautioned his son. "Creating animals out of towels takes practice."

The boy looked up at Jenny. "How did you get good at it?"

"I learned from my mistakes and practiced."

"I want to be good at it, too."

Jenny smiled. "We'll learn from each other and have fun."

"You're extraordinary, Jenny." Christopher gazed at her with a tender expression.

"Thank you." She tilted her chin up and settled back in her seat. He had always charmed her.

Christopher glanced down the hall. "Where's Scooby-Doo, Sebastian?"

"Probably gulping down water from his bowl." The boy held the towel snake protectively over one shoulder.

Before she could inquire who Scooby-Doo was, Christopher interjected, "I plan to enroll Sebastian in the island school come fall. For now, I'm homeschooling him. There's an excellent virtual academy based on the mainland."

"I like learning from you. It's more fun that way." The boy scrunched up his nose. "I'm not a fan of real school."

"You're in second grade, correct?" Jenny questioned.

"Uh-huh."

She brought her hands together. "Second grade is such fun, Sebastian."

Christopher smirked. "You remember second grade, Jenny?"

"If I did, I probably blocked it out." She'd struggled throughout school and hardly kept up with the other students, no matter the grade. She well remembered the finger-pointing and blond-airhead comments her classmates had joked about her.

"I attended so many inner-city schools on the mainland, I lost count. Don't even get me started on middle school and those rows of dented lockers covered in graffiti. Mine never seemed to close properly. And that outdated linoleum and those narrow hallways ..." Christopher shook his head. "I was frequently the new kid, and adolescent guys aren't the friendliest."

Christopher and his father had drifted from town to town during the school year as his father searched for opportunities as a mechanic. Occasionally he was successful, but often he came up empty-handed. Summers on the island proved lucrative, as he repaired expensive motors on cars and yachts.

33

Sebastian skipping off immediately drew Jenny's attention back to Christopher. "How many children attend the school here?" she asked.

"Presumably the same as when you were young." Christopher laid a hand on her chair. "A trickle of kids at most."

She offered a slight smile and tried not to zero in on his irresistible lips. "This island has its very own private bourgeois school."

"Bourgeois may not be the right word."

"What is?"

He reciprocated her smile. "How about a two-room schoolhouse that lacks a science lab, gym, or library?"

"I have a romantic notion about old-fashioned schoolhouses."

"If you're keen on a school that hasn't evolved in half a century, you're in luck."

Her mind mulled over several responses. "I received my entire elementary education there, and look how I turned out."

"You're both pretty smart to me," Sebastian chimed in.

"Flattery will get you nowhere." Christopher chuckled and beckoned his son closer. "Sebastian, offer my dearest friend, Jenny, a proper handshake."

The boy extended his hand. "Pleased to meet you, ma'am."

"If I'm your father's dearest friend, I prefer you call me Miss Jenny." She finger quoted 'dearest friend,' then shook the boy's small hand. He seemed so confident of himself and older than his years. However, he was as thin as a blade of reed grass.

"Sebastian may not be keen on school, but he is an amateur detective," Christopher said. "He loves exploring."

"I can also count backward." Sebastian stood straight. "Wanna listen, Miss Jenny? Twenty, nineteen, eighteen—"

"Excellent!" She clapped when he finished.

34

When she lived in Italy, most children couldn't speak English. That didn't stop them from conversing with her using the universal language of body posture and facial expressions. This world was chock-full of differences, yet people were all the same in the end.

"What mysteries have you solved, Sebastian?" she asked.

"We play detective games." He tugged at his father's shirt. "Don't we, Dad?"

"Often," Christopher said, then murmured to Jenny, "Cracking a riddle burns off a boatload of energy."

"Maybe we can play detective games together!" Sebastian said.

Jenny smiled at the idea. "I used to love playing private eye when I was your age."

"We have our work cut out for us." Christopher chuckled.

Jenny turned to Sebastian. "Have you ever heard of Sherlock Holmes?"

"Sure."

"We read a book about him," Christopher said. "Sherlock was a great British detective."

"Can we solve a real mystery, like finding a treasure or catching a thief?" Sebastian asked.

"We'll come up with something," Jenny replied. "Right, Sherlock?"

"Right." The boy nodded and grinned, then took another skip around the lobby.

"I bet he'd be thrilled with a magnifying glass and sleuth hat," Jenny said.

"He would, indeed."

"He's adorable."

A corner of Christopher's mouth ticked up. "I think so, too."

When Sebastian skipped back, she leaned over and petted the towel snake. "I rarely like snakes," she whispered

35

conspiratorially. "But I'm fond of this one because it's pretend."

"Me, too." Sebastian put a finger to his lips. "He's friendly."

"Does your towel snake have a name?"

"Noodle, because he's in the shape of a noodle."

"If there's ever a mystery at the hotel," she dropped her voice to a whisper. "You and Noodle are my first choice to help solve it."

"Your wish is my command … ma'am."

"Miss Jenny," she reminded him. "We're not into formality here."

"At your service, Miss Jenny." The boy extended an enchanting smile—amiable yet with a twinkle of mischief.

But he was also a tad sickly looking. Just like his dad when he was a kid.

"On another note, Christopher, where is your wife?" Her attention flicked to his ringless left hand.

"Ex-wife." The abrupt shake of his head told her this was a topic he rarely discussed with Sebastian nearby. "Jocelyn is in California and got her big break while we lived in Alaska. She's an *aspiring* actress."

Jenny heard his slight emphasis on the word 'aspiring' and didn't comment. Instead, she offered a smile while she waited for Christopher to explain.

"Mom is on TV commercials," Sebastian stated gleefully. "There's one where she's selling hairspray. It's so funny. She said it was crazy because the wind was blowing hard and kept messing up her hair." He peered up at his father. "Am I telling the story right, Dad?"

Christopher flashed his son a brilliant grin. "You are."

Jenny took in a quick breath. "Congrats to her."

A loud woof made them turn and a large black dog bound down the hallway, barking, and wagging its tail. When the dog spotted Christopher, it knocked over the planter, spreading dirt across the Persian rugs. Massive paws battered the floor, its colossal size matched by its zeal.

The dog sidled up to Christopher and nuzzled its snout against his hand.

"A ..." Jenny searched for the best description. Horse, giant ... *That was it.* "A giant dog."

"He's a lovable, gentle schnauzer and my loyal companion. He's fiercely protective and always by my side."

"Schnauzers are compact dogs. They are little. Tiny."

"You're describing a miniature Schnauzer," Christopher said.

She mentally searched through her canine encyclopedia, which turned out to be empty. Her brain's understanding of dogs was about as extensive as a fish's understanding of bicycle mechanics.

"He weighs, what, seventy pounds?" she asked.

"Eight-five pounds at his last weigh-in."

Drool dripped from the dog's open-mouthed grin, in stark contrast to his harsh eyebrows and beard. The thick coat was well-groomed but still had a slightly unkempt look to it. Dark, intelligent eyes followed every movement in the room with keen interest.

Christopher stared at the spilled dirt. "Don't mind the mess. It's easy to clean up."

The odds of finding a broom in the elegant lobby weren't great. The odds of finding a broom and a shovel? Nonexistent.

Jenny blinked. "Is the dog still growing?"

"He's a rescue. I believe in giving second chances," Christopher replied. "The vet estimates he's well over two years old, so he's probably done growing."

"Does he have any special skills, like fetching the newspaper or doing laundry?"

Christopher chuckled. "He's not quite that advanced, but he can sit, stay, and shake. And is a great cuddle."

"Does he create chaos often?"

"Typically, he's a furry tornado."

"He's certainly a handsome fellow." She scratched the dog's ears, and he leaned into her touch with a contented sigh.

Christopher smirked. "He's got a bit of an ego."

"Well, I can't blame him. He's quite the catch."

The dog barked, and Christopher raised an eyebrow. "He agrees with you."

CHAPTER 3

"*H*e's just too lovable." Christopher nudged Jenny's shoulder. "Greet Scooby-Doo, our Velcro giant schnauzer."

The dog emitted a soft snort as if to say, "What do you want from me? I can't help my size."

Jenny leaned forward. "Velcro?"

"He wants to be as close to us as possible. Sometimes he forgets how big he is and crawls on our laps for hugs."

"Or when he's bounding through a hotel lobby," she said.

"My dad gives Scooby-Doo piggyback rides." Sebastian jumped up and down. "Show her, Dad."

Now that was a visual she wasn't at all eager to see.

"Some other time." He chucked his son under the chin, then rested a hand on the dog's head. "We rescued Scooby-Doo in Alaska."

"We saw him tied to a tree on the side of the road. Dad slammed the brakes and leaped out of his truck. He said it was important to help an animal in need." Sebastian's voice trembled. "The dog's ribs jutted out. He hadn't eaten in days."

Christopher gave a solemn confirmation.

Sebastian set his towel snake on a chair. "My dad is a hero, Miss Jenny."

"Hardly." Christopher extended a smile to Sebastian, then redirected his attention to Jenny. "You may recall that I was obsessed with the cartoon."

"Scooby-Doo, the cowardly dog," she uttered to Sebastian. "His companion was Shaggy Rogers. That's a good detective's name for you."

The boy bobbed his head. "I like it. What about you, Dad?"

"I like the name, too."

"You watched Hanna-Barbera cartoons when your TV signal was stable," Jenny said to Christopher.

"You mean when the TV had no static or distortion? When did that ever happen?" Christopher's boyish grin nearly melted her insides. "The days of my youth are all coming back to me."

"That is when you weren't studying math, designing, or writing," she said.

"Rings a bell."

"Usually, you ignored me."

He grinned. "I did nothing of the sort."

"Oh, but you did."

"Is that where this conversation is headed?"

"Depending on our perspective, we all recall different things." She gazed out at the ocean, lost in memories of the past. "Everything is shaped by our point of view."

Did he remember the way she used to laugh at his jokes? The way he held her hand? The way they'd talked about their dreams? They had felt invincible, as if anything were possible.

A million questions, each vying for attention, swirled through her mind. She couldn't bring herself to ask, not wanting to spoil the moment with awkwardness or disappointment.

"I like to play checkers!" Sebastian piped up.

Sebastian had swiftly eliminated any tension in the air. The perk of being a child, Christopher supposed.

He grinned as Jenny laughed so hard, she held her stomach. He flashed back to the melodic, joyful sound of her laughter when they were young. He could never get enough of it.

As he grew older, he realized Jenny was the only person who ever truly understood him. He'd spent countless hours with her, sharing his deepest fears. He could be himself around her because she accepted him exactly the way he was.

"Christopher, your son is the best!" Jenny exclaimed.

"What's so funny?" Sebastian cocked his head.

"Nothing," Jenny and Christopher chorused.

"Can I get my checkers set, Dad?"

"Tomorrow." Christopher went with the pulse of humor and turned to Jenny. "People say my son resembles me."

"By playing checkers?"

"By being impulsive."

"I think that's a good thing sometimes. You're not afraid to take risks."

"Is that what impulsive means?" Sebastian nodded vigorously. "I like taking risks."

"Oh, do you now?" Christopher asked.

"Yeah. Remember the time I snuck into our neighbor's yard to play with his dog? He was so cute I couldn't resist." Without missing a beat, Sebastian went to reach for Christopher's cell phone. "Can I look up the word? I want to be sure I'm impulsive."

"You are, I assure you." Christopher scrubbed a hand over Sebastian's wavy hair, and he twisted away.

"I'm not a dog, Dad, I'm your kid. Is it okay if I play outside now?"

"There are no lifeguards on this stretch of the island."

"Or on any stretch," Jenny stated. "Though playing on the beach is safe."

"Is it?" Christopher asked. "Sebastian is a city kid."

"You've both lived here a while. Haven't you gone swimming yet?"

"We're a team, but Sebastian doesn't go near the ocean alone. It's unpredictable and dangerous. There are undertows and jellyfish and sharks."

Jenny nodded. "The currents are very strong."

"It's not worth risking any lives for a swim." Christopher glanced at Sebastian. "And d-r-o-w-n-i-n-g could happen quickly."

"I won't drown," Sebastian interrupted. "I swam the butterfly stroke on the swim team in Alaska."

Christopher didn't back down. "A swimming pool and the ocean are considerably different."

"My friend Maria is by the pool." Jenny pointed outside. "She's the bathing beauty sitting in the lounge chair and soaking up every ounce of the sun on the island. Oliver also hired her."

Hmm. Christopher noted to himself to consult with Olive, a nickname for Oliver his army buddies had pegged him with, because he was calm, cool, and smooth like an Olive. The guy had obviously made a few hiring decisions without Christopher's input.

"Hang on. I'll go confirm with her." Jenny waved madly at the dark-haired woman by the pool to garner her attention, then sprang to the door. The woman met her there, lifting an eyebrow as Jenny motioned to Sebastian and Christopher.

"All set. Maria will watch him," Jenny announced when she rejoined them.

Christopher scratched at his collar. "Maria is—"

"A gentle reminder," Jenny specified in a tone suggesting he hadn't listened to her. "Maria is a reliable, full-fledged adult, and I vouch for her."

"Okay." Christopher inclined his head toward his son. "Go on, then."

"Yay! Can we build sandcastles?"

"If you find a shovel and pail. If not, there will be other sunny days."

Sebastian dashed through the doorway with the giant dog barking at his heels. The bond between the two was unmistakable.

Christopher was conflicted. He had no intention of restricting the boy's freedom, but this island was famous for the unexpected, even if it didn't seem so to those who hadn't lived here before.

The islanders embraced a unique folklore passed down through generations, some of which was in direct opposition with scientific reasoning.

He recalled an island family who plastered newspaper on their outside walls, believing that a spirit must read every word before entering their home. Thus, the spirit would be deterred.

Newspaper, of all things. There were so many gaps in that theory, beginning with ... well, was it widely believed that spirits were literate?

Display the evidence, he thought. Challenge me with facts. Then I may be open to changing my views.

He was a judicious thinker and cautious, refusing to take any risks with Sebastian. He wasn't a tough kid. If anything ever happened to him ...

For a few seconds, neither Christopher nor Jenny spoke. Her gaze shadowed his—first the ceiling, then the floor—anywhere but directly at each other.

Now that he was beginning to assemble his thoughts, he couldn't believe she was on Pink Coral Island. This was truly a miracle he'd never foreseen.

A divine hand from above, shaping and molding their lives.

He blinked, steadily processing the delightful turn of events.

For years, he had yearned for a chance to see her and engage her in conversation. Occasionally, he followed her social media and discovered that she had traveled to Italy. He gathered a rough understanding of the happenings in her life, even though they weren't connected as "friends" on any of their accounts. He had composed many texts to her, but each time, he deleted all the messages before sending them.

The opportunity was here; the occasion was now. However, he wasn't certain how to begin.

He peered at the beach and the bottomless blue ocean beyond. Sebastian, Maria, and the dog were chasing each other on the sand.

He fixated on Jenny's face. She sensed his scrutiny and gazed up at him.

He reached out and tamed an unruly ringlet from her forehead, protectiveness and affection overwhelming him.

And there it was. The strength of their connection.

"I have thoughts to share." His mind overflowed with words, encompassing both the past and the present.

"What kind of thoughts?" she inquired.

"Thoughts concerning us, and what happened. I remember ..."

Ten years ago, they stood on that very same beach. Glossy light from a round moon had outlined her ethereal figure, her white skirt and blouse rippling in the wind. They remarked on the tides along the shoreline and he spoke of the sun and the moon's gravitational pull, causing waves.

"Yes, Christopher, but what about us?" she'd asked.

She was an idealist and believed that their friendship and budding romance would conquer every obstacle. He didn't. He was the opposite. An analytical guy, an architect who dealt with straight lines and math.

They'd been too young, too poor, and their impending separation by physical miles was the proverbial last straw, sealing an end to their future. He had convinced himself that their relationship wasn't meant to happen. He believed she deserved someone better than him.

Ultimately, he had reached the conclusion that letting her go was the most mature choice.

Now that he saw her again, he realized she'd been the one who'd slipped away. Or rather, that he'd stupidly encouraged her to leave.

"What do you remember, Christopher?" Jenny kept her gaze on him.

He came nearer. "I'd like to discuss why we didn't stay in touch. I often thought about you, but I was wrapped up in my own little world. I messed up, but I had a lot of issues to deal with."

"Why did you come back to the island?"

"I've always felt I had to prove myself, to be successful, in order to show my mother what she missed after she left."

He recognized the need to confront the emotional obstacles stemming from his mother's abandonment. Now he had to navigate the complexities of his relationship with Jenny and address any misunderstandings that led to their separation.

He had an unsettling feeling that something was coming, poised to disrupt the delicate tranquility he had rediscovered on the island. He knew that even in this idyllic paradise, the slightest misstep could lead to disaster.

"No strolls down memory lane. Thank you very much."

Jenny was saying. She held up her hands. "I'm not expecting an apology, if that is the direction this discussion is taking." She brushed aside a blond tangle from her face and appeared to mentally shake herself. "I assumed it was because your father wasn't keen on dogs."

He blinked. "What?"

"The reason why you rescued Scooby-Doo?"

Oh, point taken. Their previous conversation.

He knew it was wise not to interrupt her, and waited.

"Lots of people say they don't want something, and then they do." Her eyes landed on Sebastian.

The inflection in her tone suggested this dialogue wasn't about dogs. She'd reflected on Christopher's declaration from years before that he didn't want kids. And now, voila, here was Sebastian.

"Where are you living?" Jenny inquired.

"Right here, in an owner's suite." His gaze drifted toward the windows and the sweeping views of the ocean. The resort was indeed a luxurious place, with its pristine walls and spacious rooms that were filled with modern amenities. The faint scent of saltwater wafted in from the open doors. It was a world away from where he'd grown up on the island, in a small, rundown cottage on the outskirts of town.

"Owner's suite?" She echoed his words as if she'd never heard them before. "There are only two, and we reserved one for Oliver."

"Oh yeah, that's right." As his gaze returned to the endless ocean, a bitter taste filled his throat. Somewhere along the line, he'd lost touch with his roots and felt like he didn't belong in this world of lavish extravagance.

"Wait, a minute." She squared off. "Uh, no, you're not living in a suite. We don't allow animals."

"For me, you do."

"The dog will claw at the curtains and chew the bedspread, and that's only the start."

"Scooby-Doo won't do anything of the sort. He lives to serve and please."

"You're kidding, right?" Her voice sounded steady, and he almost agreed with her that indeed, he was. Only he wasn't.

"For an animal rescuer you don't mess around. No hamsters or parakeets for you, only the biggest, most impressive dog you could find."

"An English Mastiff is bigger," he corrected.

"Are you trying to get me fired?" She didn't exactly shout, but she certainly displayed a temper. In alarming detail, he recalled her fierce independence and refusal to back down from a challenge. Those traits hadn't been quite as endearing as her sweet nature.

"I have no savings. I need this job, and I can't fail," she said.

He inhaled a bracing breath, processing the impact of seeing her, conversing with her, and realizing she would live here. He didn't handle curveballs with finesse, even delightful ones. He planned out life's progression smoothly and predictably.

"I arranged everything." He reassured her with a flick of his wrist. "I cleared my living requirements."

"You have living requirements?" She fixed her hands on her hips. "Oliver is in another country, and I'm fortunate to hear from him twice a week. You, however, act as though you have a direct line to him. Therefore, it's a valid question. Who allowed your occupancy in one of our owner's suites?"

Her high-pitched tone gave him pause. She acted as if he'd committed a crime.

He sighed. "And I'm giving you a legitimate answer. Again. The big boss consented."

She flushed at his staccato-like reply, and remorse rushed

through him. "I'm sorry, Jenny. It's been a long day, and I imagine even more so for you. I'm still shocked at seeing you."

She glared at him with those deep-green eyes. Her features held plenty of confusion. Or was it panic?

Why? It was only him. Her once-upon-a-time best friend.

He had a lot to learn about what truly mattered in life. Maybe, just maybe, this reunion with Jenny was the catalyst to discover those lost values.

Olive had mentioned that he'd hired two women for managerial positions. Their names were never a concern for Christopher. He assumed they were from the mainland.

Come to think of it, Olive had been overly casual and absent-minded when Christopher requested to see their files. After all, the manager, the head of the kitchen, and a media person were key posts.

At Christopher's inquiries, Olive had swiftly changed the subject.

Christopher pondered these facts. He'd often mentioned Jenny when he and Olive had served overseas. Had Olive tracked her down, placed an online ad, and engineered all this when it was time for new hires?

He took in Jenny's oval-shaped face and her lithe figure. As a teen, her slender, willowy frame, bathed in the moon's light, was the image of his dreams. But this woman, with soft red lips and impossibly long legs, was the only woman who had ever attracted him.

The only woman he'd ever loved.

Why are you revisiting a matter that twists you into knots? It's over.

He retreated, admiring her flawless figure in a tight-fitting pencil skirt and no-nonsense brown flat sandals. She used to make him weak-kneed with a glance or an eyebrow raise, and she still had the same effect on him.

She finger-combed her ponytail, creating waves of blond hair. "Apology accepted."

He nodded and smiled. At least, he assumed he did. "Olive is pleased with how the suites turned out."

"Olive? Well, excuse me. On a nickname basis with the boss, I take it?"

"We served together." Christopher's smile faded. "When you're in the military, you develop a reliance on each other. You learn commitment. We became friends for life."

"I envisioned Oliver as a man in his sixties."

"He is sixty-two. He was an experienced, non-commissioned officer who moved to Wales after he retired from the service. Olive inherited a substantial amount of money from his uncle."

With a nod and her tote bag in hand, she glided behind the counter.

Christopher followed her. "The breakroom for employees is located to your right." He peered out the front window to ensure his son was in sight, then ushered her to a bright, spacious room painted in vibrant orange and teal blue. He strode to the refrigerator, stocked with energy drinks, and a sink beside it. A cooler spouted chilled water infused with cucumber and mint. A popcorn machine was available for mid-afternoon snacks.

"Fabulous." She observed the plush couches, a fully equipped kitchen with a silver espresso coffeemaker, and a bookshelf with a variety of books, including bestselling novels, travel guides, and books about the Gullah culture and Low Country. "Did you design it?"

"An interior decorator came in while I was off the island for a few weeks. The table and chairs were my idea." He indicated the set at the far end of the room, a contemporary style with a sleek surface.

"Impressive." She admired the ceramic vase blooming with creamy-white and yellow azaleas. "I love these flowers."

He remembered and nodded slightly. "The hotel is coming together nicely."

"You're not a bellboy."

"I'm not a bellboy. Water?"

At her grateful nod, he swiftly dispensed water from the cooler, two chocolate chip cookies, and napkins before handing them to her. He had visited the Sun-Kissed Treats bakery on the island that morning and purchased a box of cookies.

"I'll regret this later," she said, thanking him. "Eating sweets before a proper meal is never advisable."

"Ah, the sweet life. It's always worth the risk. You'll be on a sugar high, then expect a crash."

"I'll take that chance. I'm starving."

"What? They served no delicious gourmet dishes on the ferry? I bet you were hoping for caviar and crumpets."

"Has anyone ever told you that you have an innate talent for painting fantasies with words?" She collapsed into a plush chair, adorned in luscious velvet, accompanied by an array of cushions and cozy throws. The pillows boasted a kaleidoscope of colors in nubby fabrics and textures.

After a prayer of grace, she bit into the cookie and groaned with pleasure. "I adored these when I was growing up, and I still love them."

Perfectly baked, with a crisp outer layer giving way to a soft, chewy center, bursting with chunks of chocolate. Christopher had eaten two that morning.

"Regrettably, the bakery is closing its doors," he said.

Her eyes widened. "What? How can ... That can't be true."

"It's not often you're at a loss for words."

"Last I checked, the bakery was doing fine."

"That's what everyone assumed, but they are drowning in debt."

"They sell the most delicious baked goods in the entire US. They're the heart of this community."

"I agree, but the Gullah owners have cut their losses and retired."

She set down the cookie and straightened. "I can't bear the idea of this island losing such an important part of their history."

"The owners are in their seventies, plus business is scarce, with only four hundred full-time residents here. Frequently, the major grocers on the mainland undercut their most profitable baked goods, putting them at a disadvantage. Who would've imagined the bakery surviving these past fifty years?"

"But they shipped their products everywhere in the state."

"The boat transportation is too expensive and erratic to depend on a profit."

"Can't anything be done?"

"Sometimes an owner is too tired to continue. The world doesn't change its course for our benefit. No one wanted to toil away during those pre-dawn hours for meager gain."

Jenny blew out a beleaguered sigh. "In an email, Oliver said he expects us to win Evelyn Ekard's golden spoon award. How will we ever accomplish that now?"

Evelyn was the foremost hotel and food reviewer in the United States, and her article about the hotel in leading travel magazines would place it on the radar of moneyed travelers. Success hung in the balance, as a negative review from her yielded serious consequences.

"The mysterious Evelyn Ekard." Christopher briefly looked away. "Ah."

"Ah? Her review could affect the hotel's reputation and, therefore, its profitability. Maria and I were fortunate that

Oliver offered us positions so quickly, and I'm determined we get a chance to prove ourselves."

Christopher waved a hand around the room. "Where else will you find a more favorable work environment?"

She retrieved a printout from her tote bag. "Would you like to hear what Oliver wrote to me in his latest email?"

"Do I have a choice?"

"Dear Miss Jenny," she began, ignoring his comment. "I'm certain you will contribute valuably to my third venture into the world of hotel hospitality. One of my requests is that, as the manager, you ensure Evelyn Ekard awards us the coveted golden spoon award."

"Coveted doesn't begin to explain it." Christopher chuckled.

"What's a better word?"

"Impossible."

She threw him a sidelong glance and continued reading. "Evelyn spends a couple of nights at various hotels, provided they offer fine dining and baked goods. However, she has given no hotel the golden spoon award."

"You should never believe every request from Oliver," Christopher said.

"He's a liar?"

"He's a dreamer."

Jenny went on. "Evelyn arrives anonymously, dines at the restaurant, schedules room service, and then will post her discoveries on social media. She invariably finds something wrong—the croissants weren't flaky enough, the cookies were dry, or the bread was stale."

"I'm well aware," Christopher concurred.

Jenny picked up her cookie, examining it for imperfections. As usual, there were none. "I intended to purchase our sweets from the Gullah bakery."

"Evelyn's appearance and existence are shrouded in mystery," he said. "It's uncertain whether she actually exists."

"She's a single female, traveling alone, and easy to spot."

"There goes that theory. Lots of women travel by themselves."

Jenny took another bite of her cookie and chewed. "Sun-Kissed Treats would've assured us of five stars."

"Not necessarily. From what I've gathered, Evelyn's research extends beyond desserts. She examines the overall ambiance of a hotel, not just its culinary offerings." He leaned toward Jenny and inhaled, and her familiar perfume of lemon and lavender triggered a tidal wave of sentiments. "You were obsessed with baking and created some amazing cobblers and puddings. Why don't you bake the desserts?"

"For the entire hotel?"

He baited her, unable to resist. "Why not?"

"First, baking isn't a talent."

He provided a wry smile. "Of course it is. You were a pro."

"Second, I'm here to manage a hotel." She polished off her cookie and placed another on her napkin. "Are you expecting me to bake cookies during my off-hours?"

He grinned. "Only until you're out of flour."

"I'm not telling *you* to bake anything."

"Fortunately for everyone on the island," he quipped.

"I'm serious, Christopher. What if Evelyn checks in?"

"Nobody can predict if she'll even set foot anywhere in the southeast. Besides, word on the public hotel forums is that she uses an alias."

"That's worse. We'll only find out once she leaves and shares a negative review of the Grand Michelangelo. The hotel's reputation will be damaged by then."

"C'mon, Jenny. Multi-tasking is a skill, and you can do both. Manage this hotel and bake the desserts." He smiled. "There's no shame in being ambitious."

She scowled at him. "Do you recall when you used to be considerate?"

He chuckled. "Nope."

She slumped in her chair. "I still picture the times when Anyika saved these cookies for me whenever I visited her. She told stories while we ate."

"What kind?"

"Entertaining tales about animal pranksters. For instance, Brer Rabbit's cleverness and how it applied to resourceful and self-assertive slaves. All the fables had a moral lesson."

"Proof that a limited, oppressed underdog can triumph over a larger authority."

"Absolutely."

Any speck of humor faded. The island's dark past of slave labor was a stark realization.

Jenny lifted an eyebrow. "Have you seen Anyika since you arrived?"

"Once. She and Sorie, her grandson, are a few miles down the road."

"She was raised in the same house she is living in now." Jenny's lips curved into a smile. "People claim that your home is where you feel the most loved."

"Sometimes." He picked up his water and settled opposite her. "Sorie is a cute kid. He is close to Sebastian's age, and Sebastian will enroll in classes with him in the fall."

"Who is the teacher?"

"They hired Mr. Evan Farrenway, a man from out of state. He teaches elementary school, whether two or twenty attend. Once the students are in middle and high school, they travel by ferry to the mainland."

"Time stands still here. Nothing changes." Jenny's lips trembled ever so slightly. He wondered if she'd missed the island as much as he had.

"Mr. Farrenway lives in the teacher's house next to

the school," he continued. "People say he keeps to himself." He expected her to question the teacher's qualifications and experience. When she didn't, he added, "He travels back and forth to Hilton Head, especially on the weekends. Folks claim he's involved in another profession."

"Let me guess." She put her chin in her hands. "He's really a physicist."

"Why that?"

"Presumably to write a hypothesis on his latest experiment." She grinned. "Is he single?"

Why this particular question about this schoolteacher?

"As far as I'm aware. Why?"

"No reason."

Her queries nearly slayed him. She had only been on the island for a couple of hours, and another man had already sparked her curiosity. From her social media accounts, she was seeing an Italian guy. She hadn't brought him up.

"Are you dating anyone?" He inquired anyway, merely to make sure.

"Not anymore, nor do I intend to. Never again."

He stood, bent over her, and lightly kissed her cheek. "Never say never."

She pulled back. Her message was loud and clear. The subject of relationships was off the table.

Body language was such a powerful thing.

"The house and school are on a quiet part of the island near a patch of indigo," she said. "The islanders always revered the teachers here."

"Still do."

"What about Anyika's daughter?"

"She wasn't keen on island life and scurried off to parts unknown." Christopher clasped the chilled water cup between his hands. Since relocating from Alaska, he hadn't adjusted to the island's heat yet. "She's been gone for over a year, and Anyika hasn't heard from her."

"Anyika must be in her sixties."

"She is. Plus, she's trying to raise Sorie on her own."

"Trying?"

"It's challenging to bring up a kid when you're a single grandparent or a parent."

"You sound regretful."

"I am, about a lot of things." He took a long swallow of water. "I might as well say it again if I haven't made myself clear. I'm delighted we're both back on the island together."

"Many years have passed, Christopher. We've matured."

He grimaced. "I guess that's one way to look at it." She'd dashed his hope that she was as elated as he was. "However, we can learn all over again."

"Learn what?"

"Learn to be friends. Don't you remember how close we were as kids?"

"Of course." She nodded. "You questioned if I was in a relationship, and I replied. Are you?"

"One divorce is enough for me." He observed Jenny. She frowned, a revealing sign that the discussion of his marriage had upset her. "I have sole custody of Sebastian."

She raised a questioning eyebrow.

"I'm still trying to figure out a way to navigate the trials of parenting." He tapped his fingers on a side table. "A kid needs two parents, although who am I to judge?"

"The courts rarely grant the man exclusive custody."

"Depends on the circumstances. Mine is final and legal."

His mind refused to dwell on the breakup with his ex-wife, though he was sorry his marriage hadn't worked out. He was thankful his ex was out of his and his son's lives, after he discovered Sebastian had been neglected. The memory of Sebastian's asthma attack and how he'd been unattended still caused a chill down Christopher's spine. What kind of mother left an asthmatic child alone while she rehearsed for an online television audition?

Fortunately, Christopher had arrived home in time and found Sebastian wheezing and struggling for breath. He had remained composed, although inwardly he'd been shaking like a leaf in a hurricane. He'd sat Sebastian up and prompted him to take several puffs of his inhaler.

"I was finishing my script," his ex had later defended herself. "I shut our bedroom door. Filming requires absolute silence."

Yeah, sure, while her son couldn't breathe downstairs.

And then she had the audacity to bid Christopher farewell. Deserted him and Sebastian, leaving them to pick up the pieces. Similar to how Christopher's mother had left him and his father. What was it about him that caused the women in his life to abandon him and the families they supposedly loved?

He stood, pushing the difficult recollections from his mind.

He underestimated the struggles of raising a child alone and sought a perfect partner to build a family. Only one woman came to mind, and she was sitting directly across from him.

"Kids need parents who are invested in them," Jenny said.

His heart sank as he realized that their first conversation in ten years had taken a completely unexpected turn. This wasn't what he had hoped for or imagined. He wanted to discuss *their* relationship.

Past, present, and future.

Jenny's wistful tone tugged at his heartstrings. If only her emerald-colored eyes didn't stare straight at him, as if assessing him.

"All people yearn for others to care about them." He

thought to add a grin, hoping to lighten the mood. "No one should stand alone."

She placed her cookie on a napkin and reached for her water. "After my family left the island, my father deserted us. Did you know?"

"No, I didn't." He'd heard a great deal about Jenny's relocation and how she'd triumphed while attending a modern high school in the Carolinas. Anyika had reported that guys flocked around her.

He wished to celebrate Jenny's successes, even if it meant silent suffering, but jealousy had welled up inside him. The thought of being left behind pained him, despite his genuine desire for her happiness.

His gut had churned, and his heart had fallen to pieces. The practical part of him reassured him of his goal—Jenny living a good life without his destitution encircling her. She'd gone her way. He'd gone his.

"Ironic, isn't it?" Jenny mused. "My parents stayed together for my entire childhood, then divorced when I was in my teens."

In the soundless beat, thoughts swam and surfaced. Christopher had learned in the military that staying calm was important in tough times, and her parents' split was clearly difficult for her.

She lowered her eyes to her water before taking a sip. "My father was a stellar gardener."

"That he was."

"Unfortunately, he wasn't a stellar husband. The landscaping company he worked for had ceased operations. That much was true. However, he failed to mention that he'd been unfaithful to my mom for years with a woman who was one of the company's biggest clients."

A razor-sharp sadness cut through the stillness.

"Of course, my parents gave me no choice but to leave the

island." She placed the water beside her cookie. "Though my mother was ecstatic. She never liked it here."

"And you?"

"You know it devastated me."

A shudder ran through him for all that she'd endured. His decision had only precipitated her aloneness. He knew all too well the pain of being uprooted with his father's constant moves.

He viewed the lobby and beach beyond. Sebastian and Maria knelt in the sand, digging for seashells. Scooby-Doo raced in a loop around them. "At least you were older when the split happened."

"No matter the child's age, when the home is in turmoil, the situation is hard."

"Divorce is never easy, but sometimes necessary."

"Are you referring to your divorce?"

He affected a smile. "Yeah, mine."

"Why?"

"I tied the knot at a relatively immature stage, but as time went on, my ex-spouse and I drifted apart, reaching a point where there was no hope of salvaging our relationship. We experienced a complex divorce that led to our parting ways."

"Complex how?"

He shifted uncomfortably. "We just weren't right for each other."

"I'm sorry, Christopher."

"It was for the best."

"Kids are resilient, though." She spoke around a mouthful of cookie, then dabbed at her lips with a napkin.

"Hopefully." He had meant to fall into silence, but his voice had other plans. He couldn't resist talking with Jenny. He had always considered her a true blessing to confide in, knowing that she possessed a remarkable ability to focus and truly listen. "After the divorce, Sebastian mourned because our family was no longer intact. He was quite vocal about it, however he's since adjusted. It's certainly better than my ex and I being together. We fought a lot."

"About what?"

"A lack of meaningful dialogue, for one. In the military, I got used to giving and receiving orders directly. I admit, it was difficult for me to adjust to open communication, and it created a shipload of frustration and tension in my marriage."

"Were you married long?"

"A few years." Briefly, he closed his eyes. "Jocelyn insisted she didn't want kids, so her pregnancy was unexpected, and she told me about it while I was deployed overseas. She swore she was as thrilled as I was. Thinking back, I have my doubts."

"I'm not following."

"Although we clashed over everything, she wanted to stay married to escape her situation at home and used the baby as an excuse. I heard her demands and tried to understand. I looked for common ground, showed my gratitude, and took responsibility. Nothing helped. We finally realized we were incompatible."

"Fathers rarely get sole custody," Jenny remarked for a second time.

"There was ... evidence Sebastian wasn't being properly cared for by his mother."

"I'm sorry."

"It's over. My son is safe, and that's all that matters."

"Circumstances have certainly changed for both of us." Jenny sighed. The same pensive sigh, the same reflective pose.

She tossed back her hair, and he noted the sadness in her eyes.

Surely, she didn't blame him for his divorce or for having a child.

In his journey as a father, he had learned that unforeseen twists of fate could turn into extraordinary miracles. His heart swelled with pride, finding boundless delight in witnessing his cherished son grow and thrive. He couldn't imagine navigating through life without him.

He cleared his throat. "What have I done, Jenny?"

"Nothing. All your choices were the ones you believed were right."

He reviewed a quote he'd read by James Collins. "Bad decisions made with good intentions are still bad decisions." With Jenny Ormani, the quote rang true. He should've never let her go. But what eighteen-year-old guy was wise?

He detected tears in her eyes, though her stance was confident and self-assured. However, she exhibited an endearing shyness and vulnerability despite her outward demeanor.

Connection. Longing. He could never get enough of her.

What upsets you, Jenny? Is the reality of seeing me again breaking your heart, as much as it's breaking mine? We've lost so many years.

He stood and strode to a white rocking chair, lowering himself into it. He couldn't contain his restlessness. From his vantage point, the dog sat near the lobby door, keeping a watchful eye on Sebastian.

Christopher offered a wave, but Sebastian didn't see him. He was looking up at Maria. At something she said, he giggled.

The sun lowered another notch in the cloudless sky, shooting rays of soft light through the glass and promising a spectacular sunset. The slightly sweet scent of azaleas drifted through the air-conditioned room. He and Sebastian had clipped branches from a bush and arranged the bouquet in a vase. The memory of Jenny proclaiming azaleas as her favorite flower had never escaped him. Fate seemed to play a hand as she, coincidentally, had arrived on the island that same day.

He enjoyed doing activities with his son. He hoped that this raw, remote island would bring a promise of resolution, tranquility, and serenity.

Jenny stretched her arms over her head, then stood. "I am exhausted and more than ready to see my room."

"Up one flight of stairs. First door on your right."

"No elevator? I thought I spotted one on the other side of the stairs."

"That's our imaginary elevator. For now, there's no *working* elevator. We can't pinpoint what the issue is exactly." He accompanied her to the lobby, where she shouldered her tote bag while he retrieved her suitcase. "In the meantime, we'll climb the stairs. It's a good workout. Think of it as our way of promoting healthy living."

"Is everything else functioning properly?" she inquired as they climbed to the second floor.

"Mostly." He rubbed the back of his neck. "Unfortunately, hotel renovation is complicated."

She spun toward him when they reached the landing. "Don't tell me the lights in my room are out."

"No, the lights work fine." He handed her a key to her room. "Although the air conditioner might make a suspicious rattling sound, and the hot water doesn't seem to come out … hot."

Her eyebrows furrowed. "How is it coming out?"

"Lukewarm in the morning. Often cold. But hey, at least it adds character to the place."

She glanced around the hallway as if searching for a better explanation. "Christopher, I was looking forward to a relaxing soak in a hot bubble bath."

"We should resolve the problem by ... I wish I could give you a simple answer."

"Try me."

"It's a combination of factors."

"Like what?"

"Having employees who take naps during the day and workers who quit after their first hour on the job."

"When will someone fix the hot water?"

"Well, that's a mystery. I've tried calling in the plumber, the electrician, and even Anyika, the resident psychic, but so far, no luck."

At her scowl, he wrestled with the truth. A cold sweat trickled down the back of his neck. "I'm expecting by opening day."

CHAPTER 4

Time slipped through Christopher's fingers like sand. It was May, less than two months before the grand opening.

In his hotel suite, he showered and dressed in cargo shorts, a striped polo shirt, and sandals. He carried a folder of notes and ducked under plastic sheeting to avoid a ladder. He intended to swing by the lobby on the way to the patio.

Pausing, he reviewed his records from a recent phone conversation with Olive. Because of the five-hour time difference between Wales and Pink Coral Island, they scheduled their calls and video chats in advance.

Christopher had been overseeing renovations since January, finding them to be more chaotic than expected. The guest rooms were converted to king-sized suites featuring four-poster beds, premium white linens, flat-screen TVs, coffee, and hairdryers. He'd encountered several roadblocks, including ongoing plumbing problems and electrical and HVAC complications. While additional costs were unavoidable, navigating through them was tricky. The overrun was close to 30 percent and escalated with each passing hour.

As he entered the lobby, he admired the shiny grand piano taking up an entire corner. Delivering a piano from the mainland hadn't been easy, but it had been worth it. If only he could find a pianist. He and Olive had discussed hiring a keyboardist to provide live entertainment.

Christopher wanted to mix Mozart with show tunes, as visitors enjoyed margaritas and the lovely sunset. The flicker of lit, perfumed candles would create a delightful aura, carrying the spicy notes of cloves and cinnamon on the gentle breeze.

Despite Maria's efforts to find a pianist through a full-page ad in the Main Island Docket, they found no one.

An unseen stereo system was playing traditional Gullah songs with percussion accompaniment. He wondered where Jenny had tracked down the music, which wasn't readily available at any record shop.

Unlike him, she seemed more competent at going with the flow and managing the disorder. She mentioned she thought strict routines were stifling.

She certainly shouldn't worry about a stringent schedule here. Disarray was a normal occurrence, and rarely a day passed that Christopher's handful of workers didn't rush past him in a hurry or quit without notice.

Loud and chaotic power tools and drilling resounded. Disruptions of sawdust and debris happened frequently, and the rear section of the hotel was currently inaccessible.

Talk about stress.

He preferred tidiness and organization. The disciplined and uniform rhythm of his past military experiences resurfaced in his thoughts. Yes, that was his preference.

He strode through the open seating area. Jenny was overseeing hirings in the back room, and he hadn't expected her to be standing behind the service counter. She wore a long, flowy skirt with bold flowers and a light magenta shell. Her bare arms showed the beginnings of a honeyed tan.

He studied her flawless complexion, his gaze dawdling on the enticing contour of her lips. Her golden-blond hair lent a touch of brightness and sunshine to the beautiful May morning. Her green eyes were a remarkable contrast to her hair, and the singular combination created a breathtaking picture.

As he drew near the counter, she sang the opening measures of "Kumbaya" in a lilting soprano voice.

Maria appeared and yanked her headphones out of her ears. Her breath came in puffs, and her tank top and leggings were damp with sweat. She'd gone for a jog on the beach every day since she'd arrived.

"What's up with singing that?" Maria bumped Jenny's arm. "Are we supposed to gather around a campfire and toast marshmallows?"

"'Kumbaya' is a Gullah phrase," Jenny replied.

"Good morning, ladies," he greeted the women with a smile.

Maria swiped a hand through her sweaty bangs, sending droplets of perspiration flying. "Good morning."

"Morning. Praise the Lord." Jenny echoed a typical Gullah greeting.

He braced his elbow on the counter. "'Kumbaya' is a spiritual tune meaning 'come by here.' Harmony, peace, unity, and all that positive stuff."

"The song is sung here frequently," Jenny replied. "The Gullah say it is from their culture, although the original origin is disputed."

"This island is such a contrast between privileged and impoverished," Maria commented with a sigh.

"Property was pricey before everyone hightailed it back to civilization," Jenny added. "Many former residents wanted more modern conveniences."

"Ah, the simple pleasures of life, such as running water."

"Funny. Not." Jenny smiled. "Don't forget up-to-date luxuries like cars."

"Okay, then. That settles it," Maria said. "We prohibit horses and buggies from now on."

Christopher laughed. "Bicycles and walking are healthier modes of transportation, anyway."

Maria's lips flattened. "I've been thinking."

"Always dangerous," Christopher and Jenny declared in unison.

"I've come up with a couple of hotel slogans. Do you want to hear them?"

Jenny grinned. "Certainly."

"The first one is: *An Island Paradise Awaits at the Grand Michelangelo Hotel.*"

"Don't keep us in suspense," Christopher grinned. "What's the other?"

"*Relax in Style: The Grand Michelangelo Hotel—Where Every Moment is a Work of Art.*"

"I prefer the first," Christopher said.

Jenny leaned forward. "The second is my favorite."

Against a wall, an enormous clock chimed the morning hour. Carved into the timepiece was a mahogany tower depicting the schoolteacher's house. Mainlanders might think that peculiar, but there'd only ever been one teacher's residence.

Mr. Farrenway, respecting tradition, had told Anyika that he wouldn't live anywhere else. They painted the house blue, a tribute to the Gullah culture's *hain't blue*. Spirits didn't like water, and painting spaces blue to resemble water kept the spirits away.

Christopher had painstakingly enhanced the house with a screened porch.

Pink Coral Island boasted a long history. He hung black-

and-white photos of the old buildings, detailing the island's beginnings. Plantations and coveted cotton crops dotted the land. He pledged to honor the island and bring it to the attention of the world. He'd carry on their traditions because the Gullah preserved their African American culture more than any other community in the US.

"Busy morning?" He directed his question to Jenny.

"The phones are ringing off the hook, and the Internet has quit twice already. When it finally reconnects, the Wi-Fi is slow. Why?"

"Oh, it's a magical force we can't quite comprehend," he replied. "Some say it's the result of a curse put on the island by a disgruntled tourist. Others suggest it's the universe testing our patience."

"And what do you say, Christopher?"

He smiled. "It's temporary madness."

"So, everything will settle once we open, correct? Or am I not correct?"

"Well, if it isn't Miss Optimistic."

He glanced away from her glare. *Alrighty, that probably wasn't the appropriate response.*

He either needed to switch the topic or secure a safe hideout on the other side of the island.

Since their discussion on the day she arrived, Jenny had given him a wide berth, save for a fleeting bob of hello. He suspected that she would duck into another area of the hotel if she saw him coming, although he could never prove it.

Though his glimpses were quick, his senses always zoomed in on her.

Only her. Everything else around him would disappear.

Once, they'd run into each other in the hallway. She'd emerged from the breakroom with a graceful step and friendly grin as she greeted a recently hired maintenance person.

"Sorry!" Christopher sidestepped her. He'd been gripping a ceramic planter with both hands. He almost dropped it.

Jenny's grin had changed to frustration, and her eyes flashed with annoyance at seeing him, slicing a hole in his heart.

Maria, who stood adjacent and missed no person's emotion, no matter how slight, had offered him a supportive look. Maria had come to the rightful conclusion in a short while. He still had feelings for Jenny.

Love? No. He couldn't be falling in love with her again.

Love, Love, Love, a refrain from a song by the Beatles, played in his head.

Would his feelings for her vanish, the way some people hinted the Gullah culture was relegated to the past? Could he ever chase away his sadness over their lost decade?

Was it a mistake for him to stay?

No.

Christopher was a part owner of this hotel and wasn't going anywhere.

The island was significant to them both, as it had served as his summer sanctuary and her year-round home for many years. His son deserved the chance to immerse himself in the enchanting ambiance.

Enchanting.

Just like Jenny.

However, her curt tone and avoidance of eye contact were blatant indications that she wanted nothing to do with him. He couldn't come up with a valid excuse to schedule an official meeting with her, so things remained at a stalemate.

"Jenny and I love our fancy rooms, even if we're forced to take the fastest showers on the planet because the water is freezing." Maria's remark jolted Christopher back to the present. "Sometimes I wonder why we came."

"You applied for the job before I did," Jenny reminded. "We wanted more opportunity for advancement."

"The word 'island' momentarily sidetracked me," Maria said.

He had no intention of inserting himself into their conversation. If only he could find a licensed plumber.

He sauntered into the breakroom and poured himself a tall glass of orange juice. He took a long sip, feeling the cool liquid refresh his parched throat, then stepped into the lobby. Once outside, he fended off his frustration. Maybe it was the lush tropical surroundings or the energetic buzz of an exciting business venture, but his mood lightened with each step. Overhead, an osprey's wings spanned the sky with each turn and swoop, and the scenic view of the morning sun shimmering on the ocean encouraged him.

Maria materialized a short while later. The hem of her ankle-length skirt brushed against the edge of the beach, sending up small puffs of silvery sand.

"Cheers!" With a broad grin and gleaming eyes, she raised a crystal flute.

He set down his file folder beside his glass of juice. "You changed quickly."

"Yup, speaking of which, my luggage actually arrived."

"All because of the dependable ferry service." He grinned, then frowned at her glass. "What is that?"

"An orange juice mimosa." The sleeves of her flamboyant red top fluttered with her quick motion of lowering her glass. "Don't throw a fit because I'm drinking on the job."

"Does your drink have alcohol in it?"

She clinked her glass with his. "A little dabble of prosecco."

"Before nine o'clock in the morning?"

"I'm conducting daring experiments with recipes." She

waggled her eyebrows. "It just so happens that I rule over the realm of food and beverages."

He wanted to say more because an orange juice mimosa wasn't a daring recipe, but he kept his expression neutral. He had no desire to lecture an adult, especially one who harbored strong opinions and articulated them freely.

"In its heyday, this hotel was renowned for crab delights," he said.

"What's a crab delight?"

"Crabmeat salad on a fresh bun."

"It sounds like a fancy way of saying tuna salad." Maria bobbed her head. "Salifu mentioned it, and I thought he was just trying to impress me with his culinary knowledge. He insisted it was the only food capable of luring him away from beach parties."

"Beach parties? When?"

"After sunset. Some islanders meet and party. Our gatherings have mushroomed into quite the scene."

"Whereabouts on the beach?"

Her head tilted. "The sandy part."

These parties were a surprising disclosure to Christopher, as he rarely went anywhere after hours. However, word on the street was that Maria was a social butterfly, fluttering from one fun-filled gathering to another.

"She is like a carnival," Salifu had told Christopher. "Always with an extra attraction that leaves you breathless and wondering what comes next."

"Are these parties every night?" Christopher mimed a drinking motion.

"Are you taking a poll?"

He extended his coolest smile and navigated to a safer topic. "How are the advertising campaigns for the hotel going?"

71

"Hashtags and timing, tweeting and retweeting," she declared. "Have you checked social media lately?"

"The Internet here is unpredictable."

She gave a consoling smirk. "I don't want to divulge a company secret, but I guess I will."

"Please go on."

She lowered her voice. "I get a better Internet connection up in a tree."

"Helpful, but not at all convenient. You're telling me you're part monkey and part tech genius?" He grunted in disbelief. "No wonder the Internet is inconsistent. You're hoarding it."

"Ssh." She put a finger to her lips. "Trees are a favorite of mine. And somehow, I have to keep the stampede of islanders with computers away. They're constantly trying to get their Instagram fix."

"Big job, I'm sure."

"You have no idea. Just call me the Internet Tree Whisperer. It's a tough assignment, but someone's gotta do it." She gave a humorous wink. "While up in the tree, I created a hotel profile and uploaded some magnificent coastal shots for our website."

"Don't forget an old-fashioned press release in the Main Island Docket."

She stood up to her full height, although, at nearly six feet, three inches, he towered over her petite frame.

"I'll stay in my lane, Christopher," she said. "You stay in yours."

He stepped backward.

Alrighty then.

However, she *was* proficient in social media. The problem was that most of the islanders and many mainlanders were not.

She motioned to Sebastian, who occupied a table on the

patio's outskirts. He perched over a checkerboard set with paper, a pencil, and a glass of tomato juice. He played checkers against himself and listed the moves.

A fluffy white kitten lounged beneath his chair.

"Where's your gigantic terror of a dog?" Maria sluffed off cat hair from a patio chair using a lint brush conveniently placed at a nearby table.

"He is enjoying life in his air-conditioned suite," Christopher joked. "He's a late riser."

"Sebastian is an excellent player." Maria returned the brush to its place on the table. "He's beaten me four times since I arrived."

Christopher beamed. "He loves the game, and it occupies him and keeps him out of mischief."

"Now if only your dog played, as opposed to knocking over furniture."

"He's friendly and playful. It's hard not to watch him and smile."

She tipped up her chin. "What are you doing about school for him?"

"Scooby-Doo has the IQ of a two-year-old. Math is a challenge, though."

She smiled. "Your son. Not the dog."

"I'm homeschooling him for the rest of this year, and we complete an hour of assignments each morning. Thanks for keeping track of him when I'm not available."

"My pleasure. Jenny spends her spare time with him, too. During lunch, they settle at a table in the breakroom, and she shows him how to fold towel animals."

"She does?" Christopher hadn't noticed. The number of tasks needed to get the hotel going innundated him, but the news lightened his burden.

Maria observed him with sly speculation. "What's in that folder that's got you so unbalanced?"

"Nothing. Just some paperwork."

"Okay." She smirked. "However, the two people in the world you care most about—your son and the woman you—"

"Let's not go there," he interrupted, cutting her off. He knew where that sentence was headed. "I have a meeting with some hires, and I'm already behind schedule."

"I won't mention her name," Maria whispered.

He looked around the patio, his restless feet betraying his unease. His feelings for Jenny were too powerful, and the nature of their relationship was too unsure. He didn't want to discuss the fragility of their connection with her closest friend. "Anything else?"

"Oh, about thirty more pages of things, but they can wait." Maria downed her mimosa in three gulps. "You're a guy who is always on the go. Busy, busy, busy."

"I need to get started on my next project," he said.

"Which is?"

"The hot water issue."

"What about the menu issue?"

He clutched the folder closer to his chest. "What about it?"

"Well, initially, I planned to serve ravioli and meatballs as dinner options, but I'm a pescatarian."

"You are? You're responsible for all the food served here."

"So?"

"So, you're not exactly building my trust."

However, she was evidently successful in the beverage department, and he imagined happy customers at the bar when the hotel opened.

"How long have you been a vegetarian?" he asked.

"Pescatarian. The second we landed, I made up my mind, and that's a rare occurrence. I mean, I don't have the bandwidth to decide what to wear daily, but for food decisions, I'm all in."

74

He contemplated his reply. There were an abundance of responses to choose from. He settled with, "Ah, that explains your preference for holding a glass instead of a fork."

"Jenny remains adamant about seafood," Maria went on, disregarding his observation.

"I'm curious. Can a pescatarian indulge in a cup of clam chowder?"

"Absolutely."

He tried to contain his smile. "This island is right up your alley, then."

"In Italy, I learned how to prepare homemade fettuccini, greens and beans, and ravioli." As she spoke, her fingers illustrated the art of pasta-making.

"Sounds ideal for Venice, but I wouldn't recommend that type of selection here," he replied.

"Jenny shares your views." Maria waved her hand, her vibrant red fingernails adding flair to her statement. "Italian peasant dishes are not only delicious, but also quite economical."

"What about the Gullah influence Jenny is striving for?"

"Can't we offer both types of cuisine?"

"We can try." He spread his arms far apart to illustrate a large menu.

"Shipping any list of groceries is a daily experiment in patience, and we're not fully operational yet," Maria said. "If we can't get pasta, how do you expect us to acquire seafood?"

"Anywhere on the island." He tempered his response with a grin. He didn't want to overwhelm her. "Transport hiccups will ease as the temperature increases and the ocean is calmer. Gumbo and okra are also staples."

"As well as lima beans with slices of ham hock, goes the lecture from Jenny. Done here?" She indicated his nearly empty orange juice glass.

"I guess so."

"Alright, I'll bring it back to the kitchen." Maria copied his grin before stepping past.

As Christopher approached Sebastian, the boy radiated an ear-to-ear smile.

"Hi, Dad!" His back straightened. The kid had impeccable posture.

They'd eaten breakfast together—juicy grapes and fluffy, buttery pancakes. Sebastian had been a sticky mess, with syrup smeared on his hands and chin.

No one would have guessed it. He'd freshened up at the hotel's sink in record time.

Sebastian was neat and conscientious and insisted on dressing himself. He meticulously combed his brown hair. Today he'd selected a checkered shirt and navy-blue cotton shorts, free of any wrinkles or stains. He displayed poise beyond his seven years and was a delight to be around. He captured the epitome of childhood—innocence, yet his thirst for learning was boundless.

"Look at this!" Sebastian pointed to a folded gray towel resembling an elephant, arranged on the chair beside him. "Miss Jenny made it for me."

"Nice." Christopher placed his file folder on the table, bent down, and examined the towel. "I like the trunk and the head."

"Me, too, though the snake is still the best. Miss Jenny showed me how to fold it, but I still need more practice."

"Snowball and Scooby-Doo are starting to get along." Sebastian flapped his hand toward the kitten. "At least she doesn't hiss at the dog anymore. I'm glad we introduced them a little at a time."

Snowball had wandered into the hotel a few days earlier. Despite Christopher's initial objections, they adopted her when no one else claimed her.

Sebastian suffered from a mild case of asthma, and they

traveled nowhere without his inhaler close at hand. As a former asthmatic himself, Christopher understood that asthma could be serious and must not be taken lightly.

Choosing hypoallergenic animals was another challenge. Fortunately, Scooby-Doo, being a giant schnauzer, was hypoallergenic. Unfortunately, a cat was not.

Sebastian's strong-willed personality meant that attempting to change his mind was futile. Christopher had finally agreed to keep Snowball, provided she stayed outdoors, and Sebastian washed his hands after he petted her.

Christopher got to his feet as Scooby-Doo galloped over. He toppled over a beach umbrella stand before plopping himself onto Sebastian's toes.

Affectionate and good-natured, the dog wagged his tiny tail. He didn't appear thrilled that Snowball had become part of their little family. An open book regarding his emotions, he guarded his food and toys and exhibited a reluctance to be near the kitten. When she ventured too close, he raised his hackles, and his tail stiffened.

Christopher hoped the animals would develop a friendship with positive reinforcement and patience.

Scooby-Doo burrowed his nose into Sebastian's face, craving attention. In response, Sebastian laughed and scratched his ears.

The kitten stuck low to the ground and darted away, seeking refuge under a faraway chair. She opened a distrustful eye and glared at the dog.

Okay, well, the dog and the kitten weren't friends quite yet.

CHAPTER 5

A group of boisterous men sitting at an outside patio table beckoned Christopher over. They downed buckets of coffee, and a fresh carafe rested in the center of the table. Gullah pecan brownies and nut bread provided by Sun-Kissed Treats were being devoured at a rapid rate.

"You're late for the meeting that you arranged," one man called out.

"I'm coming." Christopher strode toward them and eyed the baked goods. What a shame Sun-Kissed Treats was in its last days.

Reminiscences transported him back to when he and Jenny were teens. Jenny had spent hours measuring ingredients for pudding in Anyika's tiny kitchen. The kitchen showcased brilliant yellow cabinets, wooden shelves, and a dish rack next to the sink. A solitary window allowed in a stream of cheerful, natural light.

After a lengthy taste test, Christopher had praised Jenny, and Anyika concurred.

"I've graduated, Christopher, to creating my own recipe," Jenny *had laughingly declared. "I added peaches, real cream, and butter to*

78

the bread pudding." She'd forked off a piece, still warm from the oven, and urged him to take a bite. The room was alive with laughter and the aroma of home-cooked desserts.

They unanimously agreed, after devouring half the pan of pudding, that traditional dishes were best.

Christopher yearned for the warmth of Anyika's kitchen and his childhood days with Jenny.

"Aren't you going to join us, man?" Salifu shouted at Christopher.

Salifu was a cousin of a cousin who lived on the island. Two other men seated at the patio table, Jah and Lomboi, were siblings from another family. Jah was thirty, Christopher's age, and Lomboi was eighteen. Lomboi was a problematic youth who idolized Jah, his older brother.

Lomboi repeatedly trespassed into the restricted areas of the hotel and shoplifted on the mainland. He'd never graduated from high school.

Christopher rationalized that providing a job was a beneficial first step in addressing Lomboi's inappropriate behavior. A steady income would boost his self-esteem, ending his stealing and allowing him to pursue constructive activities.

Times were tough, employment was hard to find, and Christopher was pleased to hire the men.

Another local sitting at the table, Francis Grant, had joined Christopher in his youth for the odd jobs of painting homes and fixing screens. A wide-brimmed straw hat shaded the grooves on his face. Francis appeared older now, but then again, everyone got older. The clock was ticking for each of them, and rather loudly.

Jah and Lomboi enthusiastically debated the ideal arrangement of extra chairs at the African Baptist Church, a historic landmark on the island.

Christopher found the Gullah had chosen to live in isolation, deeply rooted in African culture.

As he advanced to the table, an empty chair, along with a steaming mug of coffee, awaited him. He set down his folder. "Hi, guys. It's a pleasure to meet you newcomers."

Lomboi's flinty gaze, remarkably jaded for someone so youthful, countered, "None of us are newcomers.

"I mean, you're new to the staff."

"What about us old-timers?" Jah scratched his chin and turned to Christopher.

Christopher chuckled in response. "I'm an old-timer, too, but your brother isn't." He shook hands all around and then seated himself. "Welcome to the Grand Michelangelo Hotel. I hired several of you as either bellboys and porters or for housekeeping and wait staff."

The siblings burst into insolent laughter. "Housekeeping? You're kidding, right?"

Men's labor versus women's labor. The clash of traditional practices and values revealed a struggle that refused to fade, even in the face of changing times.

Christopher debated how to respond.

"What do you think of the Sea Lion's season dis year?" Francis interjected, thankfully steering the conversation in a safe direction. His eyes reflected a wealth of wisdom and experience. "They're a great team."

The Sea Lions status as the varsity high school football team on the mainland prompted all the men to watch them closely. Football was invariably a popular topic.

"Their top senior player graduated and is attending college out of state," Christopher said.

Salifu sneered, waving his arms in disbelief. "How are they supposed to replace a star athlete? That kid put in a lot of effort."

Case in point? These were honest men of every age, adhering to their family principles. Hardworking and refreshingly straightforward.

Christopher turned to Rusty, a veteran army buddy, hoping to engage him. The man contrasted so differently from the young, energetic guy Christopher had once served with. Rusty's blue eyes peered out from behind thick horn-rimmed eyeglasses. Injured during battle, he was not blind but had difficulty seeing.

The glasses, combined with Rusty's sparse gray hair, gave him an Elvis Costello look.

Buddies had speculated that Rusty was a musician, a pianist who had once played in Memphis, Tennessee, clubs, yet he mentioned nothing. Briefly, Christopher wondered if he should show him the piano in the lobby, but, of course, Rusty must've seen it.

An idea emerged. Perhaps he could encourage Rusty to play for the hotel guests.

Christopher choked back a quiet laugh. Like that would ever happen.

As usual, Rusty shifted, as if wishing he could disappear. He finished his glass of juice, then drummed his fingers on his thighs. From what Oliver had told Christopher, Rusty had experienced a mental breakdown.

Taking in Rusty's weather-beaten face, the creases at his temples, and his rough cheeks, Christopher battled the ache in his gut. Rusty was the most exceptional soldier imaginable and a guy the other men always relied on. He was courageous, selfless, and honorable.

"I'm on your side," Christopher had reassured him when a tense and irritable Rusty arrived on the island, carrying only a timeworn backpack. "Thanks for agreeing to my request to join us."

No response. Just a grunt.

"I was stunned to read dis press release." Francis jolted Christopher out of his musings with a firm clap on the back. He raised his reading glasses, perched them on his nose, and scrutinized Christopher with a probing, dark-eyed assessment.

"What press release?"

"Our resident math whiz has succumbed to the magnetism of the island."

"Are you referring to me?" Christopher joked.

"Who else?"

"I've hardly seen you since I arrived," Christopher said. "Where have you been?"

"Busy doing what I do best. Helping the missus." Francis patted his bulging waistline. "My wife is feeding me too many fried oysters and red field peas lately."

"From what I remember, she's a first-rate cook."

Francis motioned toward the lobby. "The pretty kitchen manager might find my wife's Gullah recipes and suggestions useful."

"You mean Maria?" Christopher smiled, enjoying the exchange of light-hearted banter.

Francis nodded. "The very same."

Francis was a devoted friend if he liked you. A big *if*, for he held only a few people in high regard. Christopher assumed that being Francis's friend gave him a decided edge.

"How's your father?" Francis asked.

"He passed away a while ago." Christopher suppressed the hollowness in his chest whenever his father was mentioned. Despite his faults and blustery ways, Christopher missed him. Who among them was perfect? Certainly not Christopher.

Regrettably, his father had never met Sebastian, his grandson and namesake.

"No word about your mother?"

Christopher swallowed his resentment. "Nope."

"You were just a little kid when she vanished," Francis said.

"Yup." A broad range of emotions pulsed through Christopher.

Sadness. Anger. Abandonment. Confusion. Why did she leave? She'd caused him and his father tremendous heartache.

Christopher searched social media and found she could be alive, used a different surname, and traveled a lot. Perhaps it was really her, perhaps not. Regardless, he'd never caught up with this woman.

He explored the famous graveyard near the Baptist church, taking in the unmarked graves and the smell of wildflowers. Colossal oak trees surrounded the graves, their branches extending like skeletal fingers adorned with wispy moss. As he walked, the ground yielded beneath his steps, its softness and sponginess a reminder of the recent rain.

He wrestled with his conflicting emotions in a constant battle between resentment and longing, anger and love.

The thought crossed his mind that she might have passed away. In some twisted sense, that may have been better than her abandoning them.

He shook off the sting of pain and quickly dismissed the notion. What he truly longed for was her existence, the chance to lay eyes on her once more.

Ultimately, he reassured himself that it was all inconsequential. She had scarcely been a presence in his life, even though, deep down, he acknowledged the void she had left behind—forever hoping for completion.

Much of his memory of his mother was a blank space. In flashes, he summoned up a lovely woman with caramel-colored hair who hugged him and spoke in a jittery voice. She'd fretted about his asthma. She'd been anxious about their meager lifestyle.

Often, she'd sit alone with a pen and paper. He was unfamiliar with her words, and his father mumbled that she liked to write, particularly poetry. However, her poems were rough and melancholic, penned in her messy scrawl. Perhaps they were a mirror of her somber perspective.

In her last weeks on the island, she'd worn an amulet, an intricate necklace crafted from shells and beads, a gift from an ancient woman from the Lowcountry. The woman claimed that the amulet had the power to bring peace and happiness.

For a time, it seemed to have delivered on its promise.

Christopher recalled the shifts in his mother's attitude and the serenity in their home. She'd even sat with him and encouraged him to write. Sometimes, they'd compose verses together—mostly poems about the island.

His father referred to the amulet as a trinket, dismissing any superstitions. He viewed his wife's anxiety as a weakness and attributed her edginess to mere nerves. He was down-to-earth and not one to accept the power of shells and beads.

That was it. That was all. And soon afterward, Christopher's mother went missing.

It left many questions.

Speculations arose; she had been grappling with personal difficulties, leading her to abandon her family in search of help. But where? The puzzling absence of a note added to the mystery, and to make matters more perplexing, her clothing and cherished amulet had vanished along with her.

Afterward, Christopher observed changes in his father's behavior. He no longer shaved and spent hardly any time with Christopher. He withdrew, pausing regularly, as if considering his words before speaking. He'd once tended a small garden and didn't anymore.

As he aged, his hands shook more and more until he needed to ask Christopher to pop the caps off his beers. Right up until the end of his life, he wore his wedding band, though he never spoke of Christopher's mother again.

Francis glanced at Sebastian, who was engrossed in his checkers game and taking notes. "You traveled with your son and dog from Alaska? Is the climate cold enough for you up there in the Arctic?"

Christopher chuckled. "In the winter, yes."

"How long does the winter last?"

"Six months."

"I don't handle frigid temperatures well." Francis cradled his hands around his mug. "I'll take warmth over cold any day."

"Me, too." Christopher shuffled the papers in his file folder. "I'm more awake and alert."

But there were other motivations.

Here, Christopher hoped to uncover the truth about his mother's abrupt disappearance. He had no desire to reach out on social media.

Whenever he roamed the familiar paths of the island, he remembered the amulet and the talk of the ancient Gullah woman. Serenity and understanding would wash over him, and he instinctively realized that he was going in the right direction.

Francis topped off his mug with more coffee and a splash of sugar. "Town gossip has it you're divorced."

"My divorce from my ex, Jocelyn, was finalized less than a year ago while we were still living in Alaska, and then I retired from the military," Christopher confirmed. "She rents an apartment in California."

Which was, thankfully, on the opposite side of the country.

"Along the way, you inherited a kitten and a cute kid."

"Yup."

"And a giant dog."

Christopher smiled. "Everyone needs a rescue dog."

"I prefer a cat," Francis said over the rim of his mug. "They're lower maintenance."

"As of now, I have all three."

Francis pressed his palms together and declared loud enough for every man at the table to overhear. "Chatter around here says you're the latest owner of dis swanky hotel."

Did anyone on this island ever mind their own business? Rumors often ran ahead of the truth.

Christopher sifted through the volley of questions thrown at him by the other men and fused his features into an unreadable frown. "Where'd you hear that?"

"Oh, here and there. The Gullah chatter, especially our womenfolk."

"Fatu is the ultimate queen of gossip." Salifu chuckled, taking over the conversation. "If there's any juicy news to be had, she's got the scoop. Her information network is second to none."

One man raised his mug, then seized the remaining pecan brownie. A solitary slice of nut bread remained, tempting Christopher like a forbidden treasure. He plotted to smuggle it back to his suite to savor while poring over the ledgers.

"You and a wealthy guy from England closed on the hotel deal last year," Francis was saying.

Olive lived in Wales, but there was no point in correcting Francis.

"I hope you don't mind me prying, but are you a part of the millionaires' club like myself?" Francis quipped.

"Nope, sorry to disappoint. The only club I'm part of is the 'living paycheck to paycheck' club," Christopher replied with a wink.

Rusty, sitting on Christopher's left, muttered a disparaging remark about wealthy people and lit a cigarette. Christopher chose not to tell Rusty that no smoking was allowed since they were outside. No need to rattle the guy's short-tempered chains.

"I dream of being rich." Lomboi picked at a callous on his palm. "Like you, Christopher. You must have a lot of smackeroos."

"You were a frail kid, with bony knees sticking out from raggedy jeans." Francis chuckled and pointed at Christopher's arms. "Today you're a self-made entrepreneur."

Christopher chuckled back and performed a flexing motion with his biceps. "Hey, I guess I've come a long way."

He painfully remembered the mocking from other students over his ill-fitting clothes. Sultry hot summers with no air conditioning and sleeping on squeaky mattresses with pointy springs that poked into his arms.

"Living day to day for a paycheck isn't so bad," Christopher's father had reassured him. He'd never prospered in any vocation, even though he'd tried every profession known to man.

Christopher vowed early on that he would be different. He'd attend college. Poverty would never be a chokehold, and Sebastian wouldn't experience the same type of childhood. His ex had changed the trajectory of Christopher's life, but not forever. Finally, he was making progress.

Financial victory was a goal, and he'd put in all his investments to attain it. Some of his wise moves were in stocks, diversifying his portfolio, and saving for a rainy day. Despite many trials, he refused to allow his history to define him. He had sufficient savings to maintain a reasonable lifestyle for himself and his son, provided the hotel was a winner.

However, a nagging thought occurred.

What if the hotel failed? What if he drained his entire bank account?

"Now why did you do such a reckless thing and purchase dis mess with shattered windows and walls about to cave in?" Francis nudged a lighthearted jab into Christopher's side.

Christopher was thankful he and Olive had purchased the

hotel at a steal price, which suited Christopher's plans perfectly. Over the years, the hotel had witnessed three owners who had invested substantial sums, totaling hundreds of thousands of dollars. It operated as an exclusive club for private investors owned by its tight-lipped proprietors. The third ownership venture was set back by a fire, forcing the hotel no choice but to become a budget inn.

Unfortunately, families opted for more convenient mainland accommodations.

"Who is gonna book a room on an island that doesn't even claim a full-scale grocery store?" Francis cajoled. "Tourists will think that we're tryin to promote a new fad diet where you survive solely on salt water and seaweed."

Christopher poured a second cup of coffee. "With any luck, folks will flock here for relaxation. This place will catapult to stardom."

"Geese flock. Folks come with der wallets open."

"Breaking bulletin." Christopher smiled. "I've heard through the grapevine that you've become a property mogul and bought a couple of oceanfront cottages to refurbish and rent out. Are you taking applications for tenants yet?"

Francis chuckled and wiped the crumbs off his chin. "Real estate here is selling for unbelievably low prices. I accumulated modest savings over time and couldn't resist the opportunity."

"Did you miss the memo? The last person who rented a place on a deserted island ended up talking to a volleyball for four years."

"You and I?" Francis smiled and lifted his mug. His third, at least. He drank a ton of caffeine. "We are definitely unwise."

"All it takes is a hefty loan and every cent of your nest egg."

"You're an idealist. But tell me, how do you envision this

hotel of yours transforming the community? You know this island has struggled economically for years."

Christopher leaned back, taking a deep breath as he collected his thoughts. "Tourism is its lifeline, and there's so much untapped potential. Creating an exceptional experience will attract more tourists, increase revenue, and generate more jobs."

Francis nodded slowly and set down his mug. "What about the environmental impact? We just can't bulldoze through nature and disregard the delicate balance of the island."

"You're right. Any success will go hand in hand with the island's preservation. We've invested in renewable energy and waste management services. I'm ever mindful of the hotel's responsibility to the community."

"Then congratulations are for both of us. To folly and audacious dreams." Francis raised his mug for a toast, and the men clinked mugs, the sound resonating with the weight of their shared vision.

Francis plucked the remaining slice of nut bread from the wicker basket and indulged in a healthy bite.

Perhaps Jenny could whip up another batch? Christopher's thought was fleeting and promptly disappeared. He could only imagine her snappy retort before she opted to strangle him.

"We're both business owners." Christopher cradled his mug and took a final draught of coffee. He'd mapped out his strategy and calculated the risks. He intertwined any success with the well-being of the islanders.

Reality rudely interrupted the enthusiasm of the men.

Foreclosure.

"I love this island." He focused on the glittering turquoise ocean waters. "The people, the scenery. It's all amazing. We can turn this hotel into something truly remarkable."

He was dedicated to bringing career opportunities and hope back to the community.

"I love the island, too." Francis looked around at the others seated at the table and nodded in agreement with himself. "The same goes for everyone. Ain't that right, folks?"

The men rumbled their assent. All except Rusty, who took a couple of drags on his cigarette, then extinguished it with the heel of his scuffed shoe.

"Together, we're going to create a legacy, guys." Christopher stood. "Well, notify me if you have questions, because training begins soon."

"What is there to learn?" Lomboi let out a small laugh. "I'm not saying I'm the king of this island, but what could you possibly teach us?"

"Everything," Christopher replied. They were all inexperienced. "To begin with, can anyone recommend a good plumber?"

Every man shook his head in tandem. "Nope."

"No connections? None of you?"

Francis folded his arms on the table. "We don't like to try new things."

Plumbing was hardly a novel concept, but why argue?

"My hut has an efficient kitchen and television." Salifu thrust a fist into the air. "Once, the huts only had a tiny kitchenette and a changing area. Praise God because circumstances have already improved, and I'm dancing for joy."

Christopher sensed the undeniable beat of optimism. A positive and uplifting environment fostered team loyalty and camaraderie. And, as Olive often reminded, prioritizing the employees' well-being ultimately advanced the bottom line.

"Meeting adjourned." Christopher clicked his stack of papers on the table.

What meeting? Coffee, pastries, and talking sports? He

hadn't so much as opened the file and would accomplish nothing at this rate.

He was on island time. Everything progressed slowly.

Viewing the glorious beach, he choked down his misgivings for all he'd missed over the past ten years while he was away. He always regarded the island as his true home, even if he hadn't appreciated its beauty during his adolescent days.

He offered a hushed prayer of thanksgiving.

"So, what truly brought you back here?" Francis indicated the hotel. "Besides dis sizable bank loan that you'll be paying on for the next hundred years."

"I wanted the perfect place to raise my son." Making a direct beeline to Sebastian, Christopher tenderly patted his soft brown hair. "We could ride our bikes over to the Drifting Sands in a couple of hours and eat lunch," he said.

Christopher had secured a beach cruiser bicycle with wide handlebars and balloon tires to glide over the sand. The flared fenders on Sebastian's shiny purple bike kept the water away, and training wheels were a relic of the past. His son was growing up quickly.

Sebastian perked up in his seat. "My favorites over there are hamburgers and French fries."

"I'll order the burger and fries as well," Christopher said.

"Okay, Dad." The boy peered down at his checkerboard again.

"Looks like Jenny, your old girlfriend, showed up here, too." Francis joined Christopher as he headed for the lobby. "She is as gorgeous now as when she was a teen. Thin and tall—she could be a model."

"We were friends," Christopher stated.

Francis sprang into step beside him. "You two were attached at the hip."

"Your memory is remarkable."

"Did she ever marry?"

"Nope."

"I wonder why she's here?"

"Coincidence." Christopher managed a faint smile. "It shocked me to see her."

"Is she off-limits? This is a small island."

"To a guy like you? Definitely."

"I've been hitched to my fine-lookin wife for ages." Francis chuckled. "But as far as I can tell, the schoolteacher is riding solo."

"So, he's single?" Christopher lowered his voice.

"He takes the ferry to the mainland most weekends and travels whenever there's a school vacation. No mention of a woman, but we've all wondered."

Christopher raked a hand through his hair. "I haven't met the guy yet."

Mr. Evan Farrenway. Christopher intended to meet him soon.

"All I'm suggesting is don't mess things up with Jenny this time," Francis said. "The word is that you split up with her ten years ago and shattered her heart."

"Who are you, Dear Abby? For the record, we were both in high school, and the breakup was mutual."

"You have a golden opportunity now. She's here, and you're here. What else do you need? A thunderbolt from the sky?"

"Francis, my heart can only take so much." Christopher tapped his chest lightly with his fist. "Jenny is trampling on it every chance she gets."

"I fancy Maria, the pretty party girl with short black hair and dark-olive eyes." Salifu caught up with them. "We met on the ferry. I see her at night."

"So, the story goes," Christopher mumbled.

"Is she married? She won't give me an answer."

At Salifu's offhand inquiry, Rusty's head jerked up. He

trailed the men by a few paces with a shuffling, halting gait. He pinched a cigarette between his lips.

"You're a likable guy, Salifu." Francis gave an off-key whistle. "What woman can resist you?"

"Not a one." Salifu waved his index finger in mock seriousness. "They all realize I'm a confirmed bachelor who plays the field."

Francis delightedly briefed Christopher on the multitude of beauties who often surrounded Salifu.

"If you find someone who truly captures your heart, don't hesitate," Christopher advised.

"Sage advice from the divorced guy with a kid." Tongue-in-cheek amusement glinted in Francis's eyes. "All these beautiful single women are on our enchanting island. Thank the Gullah magic for bringing us together."

"No such thing." Christopher stifled a laugh. "You can't possibly believe any of those folk tales."

"I do indeed. Don't you?" Rusty spoke up, causing Christopher to whirl around.

"Gullah magic is in the very air we breathe." Rusty quieted his tone. "But not in a spooky way. The spirits are understanding and reassuring."

"I'm sorry, but I find it hard to accept any of this." Christopher's forehead creased. "This notion is simply absurd."

"Witness it for yourself, my friends." With an exaggerated motion, Francis drew everyone's attention upward. His voice grew more animated. "When you've lived for as many seasons as I have, you'll come to learn anything is possible. Mystical energy is everywhere, in the sound of the waves, the sunsets, and the grains of sand. This place is like living on an entirely different planet."

CHAPTER 6

*P*ink Coral Island, years earlier.

An aged Gullah woman sat in a rocking chair on the porch of her tiny, weathered cottage. Her reputation preceded her as a fountain of wisdom, with deep roots in the region's heritage and culture. Guided by duty and reverence for her ancestors, she embraced the role of a mentor and an influence for those in need. She understood their challenges, having lived through her own trials. She found purpose in helping others overcome their obstacles.

Her cottage was near a sandy beach, choked by lofty grass and a few trees. Two rocky outcroppings sheltered it. Despite its age, the home was sturdy and habitable.

Her gnarled hands braided a necklace, an amulet of shells and beads honoring the traditions of her ancestors. Preserving her cultural heritage was important to her. This amulet was special, fashioned from the same materials her forefathers used to banish evil spirits and invite good luck. It symbolized protection and acted as a safeguard against negative influences.

She'd waited for the right person to come along and receive it, someone in need of its power. The human desire for tranquility, finding one's destined path, was strong in every individual.

As she crafted the amulet, the old woman reflected on her conversation with Mrs. Drake, who had approached her for help, seeking stability. Although her heart was troubled, she kept her resilience. She worried about her asthmatic son and was unhappy because of an impoverished lifestyle with a husband she didn't love.

"I am tied by the expectations of others." Mrs. Drake looked down at her feet, her mutterings barely above a whisper.

Velvety and floaty, deep, yet fragile, and lightly battered by a sun that had made its way across many skies.

The Gullah woman thought of little else as she envisioned Mrs. Drake. She trusted the amulet would bring her peace, just as it had brought peace to those who came before her. The amulet signified a willingness to seek defense against real or perceived dangers.

With a satisfied confirmation, the Gullah woman finished tying the necklace and placed it in a woven sweetgrass basket. Then she set off down the dirt road toward Mrs. Drake's home. All around her, the atmosphere was charged with reverence for the customs and beliefs that had shaped the island's identity.

An hour later, waves crashed against the shore when she met Mrs. Drake on the beach. Carefully, she moved through the sand, mindful not to disturb the fragile natural surroundings. The air seemed to carry whispers of ancestral wisdom and stories.

She placed the amulet in the palm of Mrs. Drake's hand,

closing her fingers and gently encircling it. Mrs. Drake's eyes, intense blue and alert, exhibited a quiet strength that the Gullah woman admired.

Hesitant at first and unconvinced, Mrs. Drake fastened the amulet around her neck. "I'm grateful for your kindness." Tears threatened to spill. "But can you assure me that the necklace truly holds any power? When my husband learns of this, he will be furious. He is a man of logic and reason," Mrs. Drake lamented, her voice tinged with worry and frustration. The consequences of her choices were uncertain, adding to her apprehension.

The root of the conflict between her and her husband was their divergent desires and priorities. She yearned for something beyond reasoning, a fuller satisfaction outside her current situation. Exploring other interests caused tension in their relationship. She feared her actions would strain her marriage and create an irreparable rift. Still, she hoped that by pursuing her passions, she could somehow find the happiness she craved.

"Have patience." The Gullah woman gently touched her arm, conveying understanding, comfort, and a powerful bond. "This amulet will ease your troubles and soothe your concerns."

"I've stayed on the island too long. I have other interests, other loves." Mrs. Drake swiped at her tears, her emotions raw and conflicted. She was challenged in emotional, social, and financial ways that drove her to change. "Though the idea of leaving my son crushes my soul."

The Gullah woman paused. A pregnant pause. "He will grow up and someday find happiness here. He is capable and will thrive."

A pitiless wind rustled the reeds of the marshlands. As if replying to her words, they vocalized a timeless song, a dialogue in which the active universe played a part in the unfolding circumstances. The wind was ruthless, and the world harsh, yet the reeds still sang, inspiring endurance and providing strength.

"I'll try to be a better mother. I will keep striving to learn, even if I fail." Mrs. Drake's eyes were drawn to the endless horizon with awe and wonder, the constant invitation to explore. She yearned for a point of purpose outside her expectations. Beyond, she hoped to embark on a personal and transformational voyage. "I'll keep the amulet close."

If only she could live up to her ideals. If only she could accept her imperfections. If only she had the strength needed to endure life.

"Be grateful for this island, its fortitude, and the true meaning of love." The Gullah woman's forgiving tone expressed reassurance. "No matter what the future holds, consider that time is precious and finite, regardless of your decision."

Their paths had intertwined. Two women, with two distinct backgrounds, had bridged the gap of different cultures to come together in mutual respect and appreciation.

CHAPTER 7

On a sunny morning a week later, Sebastian scurried across the sandy beach, his arms swinging freely at his sides. Carefree, bursting with energy, and frequently on the move, he explored his surroundings. His little legs were often at a trot, an attempt to keep up with his unquenchable curiosity.

Carrying a metal bucket, Francis strode beside him, pointing out every landmark along the way. Whenever Sebastian stumbled upon an unusual pebble or rock, he marveled at it with open-mouthed wonder. In response, Francis gave a nod of acknowledgment, and Sebastian eagerly dropped the object into the bucket. Looking up at Francis with hero worship in his eyes, Sebastian clasped his hand and fell in step beside him.

The dog accompanied them, barking alongside. Robust and frisky, he chased after sticks thrown by either Francis or Sebastian. A dog the size of Scooby-Doo required loads of exercise and relished the outdoors.

Christopher opted to type on his computer at a table near the pool, immersing himself in the digital world. The weather was pleasant and his outfit was relaxed—cotton shorts, sandals, and a tan-colored polo shirt.

He took in a breath of fresh air, revitalizing and refreshing. Waves thundered ashore, creating a consistent soundtrack. The sun had risen above the horizon, casting a golden glimmer on the sand and water.

From time to time, Sebastian held up a cuttlefish bone or dead coral for Christopher to see. "Look, Dad, here's a beautiful seashell. Mr. Grant said it's a symbol of good luck."

Although he didn't believe in symbols, Christopher dipped his head in approval, a mixture of pride and tenderness flowing through him. This intense love he felt for his son kindled a fierce protectiveness.

And nostalgia. He reflected on his own childhood running down that same beach. How quickly time passed.

He went back to his computer to finalize the extensive inventory of hotel repairs slated to be completed by opening day.

While he sipped a glass of iced tea, his gaze rested on Jenny. The sun shone on her bare shoulders, her hair blowing lazily in the wind.

Earlier, she'd taken a seat on the far edge of the patio, conversing with a gray-haired woman settled across from her. The woman slouched, and her responses to Jenny's questions were brief.

Jenny was desperate for applicants for the housekeeping supervisor position.

"Don't look in her direction again," he instructed himself. Be a responsible adult.

He was inevitably drawn back to her, unable to resist.

She looked gorgeous in a full-length gauze skirt and sleeveless cotton blouse, barely skimming her midriff. She fastened her hair with a silk scrunchie, emphasizing her stunning features—wide-set green eyes, lush black lashes, and desirable red lips. Her slim curves were evident in the thin linen fabric of her clothing.

He extended a friendly head bob in her direction, coupled with a charming smile. She didn't respond, her mouth drawn in a tight, anxious line.

Hmm. No sign of recognition because she hadn't seen him. She had more important matters on her mind.

He bided his time when the interview finished. Frustrated with himself for his attraction to her, he tidied up his ledgers and refocused on his computer.

The gray-haired woman rose, folded an application, and stuffed it in her oversized purse. Jenny also stood, and the women shook hands, although the older woman's handshake was less than enthusiastic. She ambled away, slinging the purse over her shoulders.

Christopher's gaze briefly met hers, and he noted her neutral expression. Weariness emanated from her. She never turned.

Jenny sat back down and steepled her fingers.

Christopher half-closed his laptop, intending to approach her. However, fear of rejection was a recurring thought, and she might not welcome him.

He attempted to make eye contact, but she ignored him while tapping her feet and reviewing another application.

Since assuming the role of a father, Christopher had learned to have more empathy. "I'm here if you need anything," he wanted to say. "I'll support you."

He hesitated. Maybe not. Maybe those weren't the correct words.

Maria sauntered over, holding what had developed into her apparent beverage of choice, an orange juice mimosa. Her bright-pink lipstick was smudged on the glass's rim.

By his count, this was her second drink today. Jenny had

indicated that neither she nor Maria drank alcohol, though this evidently wasn't true for Maria.

Maria peered at him; her black eyeliner was as bold as a permanent marker. "Another busy morning?"

He tipped his head slightly in Jenny's direction. "She's endlessly on the go. I wish she'd take a break and do something to alleviate her stress."

"Like what?"

"She can try goat yoga ... or baking. Or participate in your squirrel-watching hobby and climb a tree."

Maria placed her glass on the table and picked up his. "Stop thinking and start acting! You're not trying to launch a rocket to the moon."

"I'm fairly certain even rocket scientists face less rejection than I do."

"Just go over there and talk to her. What's the worst that can happen? She turns you down? At least you'll have a funny story to tell."

He traced patterns on his ledgers. "I appreciate your encouragement, but I can't help but think about all the recent times she's rejected me. It's not the most pleasant experience, and it leaves a mark. I suppose I'm not a big fan of putting myself out there, only to be met with disappointment again and again." His words carried a hint of vulnerability, a glimpse into the lingering wounds of past rejections. The fear loomed in his thoughts like an invisible barrier, keeping him tethered to the reluctance of trying again.

"Use your charm." Maria's dark eyes sparkled mischievously. "My favorite person is your favorite person, too. Don't let a prime opportunity go to waste."

"This is the problem with a tiny island." He swallowed a smile and reached for his glass that she held. "I can't swing around a corner without someone expressing their opinion."

She gripped his glass, holding it hostage. "Rusty and I decided that you and Jenny should be together."

Christopher arched an eyebrow. "Rusty talked to you?"

"In monosyllables. He's unsociable with the staff, and I can't understand why you ever hired him as a bellboy. Aren't we trying to attract customers with our high-quality, pleasant, and personalized service? With his sullen attitude, he's going to frighten everyone off the island." She set down his glass and used her hands to underline her statements. "And what about the coveted Evelyn Eckard bakery award?"

"Rusty doesn't bake."

"Fortunately, because then we might as well kiss that award goodbye, too."

"Once upon a time, Rusty was a different guy."

He and Olive vowed to assist Rusty after his family threw him out. His ex-wife had complained that Rusty was distant and critical, and she could no longer put up with his outbursts of anger. Christopher knew enough to respect Rusty's personal space and offered peer encouragement.

"Whatever he witnessed when he was deployed overseas changed him," he said.

"I'm discouraged by his sullenness, but men of few words have always attracted me." Maria's tiny smile indicated she wasn't completely serious about her discouragement.

"At least he speaks to you."

"In monosyllables."

"He no longer cares about anyone." Christopher braced himself for the inevitable questions about their war stories, but none came. "Are you aware there is a buzz that he's a pianist?"

"Him? A musician? I'll research the definition, but I doubt it describes him."

"Unverified and never confirmed."

"What a revelation." Her lips lifted in an exasperated

smile. "Sometimes, I'm able to converse with him for a half hour straight. He buries his hands in his pockets and mumbles. I consider it a promising beginning."

"Sounds like the title of a romance novel. Just keep the conversation flowing and avoid any awkward silences, and you'll be on the right track."

She touched her forefinger to her chin. "Salifu, however ..."

"He has a bit of commitment phobia."

"I have to date someone soon, or I'll start collecting cats and knitting sweaters for them."

"Salifu?" Christopher alluded to the man again.

"His relationships resemble a game of Jenga."

"How so?"

Maria leaned in. "Just like the game, he builds these connections, carefully placing each piece. But with one wrong move or misstep, the entire structure comes crashing down."

"What about the schoolteacher, Evan Farrenway?" Christopher intended to pawn the guy off on someone. Maria was a promising start.

"I haven't met him. Is he rich?"

Christopher stifled a chuckle. "I can't say. However, I ran into the cook at the Drifting Sands Restaurant when Sebastian and I ate there. We had a ... good ... meal."

"Good? Is that a synonym for great?"

"If you're into greasy food. It made us question whether the chef had mistaken salt for sugar and vice versa."

"If he's not married and still has a pulse, I'm all ears. I'm not saying I'm a gold digger, but I wouldn't object to a man who can buy truffles AND diamonds. Chefs earn a lot of money."

"Well, you've certainly got your priorities straight. Who

cares about looks or personality when you can have a fat paycheck? And he's a cook," Christopher clarified.

"What's the difference?"

"A cook prepares food. A chef is a professional with formal training."

"He could be a wealthy chef."

"Perhaps possible if he is a TV chef, which he assuredly isn't." Christopher chuckled. "He's a *cook* slinging together meals in a dimly lit, wood-paneled restaurant with a thirty-page menu."

"Perfect. I'm desperate and starving."

"Are you into tattoos? If so, he's your guy. I think his name is Rob, and I'm guessing he's in his early forties. You're what… in your twenties?"

"I'm twenty-eight, the same age as Jenny. You're acquainted with our mutual friend, who is sitting over there by herself."

He glanced in Jenny's direction. "Right."

"Uh-huh."

What's that supposed to mean?

He stored his question and asked aloud, "Keep me updated on your opinion of the Drifting Sands. It may dishearten you since they're not celebrated for their leafy greens. You're practically a salad expert, being a vegetarian."

"Pescatarian," she reminded him. "And you're changing the subject. I guess you could say I have a 'recipe' for success for getting what I want. Step one: get Rob to take me out on a date. Step two: steal his cookbook."

"Start polishing up your deep fryer."

His joke stalled at her sharp, "That's why I'm here."

Christopher smirked. He appreciated her feisty spirit. She always spoke her mind, no matter the consequences.

"You both can't keep your eyes off each other." Maria crooked a discreet finger towards Jenny.

"What continent do you live on, Maria? On mine, Jenny avoids me at all costs."

"The handsome architect returns to the summer place of his youth, and the beautiful island girl is still in love with him."

"Thanks for your unasked-for advice." He powered down his computer. "So many options, and so little time."

"Watching people is my favorite hobby." Maria's enthusiasm grew with every whispered syllable. "When Jenny and I lived in Italy, we attended a friend's wedding, and Jenny caught the bouquet."

He looked around. "Are you throwing me a bouquet?"

"Surely you're aware of the significance of when a woman catches the bride's bouquet?"

"She's the next to get married."

"See?" Maria gave an affirming grin. "You're not totally clueless."

He picked up his glass of tea. "Should I walk over to Jenny so she can ignore me?"

"Are you kidding? Look at me and smile. Make her jealous."

"What? You're her best friend."

She plucked the glass from his hand and set it back on the table. "Why else would I do something like this?"

Chuckling out loud, he mimicked her flirtatious gestures. She regaled him with her and Jenny's Italian escapades—no screens on windows and no ice cubes. Then she changed course and discussed business, lamenting the trial and error of posting on social media platforms.

"I begin our advertising campaigns with a hook, and end with a call to action," she declared.

"Click on the link and book a room at the Grand Michelangelo Hotel."

"Precisely." Chuckling, Maria locked eyes with him and touched the sleeve of his shirt.

He caught Jenny's fiery glare. Her eyebrows came together. Color stained her cheeks. She snatched up her forms and stormed into the lobby without looking at him.

"Not quite the response I was hoping for," Christopher leaned back, and the keen edge of the chair dug into his shoulders.

"*Exactly* the response you were hoping for," Maria replied with a sly laugh.

CHAPTER 8

Sometimes, Christopher forgot how much seeing Jenny sparked an immediate quickening in his veins.

As he stood in the breakroom and poured out the last of the espresso, his mind whirled with confusion. What was he thinking, allowing Maria to flirt with him in plain sight of Jenny? He hadn't intended to hurt her, but desperation had clouded his judgment. Didn't Maria comprehend the potential reactions of other women in a similar situation? She'd certainly been mistaken. Jenny had avoided eye contact with him all day.

He sipped, then discarded the coffee, headed to the lobby, and plucked an apple out of a ceramic bowl heaped with fruit. As usual, Maria, who oversaw the food budget, had overspent. In hardly any time, the fruit would rot. He hesitated to rebuke her, suspecting a fierce response, so instead he kept a mental note to inform her as casually as possible.

He rolled the apple between his palms. Apples were good, though seaside plums, a tart, seasonal fruit, were his favorite.

In August, he and Jenny would scour the sandy coastal

dunes, the air fragrant with the enticing aroma of ripe fruit. The shrub grew wild, delivering spring blossoms that resulted in the tiny dark-purple fruit, and they'd pop them into their mouths as they picked. Then, they would seek a secluded spot near the shore, where the cool shade provided respite from the sun. With each succulent bite, the sweet juice would trickle down their chins.

Later, Jenny would tie a white apron around her waist, and in Anyika's kitchen, she'd mix the fruit into hickory nut bread or boil a rich, tart chutney.

He smiled, cherishing each of those memories.

Baking was Jenny's forte. Why had she chosen to venture into management instead?

Intent on checking the hotel for a last go-round before he shut the lights for the night, he crossed the lobby. He'd tucked Sebastian into bed for the evening, a protective Scooby-Doo resting on the floor beside him.

Christopher carried a child monitor linked to his cell phone. He harbored reservations about leaving Sebastian alone, and the monitor enabled him to observe him sleeping.

Background music filled the lobby, and he chuckled at Jenny's selection.

Standard rock classics from the 1950s. She had mentioned her efforts to curate music that would resonate with the guests and enhance their experience. At the moment, "Tutti-Frutti" by Little Richard played through the speakers. Not exactly refined, but why not?

He'd weigh in eventually and vote for Gullah tunes. He wanted the island's heritage to shine.

Outside, a beam of light shone from a quarter moon. He recognized Maria and Jenny conversing before Maria started for the lobby.

Christopher greeted her. She simulated a motion as if she were slitting her throat and mouthed, "Good luck."

Jenny neared the shoreline. Her gauze skirt lightly clung to her curves like a second skin. She twirled, and the skirt gracefully flowed with her movements. Despite her face being obscured, she held her head high with poise and self-confidence, just as she had as a teen.

Barefoot, her feet sank into the sand with each step.

On cue, his pulse quickened. She was the very essence of an island beauty.

He considered retiring to his suite when she curved in his direction. In the process of pinning up her hair, she sucked in a startled breath when their gazes met. It was as if the world had faded, leaving only the two of them.

He was powerless to look away, and he rationalized that he couldn't leave her alone outside in the dark.

His protective instincts rose. She looked thin, her complexion colorless, despite her graceful appearance.

He stood where he was. "Jenny?" he called out.

"Christopher, you nearly gave me a heart attack!" Jenny dropped the hairpin, and her hair spread across her shoulders.

"Never underrate the element of a good scare." He placed his half-eaten apple on a patio table. "It's a surefire way to capture your attention and make an impression."

"Ah yes, the classic tactic of making people fear for their lives. Very effective."

"I didn't intend to frighten you," he said.

"Right, because randomly appearing behind someone is a totally normal thing to do." Her hair was in disarray. She combed her fingers through it, then scrambled to pick up the hairpin. "Are you looking for something? Or stalking me?"

He stiffened. "A stalker? Really? That's a smidge extreme, don't you think?"

"You're constantly around, and you're always following me." She twisted her hair up, exposing her slender neck, and his blood heated. Why had no other woman ever entranced him the same way she did?

"Purely a coincidence," he replied. *Well, kind of.*

As he came closer, her scent evoked memories of springtime rain and freshly laundered clothes—a refreshing aroma.

"You were in the breakroom last evening, in the lobby this morning, and sitting at the patio table when I interviewed earlier today." She secured her hair into a messy bun. "Everywhere I go, you appear."

"Perhaps I'm trying to find a way to approach you without you biting my head off. I'm not a stalker, just a man who thinks you're remarkable."

"I appreciate the compliment, but I suggest you seek someone else."

"We're practically neighbors, Jenny. We both call this island and hotel our home." His jaw tensed with conflict, sensing her reluctance. "But if you'd rather not cross paths with me, I'll try to steer clear."

Jenny sighed. "So far, you're doing a poor job of it." She sounded snappy and harsh, and there was no justification for it. Inwardly, she reproached herself. She was supposed to be a Christian woman who perceived the good in everyone. Who was kinder than Christopher?

"I was shutting down the hotel," he said. "I wanted to ensure you got home safely."

He was trying to explain, and she winced. What was the matter with her lately?

"I merely need to walk a few feet to get back inside." She gestured toward the entrance. "Besides, it's scarcely dark."

He seemed to sift through his thoughts and smiled. "Tonight is black as pitch. The ocean is deep, and light can only penetrate a certain distance beneath it. Once the molecules in the water disperse and absorb the light, there's hardly anything left."

"Thanks for the science lesson, professor."

His smile thinned, although he didn't offer a rejoinder.

Moonlight danced upon the shimmering ocean. The distant calls of seabirds and the swishing of tree branches relaxed her, despite Christopher coming to stand so close. His presence always affected her.

She had been around him for what seemed like the dawn of time, yet a part of her realized she had hardly scratched the surface of the man. He was enigmatic and difficult to read, as if she groped along a path at midnight, feeling her way as she moved.

"I can't help myself, Jenny." He lifted his hands. "I need to make certain you're safe."

"I've survived the last decade without your protection." Her tone was still harsh. *Calm down, Jenny,*

Why wasn't she able to pilot their relationship with more finesse? When they were teens, they'd stroll on the beach for hours, fingers interlaced, while the stars and planets illuminated the summer sky. Now and then, breakers splashed over their feet, sending a cool spray up their legs.

They walked in companionable silence, their arms occasionally brushing, absorbed in their own thoughts. With a broad smile, Christopher would often look down at her, and she'd quietly return his stare.

"You flew thousands of miles to get here." He held her attention with a firm grip. "Do you like it here?"

"What makes you say such a thing?"

"You're on edge much of the time."

She broke their connection and gazed out at the sea. Her mind wandered, replaying memories of better times. The vast expanse mirrored her mood, with waves crashing in a somber rhythm.

Initially, resistance had welled within her at the mere idea of returning to the island. It reminded her of her failed relationships, career, and studies.

What had been her goal during her stint in Italy? The answer eluded her, and she embarked on a range of roles, from housekeeping to receptionist, gradually climbing the professional ladder.

What if she floundered in her hometown and they judged her miserably inadequate? What if her bosses dismissed her from her job? Where would she go?

Certainly not Italy, with Dominick's 'I told you so,' resounding in her ears.

Well, she could always do what she invariably did. Leave.

This opportunity that she had pursued left her with a persistent restlessness. Did it align with the career she had envisioned?

Perhaps.

The man of her dreams had long ago vanished.

Or had he?

There was a void inside her. But why?

Images flew through her mind.

After his mother's departure, Christopher remained despondent throughout the entire summer. He kept to himself, mostly tinkering with motors alongside his father. He spent his spare time sketching designs, ambling the stark paths, or helping the islanders with their garden plots.

One afternoon, tears welled up in his eyes as he admitted how much he missed his mother. The longing for a mother who would cook his favorite meals and sing lullabies every evening before he drifted off to sleep.

"This was all my fault." He'd summoned up the hard conversations he'd heard between his parents, along with his father's fury. "The burden became too much for her—a sickly kid like me. The demands were overwhelming."

Jenny's heart ached for him. Her sweet, vulnerable Christopher.

She'd tried to ease his guilt. If his mother suffered from mental health issues, then she felt guilty, too, because she couldn't be more supportive and caring. If she needed treatment and support, it was a positive step that she recognized her concerns.

"I didn't think it was possible to miss someone so much who isn't here." Christopher wiped the tears from his eyes. "I'm embarrassed to cry in front of you. That's the last thing I want to do."

"It's okay. Openness is constructive."

"My father claimed that my mother was the problem, and she needed to fix herself."

"He's right." Jenny had picked up a bright blue pebble and smoothed her thumb along its surface. "I believe you'll see her again someday."

"She didn't leave me anything." His voice shook with a ragged sigh, barely above a whisper. "Not even a note."

White, billowy clouds lazed overhead, and the rocking sailboats held court in the harbor. Her and Christopher's secluded oasis amidst the infinite expanse of sand.

Jenny wasn't sure if her uplifting words made a difference, but thereafter, he avoided that section of beach, and never mentioned his mother again.

Once, he surprised her with a bouquet of azalea clippings, celebrating the onset of summer. At twelve, she gleefully exclaimed, "My favorite flowers!" as she embraced him, causing his face to turn beet red.

Then, there was the memorable moment when they shared a kiss on the beach. Awkwardness and exhilaration filled the air as two teenagers fell in love.

He told a joke afterward. She couldn't remember what. They had laughed together.

However, on another day, he'd uttered something she had never forgiven him for.

Loss and longing coiled in her stomach. Any memories they shared were just that. Memories. Time passed. Things changed. He wasn't *her* Christopher anymore.

His strength should delight her. He'd consistently been her protector. Thoughtful, compassionate, and exceedingly considerate.

But he ended their relationship abruptly, leaving her feeling ignored and unimportant.

Her brief homage to the past restored her to the present.

They had outgrown their elementary days, and they were no longer high school sweethearts. A decade had passed, encompassing ten far-reaching years. If she closed her eyes, she still felt his solid, shielding arms around her. She still heard the rhythmic thud of his heart while her cheek rested against his chest.

Her emotions threatened to overpower her. They'd been denied an important part of their lives when they should've been together.

She let go of her disappointment. She was now a grown woman who lived on her own.

"I believe being a gentleman is still fashionable," he was saying.

"I'm sure Maria would've loved your support if she were alone in the dark." Jenny pressed her lips tightly, realizing it was too late. Her words had just slipped out.

A roguish glint danced in Christopher's eyes. "Do I detect a spark of jealousy?"

"Maria is your type." Jenny was on a roll. She might as well keep going, considering she was broadcasting her envy like a neon sign. "Vivacious and stylish, and—"

"Maria is a friend," Christopher said. "More importantly, she's *your* friend."

Leave it to him to neither chuckle nor use her resentful remark as leverage. He'd never do such a thing. He was attentive, selfless, and respectful.

"You two are ideal together." She cut him off. "You're both stunning."

"I'm stunning?"

She ignored his attempt to appease her. "I'm merely an island girl who baked fruit cobblers, cookies, and bread pudding."

"Seriously, Jenny. You're an excellent baker, and baking is a skill."

Sure. Her one talent.

He took a step closer. "We're both aware this conversation isn't about baking."

"Then what is it about?"

"You and me. Our unresolved history."

"When you were eighteen, you planned to zip off to college and assumed that women would trip over themselves to date you. Truly, you are the most overconfident man I've ever known."

"When did I imply anything of the sort?" His posture tensed. "Why can't you recall the small detail that I asked you to accompany me?"

Right, yes, but she refused to respond to his questions.

When she'd related her father's job loss and the resultant move, she'd expected Christopher to cry, to hold her, and to reassure her.

"You deserve a terrific life, a family, and kids," he'd declared.

"Don't you want kids?"

He'd shaken his head. "Does it appear that I come from a family that can take care of kids? My mother disappeared without a trace, and my father—"

"You're not your father."

"He's a good man."

115

"I'm not implying he isn't."

"You won't find fulfillment by existing on this remote island forever, Jenny. Neither would I."

"Look around, Christopher. There's a special magic here."

"This is all you've ever known. We both deserve more challenges and different opportunities. I want to attend college. After you graduate from high school, you can join me."

"College isn't what it's cracked up to be."

"You're wrong, Jenny. Nowadays, to succeed, you need a university degree. I plan to apply to Carnegie Mellon in Pittsburgh. Scholarships are available."

"Why? This place is heaven."

"The world out there is too vast for us not to explore. Come with me."

"I adore this island."

"Join me," he'd repeated.

No mention of love or commitment, only the intention of a prosperous future.

As his words settled, her clogged throat uttered a single reply.

"Maybe."

It was a lie. She'd never intended to go with him. Academics had taken its toll, so what would she do while he attended classes? Flip burgers at a fast-food restaurant? The high school counselor said Jenny's grades made her unsuitable for higher education.

"Then I'll miss you, Jenny," Christopher's calm tone had cut her off, implying that she wasn't important. His goals took priority over hers.

The heat had risen in her chest and face. She stepped closer, her hands balled into fists. In anger, exasperation, or desperation, she'd swung her fist at him. Then, without hesitation, she marched away, leaving an impassable silence.

She never backtracked. She never heard from him again.

"Jenny?" Christopher's resonant voice yanked her from the past. He cupped his fingers around her chin, forcing her to look up at him. "I'm not interested in Maria. If that's what you believe, I beg your forgiveness."

Though she attempted to conceal her hurt, tears formed.

She'd spouted an outrageous amount of resentment, and the mantle didn't suit her. Besides, she couldn't be envious of him and Maria flirting. And laughing. And gazing into each other's eyes.

She clicked her tongue. Could she?

She debated apologizing for her outburst, yet she was too distressed about how badly her day had gone to think clearly.

He rubbed small circles with his thumb over her palm, his voice a light caress. "What's truly the matter, Jenny?" He brought her hand to his mouth and pressed a kiss on her knuckles.

Overcome by the conviction that she could never deceive him, that her attraction to him was stronger than ever, her lips quivered.

Perhaps she'd discovered the reason it was necessary to evade him and outmaneuver him before he got too close.

Perhaps she was unwilling to be hurt again.

She positioned a cream-colored patio chair nearer the lobby and flopped down in it. "Where do I begin?"

He sat beside her. Their knees touched. How was she supposed to concentrate when she felt a distinct jolt of magnetism at his nearness?

"The beginning is helpful," he said.

The genuine interest in his tone prompted her, and she gave a listless sigh. "Well, the morning started with the woman I interviewed for the head of housekeeping."

"She seemed a promising candidate."

"My thoughts exactly. Unfortunately, she declined the job offer later in the day, citing an unreliable ferry service.

Many other potential employees have supplied the same reason."

"Securing the right personnel is a day-to-day trial."

"That's for sure. Then, I appealed to Oliver to raise the starting salary to match the national average. He balked. Wages vary in range, depending on qualifications, and most of the jobs are entry-level positions. His focus should be on staff satisfaction to ensure the hotel's success."

"Olive is normally a reasonable guy."

"Olive. Right. I forgot you were best buddies." She glanced at Christopher, who kept a blasé expression. "What's the point of an espresso coffee machine if it's just going to collect dust? It's begging for a job. Maybe it should start filling out applications."

He grinned. "I'll email him."

Who did Christopher think he was, resolving problems with a simple email? And this mysterious direct line to the boss was wearing thin.

She'd heard whispers that Christopher and Oliver were more than friends—that they were business partners. She'd meant to ask Christopher more than once, but now didn't seem the right time.

"Best of luck with that conversation." She rolled her eyes. "I quoted a news clip to him that said competitive salaries were necessary to attract top talent. We can't rely on the same handful of islanders."

"They are the most reliable staff," he replied, grinning. "Along with my army buddies."

"Rusty?"

Christopher's grin widened. "You'll like him once you spend more time with him."

"Therein lies the problem." Jenny's frustration bubbled to the surface. "It's not sustainable to rely on the same people indefinitely."

"The islanders have been here for generations. We owe it to them to keep their trust and loyalty."

"I'm not suggesting that we abandon them. But we need to develop to meet the growing demands. It's about preserving what we have and incorporating new opportunities."

"Expanding the team without proper vetting means bringing in outsiders." His voice grew defensive, a hint of conflict emerging. "We risk losing the unique charm that will set us apart."

A loud crash reverberated through the hallway, catching Christopher and Jenny off guard as they both turned their heads in surprise.

"What on earth?" Jenny's eyes widened at the sight of a young Gullah woman covered in red paint standing amidst the wreckage of a knocked-over trolley. "Who are you?"

The woman's face blushed a warm shade of crimson, and she quickly scrambled to pick up the fallen items. "I-I'm so sorry. I'm a new hire, an aspiring painter who switched to housekeeping staff. I was trying to navigate the hallway with my art supplies, and ... well, you can see how that went."

"You certainly know how to make an entrance." Jenny laughed. "Welcome, and try to keep the paint where it belongs."

"I suppose more color around here would be appreciated," Christopher said. "Just try not to redecorate the entire hotel, okay?"

"I promise to bring creativity without chaos. Maybe in my off hours I can create a mural somewhere?" the young woman suggested.

"That's an interesting idea," he replied. "We'll brainstorm at some point and see if it fits into our plans."

Jenny studied Christopher's face, contemplating before responding. "Are you saying we're expanding our team to include a painter? I thought we were discussing hiring more personnel for the hotel's operations."

"I didn't mean to give that impression. I was just joking about the color."

As the tension between Jenny and Christopher mounted, the young painter, still wearing paint, remarked, "A work of art should capture the island's beauty."

"Very good selling point." With a nod and a smile, Jenny followed Christopher to another corner of the hotel.

"Let's set the mural momentarily aside and continue where we left off," he said. "You're upset because of the lack of personnel?"

"Yes, because this shortage strains our current staff." Her frustration resurfaced. "They've been working tirelessly. Learning the ropes and double shifts will take a toll on them."

"You're right. We can't expect anyone to carry an extra load indefinitely." He nodded, his blue-eyed gaze reflecting empathy. "Anything else?"

Jenny inhaled and organized her thoughts. "Plenty. Sometimes, I question whether I truly belong here. The challenges we face, the decisions we make … it can be overwhelming. But no, I take that back. I do belong here." She batted a hand in the air. She had already over shared. "Although a management position is quite stressful."

Christopher's gaze softened. "I know it's not always easy, but you have brought so much to this hotel. Your dedication, your passion, and your ability to see the bigger picture. You absolutely belong here."

"Thank you." Her lips curled into a genuine smile. "It means a lot to hear that."

He reached for her hand and squeezed gently. "I'm sorry, Jenny."

"For what?"

"I'm not sure, although it appears as if you need an apology from someone. It might as well be me."

Her body sagged. How were they expected to be up and running in such a limited timeframe? She put in tireless hours, and they were into the second week of May. A tunnel stretched out before her, offering no glimpse of the light at the end.

"Please don't apologize, Christopher. This isn't your fault. I'm still adjusting to you and me living on the same island."

"We've already gone down that road."

She blinked back hot tears. She was struggling with frustration, sadness, and self-doubt. And yes, the jealousy issue she hadn't made peace with.

"Hey." He lifted her chin. "You're not shaking me off that quickly."

"Let me clarify this. You're comfortable in a lavish, upscale suite with your son, along with a gigantic dog and a kitten who sprints away whenever I approach. Meanwhile, I'm living in a medieval castle, occupying a room one floor above that doesn't have a properly functioning toilet."

"At least you don't have to share your room with a dog the size of a horse." He paused. "Your toilet doesn't work?"

"The plumber must've hooked it up wrong because the water is hot."

"Hot?"

"Don't laugh." She frowned as he grinned. "The situation is extremely uncomfortable."

"You should've told me sooner. I'm your knight in shining armor."

"More like a jester in tattered sandals," she retorted. "At least my shower isn't Arctic-cold. It's more like a refreshing dip in a mountain stream ... if that stream had indoor plumbing. You always had a knack for solving problems back in the day."

"Thanks."

"You submitted an article to the Main Island Docket newspaper."

"A change of subject, but okay, you remembered." A flicker of delight ignited in his eyes. "I wrote about the practicality of Gullah homes."

"I described the homes to Maria."

"I hope she didn't nod off."

"She wasn't on the edge of her seat." Jenny studied her hands. "You were joking together."

"She told me about your Italian escapades."

"I was the woman you used to joke with."

"Jenny." The intenseness of his deep voice impelled her to look up. The muscles at the corners of his eyes bunched. He always did that when he had something serious to say. "When we were young, you were my cheerleader. I can't imagine where I'd be today if it wasn't for your encouragement."

"Past tense?"

"Present." He traced the line of her forefinger with his thumb, sending delightful quivers down her spine.

"You and I are in completely different stratospheres," she said. "You enlisted in the military, tied the knot, and completed college. I don't have a degree from anywhere."

"Formal education isn't necessary." He stood and beckoned her to her feet. "Destiny reunited us. Fate gave us a second chance."

"You had a son."

"A son I adore."

Her eyes burned. "You didn't want children."

"I'm learning to be a nurturing father." He reached out and drew her close. Part of her demanded she resist. He was trying to make up for lost time.

Or worse, there were only a few females on the island, and she was one of them, in competition with Maria.

"You've always loved him," her heart screamed.

"He let you go once. He'll let you go again," her rational mind argued.

He took her hand and guided her near the beach. "Shall we dance?" He indicated the background music playing, "Can't Help Falling in Love." Elvis Presley sang an iconic, persuasive melody. She hadn't been aware of the tune filtering from the lobby until now.

"We used to waltz." He shook off his sandals. "I would bring my portable radio."

"On the beach." She bowed her head. She remembered.

Her heart swelled with emotion as she recalled when she'd been bedridden by the flu. Christopher had shown up with a basket of peaches, touting the fruit as a moderate source of vitamin C, and a natural way to boost her immune system.

She soaked in his defined features and his soulful blue eyes, which resembled two glittering sapphires—alluring and captivating, and yet unfathomable. How did he charm her so effortlessly?

She was falling under his spell. Again.

He held her, and she welcomed the heat of his hand against the small of her back. His woodsy scent invaded her nostrils.

They danced in the fine sand, her fingers on his shoulders, their bodies touching. His shirt grazed her neck, and her skin tingled at the friction.

He completely focused on her, a tender expression on his face as he gazed down at her.

Peaceful and romantic, the island was the picture-perfect place for a man and woman in love. In this interlude, in this music, the island isolated her from everything else in the world, faraway, yet so familiar.

She closed her eyes, their shared rhythm in unison.

"You're stunning, Jenny." His lips brushed hers, and the years melted away. Oh, how she had missed him. The sorrow of the past and the promise of the future melded together. Life was complete.

She inhaled, absorbing every second of this exquisite night. The intimacy. The closeness.

She was here again. Her judgment was on point. She'd tried to deny it, but truly, Pink Coral Island was where her heart belonged.

She sniffed, paused, and opened her eyes. Ocean scent, coconut sunscreen, jasmine, and a hint of … smoke?

"Christopher?" She stepped from his arms, an overpowering panic knocking her off balance. "Is that—"

For a split second, he froze, surveying the expanse of the beach. An ear-splitting siren sounded.

"Fire!" His attention flashed to a stretch of beach where a few huts were located. They housed several employees, including Salifu, Rusty, and the siblings. In the brief period since she'd met them, she viewed these men as friends. Thankfully, Francis Grant lived at the other end of the island with his wife.

Her heartbeat sped up. Jenny's understanding of the speed at which flames spread was a product of her previous experience.

She and Christopher read each other's thoughts before the word escaped their lips.

"No."

A fire had occurred at the hotel when she was in her teens.

A nightmare from the past resurfaced, and she banished the horrific recollections before they overwhelmed her mind. She'd suffered nightmares and insomnia for months afterward.

The islanders had toiled determinedly to contain the blaze. The desperate hotel lodgers had to make harrowing leaps from their opulent rooms to escape. Others were sandwiched between the revolving lobby door and the outdoors, as the musical notes from a live band stilled.

Intense flames engulfed the ground floor, swiftly spreading upwards. Fumes billowed from each corner. Red and yellow, then roaring heat before the roof exploded.

The islanders rallied, but the fire was quicker.

Miraculously, no one died, yet scores of people were injured.

Her breath hitched. This couldn't happen again on the island, not a second time.

"Tell Maria to go to Sebastian's room and stay with him," Christopher instructed. "There's another inhaler by his bed if he needs it."

"I'll go. Do you think he'll have an asthma attack?"

"He shouldn't." Christopher slipped on his sandals. "He has shown no signs of breathing difficulties since we arrived."

Jenny lowered her head. Pinpricks of sweat crept up her arms. She had chills.

Her heart thumped madly in her chest. Surely, Christopher heard it.

"The volunteers are likely to be close by." He tilted his gaze toward the alarm sound.

"The board operates twenty-four hours a day." She thought she spoke but wasn't certain.

"I'm going over there to help." He flicked his glance between her and the smoke plume in the distance.

"Wait. What about your asthma?"

"I'm okay. The doctor said I'd outgrown it, remember?

You stay here. I don't want to risk your safety." His entire stance carried conviction, a confidence in his ability to handle the situation.

She swallowed any protests. Time slowed. She wanted to protect him, to shield him from any harm.

"Please, Christopher, be careful," she pleaded, a silent prayer for his well-being.

"Promise you won't follow me?"

Their eyes locked as his request echoed in her mind.

"I promise." She had no intention of following him. She was a coward and couldn't bear witness to another fire.

"PostScript to my list of failings," she thought.

As he raced off, her heart pounded, a combination of fear and admiration for his bravery.

She hardly finished a gasp as she hurried inside the hotel, seeking shelter from the chaos unfolding outside.

CHAPTER 9

Christopher arrived at the site of the blaze in record time. Black smoke rose above a single hut, which was engulfed in flames. Sparks and embers illuminated the landscape with an orange-red glow. The stench of burnt wood, along with screams, breaking glass, and crackling brush, was everywhere.

He surveyed the area for anyone potentially injured, but the billowing, dense haze obscured his view, hindering him from seeing beyond a few feet. The fumes irritated his nose and throat, making it hard to breathe. A slight tightening in his chest reminded him of his vulnerability during his childhood asthmatic episodes.

Panic and anxiety flooded his mind as he realized the danger the smoke posed to his respiratory system.

Perhaps Jenny was right.

However, as he continued to inhale, he noticed a shift in his body's response, and he could breathe easily. Despite his initial fear, relief washed over him. He had, thankfully, outgrown his asthma, just as the doctor had told him.

A tall, muscular man wearing a helmet, reflective vest, and firefighter boots over black pants and a shirt barked an order into a radio.

"We got here in time to prevent any other huts from catching fire." The man, who introduced himself as the fire chief, explained when Christopher questioned what had happened.

A faint, frantic gasp, a plea for help, prompted Christopher to turn. He waited, uncertain if he had heard correctly, then dashed toward the source of the cry. His heart raced with adrenaline and a conscious urgency. As he navigated through the mess of wreckage, the piercing crackle of sparking timber muffled his footsteps.

He detected a small wooden boat anchored on the sandy shore near the beach. Close by, an unconscious man lay motionless on the ground.

Christopher recognized the man as Lomboi, the younger sibling he'd recently employed. Without a moment's hesitation, he sprinted toward the scene, his heart pounding with concern.

An odor of seaweed and damp, gritty earth filled the air as Christopher lifted Lomboi's limp body. The clammy coolness of Lomboi's skin brushed against his own. Christopher adjusted his grip and hastened his steps. He pushed forward with all his strength to a group of volunteers standing by the trees.

Carefully, he laid Lomboi down, his knees sinking to the dirt as he knelt by his side. He pressed two fingers against Lomboi's neck, searching for a pulse. Relief surged through him as he detected a faint yet steady rhythm, and his breath caught in his throat as Lomboi's weak cough subsided into ragged breaths. It felt almost miraculous, a moment of optimism within the uncertainty.

Christopher rose and squinted against the relentless

onslaught of the scorching wind. The once lush leaves of the brush had discolored, scarred by the remnants of the smoldering fire. A plume of fumes billowed into the sky, swept away by the refreshing sea breeze.

The fire chief, amidst the confusion, walked with purpose and yanked off his helmet. A shock of unruly gray fuzz spilled over his forehead like a brewing storm cloud. There was an aura of authority about him, and Christopher instinctively liked him.

"I'm Michael Freid," he introduced himself, extending his hand. "We're grateful to you for saving Lomboi."

Christopher accepted the handshake, their hands firmly clasping in a gesture of mutual respect. "Christopher Drake," he replied. "My apologies for not introducing myself sooner."

The fire chief's eyes bore into Christopher's, a blend of admiration and inquisitiveness. "That kid," he began, nodding towards Lomboi, "he's trouble, the island's resident delinquent. He often wanders off on his own stirring up all sorts of pranks. So far, they've been harmless."

"He's young, and everyone makes mistakes." Christopher's gaze lingered on Lomboi's motionless form. "With any luck, he'll learn from them, and his older brother might serve as a positive influence."

Michael cast Christopher a sidelong glance. "I've heard rumors about you. Aren't you the guy who bought the Grand Michelangelo, the rundown hotel? It's looking good now."

Christopher nodded appreciatively. "Indeed. My friend from Wales is my partner."

Information traveled swiftly among the inhabitants; their ears attuned to the tales that circulated within their neighborhoods.

"A fire nearly destroyed that hotel a few years ago." A low growl rumbled in the chief's chest as he recounted the story.

"I wasn't here when it happened."

"I've lived here forever." The chief's eyebrows shot up, wiry strands of gray hair standing on end. "Hold on a second. You used to live here with your dad. During the summer months, right?"

"That was me." Christopher shook his head in admission.

"So, are you planning to stay on the island?"

"Absolutely. My son and I intend to settle here permanently."

"Will you consider joining our volunteer fire department and contributing to our modest community? I care about the residents, and I assume you do, too." The chief's gaze fixed on the volunteers hoisting heavy hoses over their shoulders. "We need men and women who dedicate themselves to serving others. Our meetings are once a month."

"Besides the siren, how do you communicate?"

"We're high tech." Michael offered a half-grin. "We use a phone tree system."

Christopher identified many of the townspeople, as well as Thomas, the gray-mustached porter from the ferry.

"Certainly, I'll join." Christopher paused. "This hut ... isn't this Rusty's hut?"

"Think so."

"Is he hurt?" Panic hit Christopher in the gut. "Where is he?"

At the hum of Gullah dialect, he swerved.

"Rusty was raging mad and spouting curse words about a candle." A dark-skinned man with a craggy appearance, reflecting a life spent outdoors, stepped over. "Francis Grant hauled Rusty away on a long walk, then brought him to his house. Salifu and several other men who live in these huts accompanied him."

"What caused the fire?" Christopher inquired.

The chief's mouth pinched. "Too soon to tell. Sure hope it

was an accident, a lit cigarette or something similar. Or maybe a bit of mischief at the worst." He swung off, dispatching the volunteers to return to their various positions. "Rusty wasn't supposed to be home tonight. He was traveling to the mainland, but Skipper Andy canceled the ferry. He suspected a thunderstorm was coming in. Apparently, it didn't."

Perhaps Rusty's careless smoking habits caused the destruction. Had he dozed off with a burning cigarette in bed?

Christopher had neglected to install smoke detectors in the huts, a decision that could have been a key factor. How could he have forgotten this important feature? He'd mounted detectors in every alcove of the hotel—the guest rooms, hallways, lobby, kitchen, and restaurant.

Christopher swore to make it a priority in the future, despite it appearing to be too little, too late.

He retreated as the volunteers gripped their gear. They advanced with practiced ease, heaving a pump and generator.

Diligent individuals banded together when a tragedy struck. Risks did not intimidate them, and they were accessible twenty-four hours a day, ready to respond to any emergency promptly.

"Out of the way!" The chief waved his hands in a semicircle. His succinct, clipped instructions cut through the breeze like a whip, and the group near Rusty's charred hut dispersed.

Christopher scanned the panicked faces, seeking Jenny's familiar one, and a wave of relief crested over him. Fortunately, she was nowhere in sight. She had listened to his advice and kept her distance.

Satisfied, he trekked along the shoreline and returned to

the hotel. When he arrived at the entrance, he stopped to regroup and shook the sand from his sandals. Then he pushed open the doors and stepped into the lobby.

Muted light illuminated two lamps that framed a chair in the nook where Jenny sat. Her gorgeous face was ashen, and her eyes were huge and fearful.

She stood and scurried over to him. "Are you alright?"

"I'm fine."

She granted a wan smile, her slender fingers brushing away tiny particles of soot from his shirt. She drew a breath. "You smell of smoke. With your asthma ... you must be careful."

"Don't worry. I'm all better and have outgrown it." He leaned in to plant a kiss on her temple. "How is Sebastian?"

"He's sleeping peacefully. The dog is staying vigilant on the floor close to him. Thankfully, no asthma attack for him, either. Maria went back to her room a short while ago."

Christopher gestured to the door. "Do you want to sit outside on the patio?"

Jenny shook her head, her eyes scanning the lobby. "Here is better. What happened?"

"Rusty's hut caught fire," Christopher recounted. "But he is safe, and the fire is out."

Her face was a canvas of emotions, each vying for dominance—astonishment, disbelief, sympathy, and concern. "Oh, no. He must've lost all his belongings."

Christopher nodded solemnly. "Yes, everything was destroyed."

"How can we support him?" Her eyes welled with empathy.

"He's staying with Francis Grant and his wife."

"Do we know how the fire started?"

"The fire chief isn't certain. But it's possible that a discarded, lit cigarette was the culprit."

"No one smokes around here, do they?"

Christopher gave a nod. "Rusty does."

"Did you have time to ask him about it?"

"He had already left when I showed up." Christopher strode to the breakroom and returned with a couple of bottles of water. "My adrenaline is still running. Do you want one?"

"Not now."

Gulping from a bottle, he set both on a table and settled next to her. "The people on this island are incredible."

She indicated her agreement with a bob of her head. "They're truly the best."

"I'm thankful you heeded my instructions earlier."

"It was easy because I'm not brave." A hint of self-doubt laced her tone. "I just remained numb and paralyzed."

"You were an adolescent when the previous fire occurred," he reminded her.

"I can't apply age as an excuse anymore." Her gaze grew distant. "The truth is, I'm a coward, too fearful to do anything else."

"You're the complete opposite," Christopher countered.

"I wish," she mumbled. "The last fire happened during Thanksgiving break when the hotel was at full capacity. The memories continue to haunt me."

"It was a scary night, but mercifully, no one died." He rested a hand on her shoulder, offering a comforting squeeze.

"Blessedly." She angled her face up toward him, tendrils of silky blond hair caressing her flushed cheeks and framing her delicate features. "I couldn't bring myself to look at anything like that ever again."

He could see the lingering horror of that evening reflected in her glimmering green eyes.

"It's only natural to be troubled and upset." He cradled her closer, and moved his hands up and down her back to soothe her.

"You're not alone," he breathed. "I'll support you through any difficulty. No matter what, I'll always be here for you. I promise."

CHAPTER 10

*R*ain fell steadily, each drop hammering out a beat on the roof of the Grand Michelangelo Hotel. The relentless downpour persisted, unabated, for two consecutive days.

The soothing rhythm had lulled Jenny into a deep slumber, shielding her from the unsettling sound of the howling wind. When she'd awoken and peeped out her window, whitecaps had formed on the sea, and a miniature ship, as if a ghostly vision, sailed on the surface.

A leak had sprung on the ceiling near the piano, and Christopher proclaimed the project the morning's top priority. Water dribbled in a tiny puddle, running in a narrow stream and into the corridor.

Jenny stationed herself in the doorway. Intently, she observed the last of the construction crew as they moved about. It was June 8, and the refurbishments were almost complete.

She and Christopher had managed a vast array of tasks, and they slated for the hotel to welcome the public on June

30. They inspected the property multiple times and repainted, replaced furniture, and added new appliances.

Several renovations were needed due to Scooby-Doo's mischief.

"Hi there, Jenny." Christopher's lips spread into a grin as he drew near. He was wearing black shorts and a red shirt displaying the hotel slogan *Relax in Style: The Grand Michelangelo Hotel—Where Every Moment is a Work of Art.*

Maria and Jenny had outvoted Christopher's selection.

Despite his casual attire, he had an air of self-assurance and strength, yet there was a tenderness to him that she found appealing.

"Morning. Praise the Lord." Jenny responded with the Gullah greeting. She was clad in a long skirt and sported a similar T-shirt, although hers was pink.

"The hotel is looking fantastic," he said. "And so are you."

The intensity of his blue eyes consumed her, and her heart fluttered. The sharp breezes and rain tousled his dark hair, and she resisted the urge to slick it back.

"Thank you." She flushed. "Indeed, the progress is quite promising."

She stayed focused on the workers as she admired the grandeur of the building. They redesigned old-fashioned elements, upgraded the pool and eatery, and fixed the plumbing issue. Christopher lowered the carbon footprint with energy efficient lighting and water saving fixtures.

All the personnel had breathed fresh vitality into a beloved and historic structure, and her chest burst with satisfaction.

Even so, unease crept up on her. Everything was proceeding as planned, yet she couldn't ignore the growing fear that something disastrous was imminent. She'd seen too many dreams crumble, including her own. They had all worked tirelessly, but now all their ambitions depended on a single triumphant launch.

Christopher patted her shoulder. "Don't worry. I'll ensure all is ready for an impressive opening." His voice rang loud and distinct, and his touch was heartening and affectionate. "Congratulations on finding and hiring a full staff."

"Happily, Oliver conceded to raise the wages." She cast a glance at Christopher. "I suspect you had a hand in influencing his shift in perspective."

"Everyone is entitled to a decent salary. I simply ensured that he consented." He gestured subtly to Maria. "How generous of her to grace us with her presence today."

In a vibrant turquoise skirt, the color reminiscent of the ocean, Maria scurried into the hallway. She paired the skirt with a figure-hugging T-shirt emblazoned with the hotel logo. Her overall effect exuded effortless beauty.

"She only missed a handful of days." Jenny surveyed the water dripping from the ceiling. "Everyone gets sick."

"She was late, three days in a row. It's not exactly a difficult commute from her hotel room to the lobby. Did you reprimand her?"

"Of course not. Occasional tardiness is to be expected." Jenny felt an undeniable loyalty to Maria, and she'd resolved any jealousy issues. After all, Maria had crossed the Atlantic with her. "We owe her a mountain of thanks because her marketing and special promotional efforts paid off. I manage the reservations and discounts, and we nearly booked the hotel for June 30. At this rate, we'll need to redirect potential customers to other hotels for the rest of the summer."

"Any mysterious bookings from an infamous reviewer?" Christopher inquired.

"If you're referring to Evelyn Eckard, nothing so far, and I'm relieved. We haven't located a better bakery than Sun-Kissed Treats."

Temporarily, they'd opted for a menu featuring straight-forward, typical desserts sourced from the mainland.

Her gaze was drawn to the hallway when Scooby-Doo collided with Maria, making the trash can she had forgotten to empty tumble. The can clattered, spilling its contents.

Jenny let out a groan. "Oh no, not again."

Maria stumbled and steadied herself by gripping the wall. She glared down at the dog; her face imprinted with exasperation. She launched into a one-sided, heated exchange, scolding the dog for his misbehavior. Even though Jenny couldn't hear Maria, she understood her friend's actions were firm yet kind. She was a marshmallow at her core.

A previous discussion sprung into Jenny's mind.

"I have zero tolerance for dogs," Maria confessed shortly after their arrival. "Especially big ones."

"Why?" Jenny had questioned.

"I'm worried that Christopher's colossal canine will leap on me and knock me down."

"Does it happen often?"

"Constantly," Maria replied, recalling the numerous instances when the energetic dog had caused turmoil.

"Has he ever hurt you?"

"No, but my hair gets messed up. He slobbers, barks, and sheds all over." Maria had glowered at Scooby-Doo, who was busily destroying a pillow. "Why does he choose to chew on everything inanimate?"

"Christopher thinks it's separation anxiety," Jenny explained.

"Why? The dog is constantly by someone's side, but I seem to be in its vicinity most of the time."

"He assured me that Scooby-Doo is an outstanding dog."

"Really? Well, he's living in denial."

"Jenny?" Christopher skimmed his thumb along her wrist, grounding her back into the moment.

She eyed the dog. "Please spare me his praises."

"Me?" Christopher's tone, however, suggested otherwise.

As Maria chastised Scooby-Doo, the dog acted the part by appearing contrite. His tail drooped, and his massive frame sagged. Maria's facial expression relaxed as she scratched the dog's head. She smirked and took his paw when he lifted it for a handshake.

"That's the only trick he's got up his sleeve," Jenny observed.

Christopher grinned. "He's a smooth operator."

Maria wiped her cheek when the dog licked her.

"Yep. An undeniable ladykiller." Jenny laughed.

Christopher feigned surprise. "He hasn't been excessively terrible."

"He gnawed on four chairs, a half dozen coffee tables, and a shipment of bedding." Jenny shook her head. "May I remind you that all the items needed to be replaced?"

The corners of his lips twitched, as if daring humanity to join in on the joke only he understood. "Dogs enjoy chewing."

"So, you've noted, and let's not get into the topic of separation anxiety. *Puppies* enjoy chewing. Hasn't he outgrown the puppy stage by now?"

"He's a slow learner."

"Dad!" Sebastian skipped over; the towel snake draped over his shoulder. He'd decked himself out in a Sherlock Holmes detective hat that Jenny had purchased for him. The tweed houndstooth hat was wide-brimmed and featured two ear flaps. It skewed to the side, lending a humorous appearance. He gripped a huge magnifying glass in one hand. In the other, he brandished a notebook. "I uncovered more clues about the fire."

"Sebastian, please, not again. The fire chief is handling the investigation."

"But, Dad, something caused it."

"Yes. The chief is assuming it originated from a burning cigarette."

"He's not positive."

Jenny was keenly aware of Sebastian's investigative endeavors. She observed him searching the charred remains of the hut, taking out a piece of wood to analyze for clues.

"What did I warn you about?" Christopher said. "Steer clear of the hut. You must be mindful not to destroy any evidence the fire chief might use."

"I'm trying. But I talked with some people when I went on a hike with Mr. Grant."

"What did you and Mr. Grant talk about?"

"Not much. He was only there for a while that night when he took Mr. Rusty back to his house. He also adopted our white kitten because she's a companion for Mr. Rusty."

"Good."

"But Dad. I spied footprints." Sebastian's blue eyes twinkled. "When Mr. Grant was sitting on a rock to rest, I followed tracks leading to the dock. The tracks led into the water where there was softer sand."

Jenny smiled. "You're developing into a real detective, sweetheart. A regular Shaggy Rogers."

The boy reciprocated the smile. He looked healthier than he had in ages. His cheeks shone rosy and plump, and his dark locks were full and shiny.

"Don't encourage him, Jenny," Christopher muttered.

"There's more, Dad."

Christopher's concentration snapped back to Sebastian like a magnet. A muscle throbbed in his jaw.

"After the soft sand, the sand got firm again." Seconds stretched as Sebastian continued. "I traced the sand to where the huts are, but people were walking barefoot, and I lost the footprints. Maybe you can figure out whose shoes made them and—"

Christopher gave a noncommittal half smile that indicated *no way* as easily as it indicated *sure, we'll look together*. He concluded with a vague, "We'll see."

Sebastian pouted briefly before a huge grin overtook his face. He flipped open his notebook, displaying sketches of footprints. "I'm keeping track of my clues."

"Fire investigations are dangerous and complex." Christopher stressed the importance of avoiding unnecessary risks. "You're a young boy. Obey me and stay away from danger."

"But I have to interview witnesses."

"Dozens of islanders were there that night. Did Mr. Grant see anything unusual?" Christopher asked.

Sebastian scrunched up his face. "Nope."

"Then the case is concluded as far as you're concerned."

* * *

THAT AFTERNOON, Jenny was positioned behind the concierge's desk. The desk was built from reclaimed wood and boasted a contemporary island design.

She spoke on the phone to a potential guest who requested an extended weekend stay at the end of July. Party of six.

"We only have a few one-night openings available, but I'll be happy to add you to our waiting list." She inputted the woman's information into the computer.

With the phone still tucked between her ear and shoulder, she peered up as Anyika and Francis's wife, Fatu, ambled into the lobby. Both women wore cantaloupe-colored scarves on their hair, emphasizing the softness of their black skin. Both had knotted aprons over their Mumu dresses and carried sweetgrass baskets stocked with seeds and spices.

Jenny set down the phone. "Ladies, what a lovely surprise!"

"My grandson is in school, and we figured you could benefit from some help with your desserts," Anyika said. "Word is that you hired a fancy chef and his crew from Charleston to oversee the kitchen."

"Yes. We're starting with Friday and Saturday evenings for dinner and a Sunday brunch."

Anyika clicked her tongue. "I heard you're planning to serve chocolate cake as your main dessert."

"What's wrong with chocolate cake? You make it sound as if we'll be serving mud pies."

"Does chocolate cake seem like an authentic Gullah dessert to you?" Anyika's strong African characteristics—her broad nose, high cheekbones, and smiling full lips—evoked memories of her kind-heartedness and hospitality. "We brought our recipes."

"Where?"

Fatu tapped her forehead. "In our minds, child."

"I'm the hotel manager, not a baker," Jenny replied. "Maria is in charge of the restaurant."

"Where is she?"

"Resting."

"You frequently baked when you were young." Anyika tipped her chin toward Christopher. "I couldn't keep you and that fine-lookin boy over there out of my kitchen. Too bad he hurt you. I didn't think I could ever forgive him."

"That was a decade ago, and things have improved since then." Jenny glanced at Christopher. He'd patched the ceiling leak. He and the electrician were hunkered down by the elevator, trying to fix the overheated motor.

Given that the elevator was scarcely used, Jenny considered that fact troublesome.

A visibly upset Maria had been stuck between floors for over an hour before Christopher rescued her.

When she emerged, appearing as if smoke was pouring out of her ears, she'd hurled her red stiletto heels at Christopher, grazing his arm. Then she stomped into the breakroom, filled an overflowing glass of white wine, and announced she was done for the day.

Face flushed and hysterical, she then threatened to find Skipper Andy and leave on the next ferry until Jenny calmed her down.

What if they couldn't fix the elevator? Jenny envisioned Rusty cursing aloud if a guest requested him to lug a suitcase up a steep flight of stairs. He wasn't particularly adept when it came to customer service. She'd have a better chance to teach Scooby-Doo how to fetch than to win over Rusty. It simply wasn't in his DNA.

Maria refused to lug anything bigger than her handbag up the stairs. Jenny was curious about what Maria would say if she had to carry something heavier. She could only imagine.

She refocused, realizing that Fatu was speaking.

"With Sun-Kissed Treats closed, you're gonna need some mighty fine desserts." Fatu positioned a hand on her hip and swung her basket. "If you have flour, sugar, and butter, we've got the other ingredients covered. Time to go get baking!"

"Go where?" Sidetracked, Jenny reached to pick up her ringing phone. Fatu pushed her hand away.

"We're going into your swanky hotel kitchen. With you."

Jenny's lips parted with an objection, but before she refused, Anyika articulated in her familiar Southern drawl, "No excuses, honey."

"Can't I take a minute to consider?" An email pinged, and Jenny's fingers stretched out to her computer.

Nothing could prevent her from completing her tasks, not even a herd of stampeding elephants or a marching band parading across the patio. She glanced at the women, who frowned at her with unruffled disapproval, their expressive eyes glowering and attentive.

Right. Okay. Maybe two persistent Gullah women could persuade her.

"Okay. I can spare a couple of hours." Jenny shut down her computer and clicked off her phone. "I'll check the emails later."

After the elevator incident, Jenny knew Maria wasn't up to manning the front desk. Presently, she was playing checkers with Sebastian in his suite while she reclined on a lounge chair.

She caught Christopher's stare, and a silent nod of understanding passed between them. She pointed to Anyika and Fatu, then to the kitchen.

"Excellent." He voiced his approval. "Everything here is under control."

Jenny threw him a dubious glance. "Sure. As if that could ever happen at this hotel."

THE KITCHEN WAS a cook's dream, a spacious, well-lit area boasting gleaming stainless-steel appliances and an array of cooking tools ready to be used.

Jenny tied her hair into a sleek ponytail, washed her hands, and slipped on an apron. "What are we making?" She studied the ingredients.

"A traditional low-country dessert. Benne Seed Cookies, or what you folks call Sesame Seed Cookies, are suitable for this stylish hotel when it's teatime." Anyika's voice had hardly changed, maintaining its gravelly quality.

Fatu was serene and more reserved. Jenny hadn't seen her in years, but the faint lines around her nose and mouth hadn't noticeably deepened.

"First, toast the seeds, honey." Anyika's hands glided steadily over the stove. "We put them in a skillet on a medium flame and stir 'em until they get nice and brown. Then we'll mix 'em up with butter, flour, and sugar, and roll 'em into little balls."

"Don't overmix." Fatu waved her squashy arms as if she was trying to flap her way out of the kitchen. Her easygoing yet firm instructions made it seem like she was coaching a sports team instead of a baking class. "The dough should be crumbly and tender, not tough. My secret is to sprinkle a speck of salt on each cookie before you bake. It'll bring out the nutty flavor of the benne seeds."

Jenny pushed up her sleeves and baked alongside them, appreciative of their collective fellowship. She laughed at the women's chitchat and the wisdom and expertise her friends contributed to the task.

"We have dozens of favorite recipes to share with you, honey. Just ask." While Anyika rolled the dough, she teased Fatu. Jenny chuckled at the ease of their conversation, interspersed by measuring spoons clinking against bowls.

When the cookies finished baking, the women assembled to sample them. Jenny savored every morsel, the delectable flavor dancing on her tongue.

Between tastings, she brewed an herbal Gullah tea by steeping and straining the tea leaves, then adding honey and lemon. As she poured the steaming tea into mugs, the older women swapped stories. They talked about their history, struggles as marginalized people, and victories.

They stressed the significance of family relationships and the essential role of women. These were the beliefs, Anyika shared with a robust laugh, that bound the Gullah community together.

"De ooman ain't got but one heart." Fatu pounded her

chest with her fist to emphasize that everyone is human and should be treated with kindness and respect.

They proudly exchanged their thoughtful insights, creating a relaxed atmosphere rarely found in contemporary society.

Christopher stepped in and flashed Jenny a smile. The aroma of freshly baked cookies saturated the room, their gooey goodness tempting all within nose distance. His glance roamed over the organized counter, taking in the neatly arranged pots, pans, and baking utensils.

"Right on cue," Jenny joked, handing him a cookie.

He eagerly accepted, taking a hefty bite. He closed his eyes in pure pleasure, relishing the taste as he chewed. Once he finished, he opened his eyes, and his face transformed into an expression of sheer contentment. As he clasped her hand within his own, he applied a firm and heartfelt squeeze, expressing his gratitude.

"Jenny, these are amazing," he said. "You haven't lost your talent."

"You're giving me far more credit than I deserve. I'm learning from the most experienced and knowledgeable bakers in the world." Jenny beamed, then motioned to Fatu and Anyika. Flour and sugar blanketed their aprons. "These are the ladies who did all the work."

"You labored right alongside us," Fatu declared with a wink. "If you want my advice, stick to baking, honey. It's your forte."

Jenny laughed and thanked her.

"Do you still dream of becoming a baker?" Anyika leaned in, her tone quiet and intimate.

The four of them lapsed into a contemplative silence, the air heavy with an unspoken weight, and Jenny revisited the carefree naivete of her youth.

"Not anymore. Those were childhood fantasies." Her voice quivered with sadness, as if she had lost something precious that had once been within her grasp.

CHAPTER 11

The sun rose and set in a never-ending cycle, and two more weeks melted away.

Jenny checked the date on her computer. June 22.

Her gaze roamed over the grandeur of the hotel lobby, taking in every detail. They executed last-minute preparations with precision, and all were ready to greet their esteemed guests.

A large abstract artwork of musical instruments was mounted on a wall near the piano, and they created seating areas with ocean views.

In addition, Christopher had replaced the concrete patio with white tiles. The tiles were cool to walk on and ideal for guests returning from a swim.

A stylish Maria pirouetted across the floor, her dress ballooning around her as she spun. "The clock is almost striking six. Time to declare a break tonight and let the relaxation begin!"

She'd been irritable and moody the entire day, although, in one of her typical mood swings, she was now in high spirits. The spunky Maria had returned.

"Are you kidding?" Jenny tipped her head up. "It'll take forty more hours at this computer before I can even consider that idea. Besides, tomorrow morning is church service."

She attended services at the African Baptist Church every Sunday since she'd arrived on the island, the same church she had attended in her youth.

The air inside the sacred walls was brimming with infectious energy, with wooden pews, an elevated pulpit, and an array of cheerful decorations. Whenever she came within earshot, lively music and singing spilled from the open doors.

She dressed in her Sunday best and joined in the hand-clapping and uplifting spirituals. Often, she'd connect with the locals and shout enthusiastic "Amens" to the minister's passionate sermon.

Christopher and Maria had yet to go with her, but she hoped they would someday.

"We won't be out late. Will we never get to have any fun?" She came to a sudden halt. "We're on an island, which is a fairly typical place for people to unwind. You can't stand behind that desk forever."

Jenny sighed. She wanted the concierge counter open twenty-four hours a day, seven days a week, to assist guests while they explored the island's history. When Jenny proposed the idea, Fatu, an island native, offered to help, and Jenny was overjoyed.

"How about if we all head to dinner at the Drifting Sands?" Christopher sat at a table in the lobby, typing out a report on his laptop. His style was informal, with a fitted polo shirt tucked into tailored shorts. "My treat."

"You? Treat?" Maria gawked at him.

He lifted an eyebrow and waved a hand in her direction. "Yes. Me."

"You?" she parroted.

149

"I'm a generous guy, and tonight I won't try to hide it."

"You're suggesting we go to the Drifting Sands," Maria repeated. "Last week, I had a perfectly delightful time there."

"What could've possibly occurred since then to change your mind?" A grin twisted at the corners of Christopher's mouth. "Please tell all. I'm officially intrigued."

"Rob, the tattooed chef, that's what happened. I'll have to disguise myself or act like I'm invisible if he's there."

"Why? Did he run off with a circus performer or something?" Christopher kept his tone lighthearted. "I'm struggling to figure out how a relationship can crumble in a week."

"They always say that dating a chef is like having a secret ingredient in your life. And then, poof, it's gone."

"He's a cook," Christopher clarified. "Not a chef. The terms are often used interchangeably, but there is a *marked* difference. Consider comparing a deep-fried food to an elegantly prepared entrée."

"You're no longer dating the cook there?" Jenny turned to Maria. "I assumed you liked him."

"Not anymore. I wish I was Einstein, so I could figure out why all the guys I date end up being jerks."

"Rob didn't have a top-secret collection of veggie burger recipes to share with you?" Christopher joked. "If no dice, I'm sure he could recommend his favorite tattoo parlor."

Maria's lips froze in a thunderous scowl.

"Are there any other attractive men on the horizon?" Jenny's spirited tone indicated she wasn't entirely serious. "What about Rusty?"

"Once, he took my hand and held it," Maria replied.

"How romantic."

"His hand felt like a handshake from an old friend—firm, dependable, and with a few calluses that could probably sand down wood. It was both reassuring and oddly endearing. But then there's Evan Farrenway, the incredibly appealing schoolteacher. My teachers never looked that good." Maria batted her eyelashes and tossed back her hair. "He's such a down-to-earth guy. Unfortunately, he invited *you* on a date with him. Not me."

Jenny glanced at Christopher. A muscle in his jaw twitched.

"Where did you two end up going for coffee?" Christopher inquired, his tone flat. "Sun-Kissed Treats? Oh, wait, they're closed. Maybe you went fishing, and he snared a barracuda with his bare hands."

"Christopher, please." Jenny knew that her cheeks had pinkened.

Evan Farrenway had dropped by the hotel a few days earlier. He had recommended the seating upgrades, along with the abstract artwork. He told Jenny that he had studied hard to become a professional decorator.

"Mr. Farrenway is the schoolteacher?" Maria had mouthed to Jenny when he'd sauntered into the lobby. The women gaped as he strode to the counter, lifted his wire-rimmed eyeglasses, and introduced himself. His blond hair complemented his compelling facial features and the tiny amount of stubble on his chin. His arms and chest were well-defined beneath a crisp white shirt and khaki pants.

"Were you the decorator who incorporated the local artisans' designs?" Jenny had asked, motioning to the seagrass lamp.

"Yes." He gave her a wink.

"I'm impressed. Your decorating is spot-on."

"Extraordinary!" Maria reached over and squeezed his biceps.

He smiled, especially at Jenny, and brushed off Maria's obvious advances. He leaned against the counter and seemed genuinely engaged in everything she said. They shared common island experiences, and he invited her out for coffee.

"You and Farrenway weren't gone that long," Christopher continued. "I guess the fish were in no mood to bite that day."

"What every fisherman dreams of hearing," she murmured with a wry smile. "Regardless, we had fun."

For some reason, Jenny felt irritated. Irritated at Christopher. Irritated at herself. These fourteen-hour workdays were finally getting to her. Why did he constantly pervade her thoughts, even when she'd attempted to enjoy her date with Evan?

"Be careful, Christopher," Maria cautioned. "That sounds an awful lot like the green-eyed monster."

"You couldn't possibly look more satisfied, Maria," he replied.

Jenny pressed her lips together. She didn't intend to tell Christopher that Evan constantly sent her flirty emojis on her phone—heart eyes or an iconic wink. Often, her thumbs hovered over her phone's keyboard, although she seldom typed a response.

Sebastian skipped into the lobby with Scooby-Doo galloping alongside him.

"I listened to you all talk." A captivating smile lit his cherubic face. "Can I join you for dinner, too?"

The dog eyed an embroidered throw pillow on the sofa, and Jenny waggled her finger at him. "Don't even consider chewing up that pillow! You've caused the hotel several thousand dollars in expenses already."

"Then it's decided." Maria sliced through the conversation. "We're all heading to the Drifting Sands for dinner."

"I can't," Jenny said. "There's a ton of work left to do here."

"Evan Farrenway might be at the restaurant." Maria cast a sidelong glance at Christopher's frown, then grinned at

Jenny. "That drop-dead gorgeous guy is reason enough to go. He must eat somewhere on this island, and the Drifting Sands is the only place unless you count the crab cake stand at the marina."

"Evan goes out of town on the weekends." Jenny's competitive streak kicked in. She peeked at Christopher and noted his deepening frown. She'd hit a nerve by referring to Evan by his first name.

"If he's not at the restaurant, then that's the most encouraging announcement I've heard all day." Christopher closed his laptop and stood, causing a wave of apprehension to wash over her. "Can you be ready by seven o'clock, Jenny?"

She hesitated. She didn't want to let anyone down, but the mounting workload leading up to the hotel's opening loomed over her like a dark cloud. The thought of taking a break, even for a short while, seemed like an impossible luxury.

"I never mentioned my intention to go," she replied.

"It'll do everyone good to get out," Christopher said.

"Please, Miss Jenny?" Sebastian tugged at her blouse, looking up at her with a hopeful expression.

She sighed and made a reluctant decision. "Okay. I'll do my best, but I'll need to shower and change first." She didn't want to disappoint any of them, yet her mind was already calculating the amount of time needed to catch up when she got back.

"Ready for a lightning-fast sprint with the dog before we take over the town?" Maria clasped Sebastian's hand. "I'll be sure he has his inhaler, Christopher, so he'll be fine. You two don't have to rush. Sebastian and I will just order everything on the menu and eat our way through the appetizers while we wait."

After a quick shower, Christopher stepped out of his suite

and ascended the stairs to the second floor. He slung a linen blazer over his shoulders and knocked on Jenny's door.

She moved into the hallway, motioned to her watch, and grinned. "You're one minute late," she laughingly admonished. "I've been pacing my room, waiting for you."

"I'm five minutes early." He checked his watch, too. "However, now that I'm aware of how eager you are to see me, I'll make it a priority to always be early."

The schoolhouse clock in the lobby chimed seven o'clock, and he shot her a what-did-I-tell-you grin.

He retreated a step to admire her. Naturally beautiful, she wore a strapless halter jumpsuit, the top two buttons unbuttoned. The fuchsia shade complemented her golden locks and brought out her vibrant green eyes and thick black eyelashes. Her complexion was translucent and flawless. She'd styled her hair into a French braid that cascaded down her back, each strand meticulously in place.

The fabric of her jumpsuit was feather-light, lending a graceful motion to her steps. A slit up one side emphasized her long, toned legs.

He couldn't hide his appreciative grin. "You are stunning, Jenny."

"I appreciate your kindness. You look splendid, too." She covered a yawn beneath her slim fingertips. "I apologize. I'm so drained lately." Her provocative smile sent a rush of longing through him.

"My apologies for encouraging you to go tonight, but I couldn't resist." He slid his arms around her and inhaled. Her faint scent was a blend between an exotic flower—a plumeria came to mind—and a saltwater breeze.

"Don't be sorry." She shook a strand of hair from her face. "I'm overworked and underpaid, none of which is your fault."

"You're working far too hard."

"Everywhere I look, there's an untouched pile of tasks,

each more difficult than the last. I find myself overwhelmed with weariness and plagued by doubts regarding my competence."

A few more stray hairs framed her face, softening her features. He lifted a silky strand from her forehead. "Do you like your job?"

"Truthfully?" She averted her eyes. "No."

"You enjoy baking, though."

"Baking is a blurry, far-off fantasy." She granted him a smile. "Go ahead. Say it."

"Say what?"

"Share any positive, uplifting slogan that comes to mind to boost my morale."

"You must make these choices for yourself." He lifted his shoulders. "However, I have a confession, Jenny."

"Let me guess. You're passionate about being an architect because it's the dream job you always wanted."

"More than that. I have a tremendous stake in this hotel."

"We all do."

Despite her unintended dismissal of his words, he grinned. She allowed him to keep her in his arms, and he was pleased.

"Some of us have more of an interest than others." He gave her an extended, meaningful look.

"What do you mean?"

He blew out a breath. "I'm a part owner of this hotel, together with Olive. As I mentioned, we met in the army, and when he was looking for an investment property last year, this place caught his eye. I encouraged him because I was familiar with the location. I had saved money for years and invested all I had into this project."

"Christopher, I heard whispers that you might be the owner, but I never got the chance to ask you." She gazed up at him. "But how? You're not a billionaire like Oliver."

"Very true, and after this venture, I'm even poorer."

"Why didn't you tell me sooner?"

"I couldn't find the right opportunity. How could I have anticipated that you would be upset with me from the very first minute you arrived?"

"You're replying to my question with a question." She stepped backward, taking herself out of his reach. "Why did you decide to invest in a completely dilapidated building?"

"You were right all along. I'm drawn to this island and all its traditions."

"Don't you dare tell me your investment is all because of me."

"You arrived unexpectedly and had nothing to do with my decision."

He didn't confess, however, that she was always in his thoughts.

"Perfect!" She knotted her hands. "Now the picture is crystal-clear. After not seeing each other for a decade, we both show up on this island. You drove a sound bargain with Oliver, and I'm pushing myself way too hard ... for you."

"Maybe this isn't your ideal job."

Her gaze narrowed. "You're firing me?"

He took the silence that followed as consent for his explanation. "No. You're overly competent. I simply want you to be happy, and you're clearly stressed."

"I'm frustrated."

"You have all the traits to excel in any career, and I'm here to lend a helping hand." He pressed a brief kiss on her cheek and guided her down the stairs, then steered her outside. A balmy breeze carrying the scent of lush vegetation greeted them.

She leaned into his shoulder as they walked. "Christopher Drake, I must admit that you're a terrific boss ... most of the time."

He laughed. "Face it, Jenny. In our relationship, you're the one who is always in charge."

Their eyes met in a spark of mutual understanding.

"Did you miss me?" He glanced meaningfully toward the beach, where they had danced together in an easy rhythm to an Elvis Presley song, the golden sand rolling beneath their feet.

"Miss you? In the few minutes we were apart today? Umm, no. I see you almost constantly."

The sun had begun its descent, painting the sky in subtle shades of mauve. The temperature cooled as they neared the ocean, and she shivered.

He tucked his jacket around her shoulders. "Do you prefer walking or hopping on a golf cart?"

"I'd prefer to walk."

He held her hand as if it were the most natural thing in the world. They strolled along the shore; the endless waves rhythmic and soothing. Recollections floated through his mind, clear and heartrending.

When they were young, they'd explored the numerous coastlines, and their friendship had been effortless. He recalled dips in the ocean, spying on snowy egrets, and collecting exquisite pieces of sea glass from the sand.

As they continued, she paused often, drawn to the tidal pools brimming with iridescent shells and schools of silver fish. The occasional seagull dove from overhead, enhancing the idyllic scene.

The sky grew darker. The constellations of stars twinkled, lighting the beach with tiny flickers. From afar, the beam from the lighthouse's lantern cast its light over the ocean.

"This is peace," Jenny murmured. "This is tranquility."

"I think you should be aware of something."

"This island isn't real," she half-joked.

He didn't hear her. What he heard was, *"Hold me in your arms and kiss me."*

Mindful of the few feet separating them, he analyzed it.

The distance was volatile, predetermined, and closable.

He chose the latter.

Slowly, he drew her to him, giving her ample time to back away. Instead, she touched his cheek and whispered his name.

"What should I be aware of, Christopher?" She laughed quietly, a pure, bell-like sound reminding him of wind chimes.

"The attraction I feel for you is powerful, Jenny."

For an indeterminable moment, they were silent, as if even a word might disrupt the spell of the fading daylight, the link to the land uniting them as one. They stood there suspended in time, as if the island itself held its breath in anticipation of their next move.

"Your smile lights up the entire island." He lowered his head, his lips grazing hers. His arms adjusted to mold her to him, and he increased the intensity of his kiss.

Affection and desire smoldered in her eyes as she followed his lead.

Minutes later, he lifted his mouth and cradled her face in his hands.

She shifted, but he tightened his hold.

"Don't move, Jenny," he murmured, his voice husky. "I want to stay like this for a while longer."

She leaned back, watching him and watching his lips. He intended to accept her encouragement to kiss her again, but an instant before their mouths touched, he restrained himself.

"Nope." His mind reluctantly fought for control. "We need more time to talk and get reacquainted with each other."

"Then talk. I'm listening."

"Unfortunately, coherent speech is impossible for me right now."

He clasped her hand once more, and they wandered along a dirt trail. Lofty, arching branches cast dabbling shadows on the ground. Tiny creatures zipped through the foliage, their cheeping creating an animated soundtrack. Now and then, glimpses of the waves became visible through the trees.

As they got closer to the restaurant, a group of Gullah women sat in a circle, perched on stools, talking energetically. Beads of perspiration gathered on their foreheads and necks, and they wiped the dampness away with their palms. They wore dazzling, loose-fitting clothing and conversed and laughed with each other. Their dialect was a combination of English and Gullah.

Two women skillfully wove fishnets, knitting and fastening the strings into complex knots. They carved their needles from pointed rushes and strung the nets together.

"To keep the fishnets taut," Jenny told him.

Several other women braided baskets using lengthy, slender reeds of sweetgrass and palmetto leaves, the symbol of the south. One woman used her teeth to slice the sweetgrass into narrow strips, then wielded her fingers to direct the strips into place.

Christopher took it all in—the squawking of the seabirds, the deep hum of the surging sea, and the mild whispering of marsh grass beneath his feet. Each was a reminder of the wild beauty of nature.

The salty tang of the ocean breeze mingled with the earthy smell of the soil, enveloping him in nostalgia. This was the place he'd been yearning for his entire adulthood. The summers of his youth brought him back to life.

CHAPTER 12

Christopher stopped beside an old, weathered structure and squinted through the grimy windows.

"Are you eavesdropping on someone's conversation?" Jenny teased.

"I'm confirming that the restaurant is up and running. This window is so dirty you can't see through it." With a mighty tug, he yanked the door open. "Sometimes this place shuts down for no—"

"Greetings from the Drifting Sands!" A server with abundant auburn ringlets and a nose piercing greeted them. "How many people are in your party?"

Jenny scanned the restaurant. "Two, but we're meeting—" The smell of beer and greasy fried food permeated the air, combined with the occasional puff of cigarette smoke. There appeared to be more patrons in the restaurant than on the entire island.

The server indicated the bar. "We're full service. If you'd like a table, wave me over." She handed them each a twenty-page menu.

Seated at a recessed booth fashioned from a thin slab of

Formica, Sebastian and Maria beckoned them over. In an opposite corner stood a pool table, scarred by extended use, and a lighted jukebox blaring reggae music. The soulful sound of Bob Marley's voice was instantly recognizable.

The restaurant had a rural atmosphere with mismatched, bulky furniture and planked floors and walls. The area was cramped but airy, with glimpses of the ocean through the windows. The owner had sketched pictures of local sports teams in black markers and framed them alongside a flashing beer sign. He'd copied the teams from a calendar, but they resembled caricatures rather than people.

Jenny and Christopher passed by the bar, which served as the focal point. The rowdy crowd and the commentator's speech resonated throughout the establishment.

"Ahh, the great American pastime. Watching sports and enjoying a cold one." Christopher gestured to the wide-screen television. The patrons rooted for either of the Carolina teams.

Jenny chuckled. "It's practically a requirement."

After they sank down beside Maria and Sebastian, the server showed up and braced her hands on the sticky table. "What can I get you, folks?"

"A fresh glass of red wine for me, please." Maria zeroed in on Christopher while she nibbled on a leftover, limp onion ring. "Don't forget, you're footing the bill."

"How can I forget anything when you remind me at every turn?" Christopher muttered.

Sebastian, Christopher, and Jenny decided on water with their meal.

Jenny slipped off Christopher's jacket, then skimmed the eighth page of the menu.

"We finished the appetizers. Now I'm ordering a salad." Maria picked at the peeling Formica. "Or the crispy shrimp."

161

"Ahh, the perils of being a pescatarian," Christopher joked. "Stick with the shrimp."

"Why? What's the specialty?"

Christopher motioned to the flashing beer sign.

"Not their salads?"

"It depends on your definition of a salad." Christopher scrunched up his face in a humorous expression. "If you drench a bed of stale lettuce in oil and vinegar, then top it with crumbled corn chips, it might pass."

Jenny scrutinized the menu. "Every item is deep fried."

"The French fries are great, Miss Jenny!" Sebastian exclaimed.

"I suppose," Christopher said with a smile. "But my arteries and my arteries alone will decide that."

When the server returned with their drinks and silverware, they ordered hamburgers and French fries. All except Maria, who requested a chef salad, despite the server's raised eyebrows. Christopher joked that Rob, the so-called cook, might emerge from the kitchen with a bag of corn chips to dump over Maria's head. Anything to avoid making a salad.

"A lighthearted jest," Christopher clarified at Maria's scowl.

"Is your favorite cook in charge tonight?" Jenny peered at the pass-through window leading to the kitchen.

"No. When I asked our server about him, she glared at me like I had just insulted her grandmother." Maria shook her head. "I suspect they're dating."

"Uh, oh," Christopher said. "She is protective of him. Careful, or she'll spit in your salad."

Maria clattered her fork on her appetizer plate. "She informed me that Rob sailed away for the weekend, along with Salifu and Mr. Farrenway. Those guys know something that we don't."

"Like what?" Sebastian asked.

"Like there's a universe of adventure out there in contrast to what's happening here."

"Why?" Sebastian splashed the ice cubes in his water glass with his spoon. "What's happening here?"

"Nothing. Cheers!" Maria indulged in a hearty gulp of wine, as if she were single-handedly keeping the vineyards in business.

Jenny murmured a quiet prayer of grace. She thanked God for food and friendship and expressed her gratitude for the meal they shared and their commitment to the island's traditions.

They sealed the evening with a cheerful clink of their glasses and a toast to a well-deserved break.

With the dinner finished and Christopher settled the tab, Maria volunteered to escort Sebastian back to the hotel, assuring an early night.

Jenny glanced toward the exit. "I'm tired, too."

Christopher noticed the weariness on her features, the subtle yearning in her eyes. Determined to ease her fatigue and bring a spark of joy into her life, he made a mental note to help her recharge. He understood the importance of finding moments of levity and lightness among the demands of a heavy workload.

"Hold on a minute." He smiled and reached for his jacket. "I've got a proposition for you. How about if we dive into a game of pool? If I win, I'll whisk you away to a secret destination where adventure awaits at every turn. Deal or no deal?"

"Is that a challenge?"

"Absolutely. I'm offering you a break."

"Where? Where will you bring me?"

"You'll see when we're done." He wanted to show her a cherished place that was close to his heart. He hoped it was close to her heart, too.

"And if *I* win?" she pressed.

He kissed her forehead. Replenishing her spirit and rekindling her energy was essential for her well-being. "We'll burn that bridge when we get to it. However, you probably aren't up to the task of beating me."

Jenny rose. "You're on."

The floor was tacky, with scattered nachos and spilled pints of frothy beer. As they walked to the pool table, their feet stuck to the floor like gum on a hot day.

"We're in for a sticky game," Christopher wisecracked, earning a chuckle from Jenny.

He strode to the jukebox and inserted some coins. The faint scent of dust and aged vinyl records gave way to the melodic notes of "Don't Stop Believin'," Journey's classic hit.

"My favorite song," Jenny said.

"Me, too." Christopher snatched a cue and rack, then gathered the balls in the center of the felt table. "Are you familiar with the rules? First is the significance of the cue ball. This precious white ball serves as your mighty tool to propel the other balls into their pockets."

"Thanks for the tip. The owners didn't permit me here when I was a kid, and you were too poor to come."

He peered up at Jenny as he leaned over the table to line up his shot.

She observed him from the other side. "Careful now. Don't scratch."

"Just watch me sink this."

"You're certainly sure of yourself."

He grinned. "If I win, I'll give you a piggyback ride."

"Just what I always wanted. By the way, that is not a rule."

"Here's how it's done." Christopher took his shot. The ball bounced off the table's edge and landed in the pocket.

"You got so lucky." She groaned in mock defeat. "If *you* miss, you play your next shot blindfolded."

"Deal."

"You'll follow the rules, I hope?"

"One can only hope." He handed her the cue stick. "Now you."

Jenny steadied the stick and peered over her shoulder.

"Loosen your grip." He hovered over her, wrested her tight fingers from the stick, and realigned them. "Keep the stick straight out and aim."

"Oh, I forgot." She lined up her shot. "There's something I neglected to mention earlier."

"Have you mastered spinning the ball?"

"Yes." The ball spun and hit a striped ball, sending it careening into a corner pocket. "I went against my mother's wishes and snuck into the restaurant to play pool when I turned fourteen. Usually by myself or with the owner's son, but I got the hang of it fairly quick."

"You disobeyed your mother."

"Yes."

"And you played anyway."

"Yes."

"Did you win?"

"Why does it matter if I won or lost?"

"It doesn't. I was merely wondering if you played properly."

"I did. The other players accepted me as part of the gang." She watched him smugly, then glanced at the cluster of onlookers at the bar, who observed them with glee and curiosity. They spoke among themselves and gestured to Christopher and Jenny, although their conversations were out of earshot.

He inched closer. "And I forgot to say." He tugged the cue stick from her hands, got into position, and sent a striped ball, followed by a red ball, plunging into a pocket. "That my father had a knack for drinking beers in countless pool halls while he squandered his hard-earned paycheck on Friday nights. Naturally, he brought me with him, and I gained some serious skills. I was a celebrated legend on the billiards scene."

She laughed. "A remarkable upbringing, Christopher."

"Hey, it worked." He laid the cue stick down, crossed to the bar, and returned with two glasses of water. He placed the glasses on a table beside her. "Did you eventually attend college, Jenny?"

"You're asking me that question now?"

"Why not? I'm eager to piece together all the years we missed."

"I never found a subject I was passionate about and didn't enjoy formal classes. After my father uprooted our family, he left my mother and me with no financial support. Every day was more difficult than the last."

He listened to her and realized a pang of empathy for her difficult past. "What did you do?"

"We contacted our cousins in New York."

"Did they respond?"

"No."

The pain of their rejected plea was etched in her voice, a testament to the dashed hopes that she had harbored.

"Believe me, we didn't pack any bags ahead of time," she continued. "Instead, my mother and I applied for positions as house cleaners. We scoured floors and filthy bathrooms caked with toothpaste stains."

"Hard jobs," he acknowledged.

"Yes, but they paid the bills."

"Have you considered culinary school? How about enrolling in online courses?"

She perched on a stool and placed her hands in her lap, as if seeking comfort and support. She cast her eyes at her water glass, then moved it aside, as if it were a topic she didn't wish to address.

"I appreciate your advice." She hesitated. He could almost see the wheels turning in her head, the internal clash between practicality and goals. "College isn't feasible anymore."

The word 'feasible' floated, revealing Jenny's perception of the limitations imposed upon her by her circumstances. Her admission illustrated a picture of a dream deferred; aspirations abandoned in the face of her harsh judgment of her abilities.

"The possibility of a change is always available, Jenny. You can attend college anytime." He wanted to say more, though the palpable tension stifled his words, and the timing wasn't suitable for pressing her further. Aware of the fragile balance between them, he didn't dare risk upsetting her.

When their pool game ended, Jenny snatched Christopher's jacket and declared him the winner.

"It seems I owe you," she said.

He grinned. "Are you ready to pay up?"

"How?"

"Hop on my back, and I'll carry you out." He stretched out his arms.

She peered around the restaurant. "In front of all these people?"

"It's all in good fun." He gave an "OK" sign to several islanders drinking at the bar. "Don't fault the player, fault the game."

He lifted her, and she climbed onto his back. As he proceeded to the door, her body bounced with each of his strides, and she broke into giggles.

Simulating a struggle, he feigned a groan. "You're not half bad as a piggyback rider."

"Hey, I'm a professional at this." She poked him in the

ribs. "You're lucky it's not the other way around. Or rather, *I'm* lucky."

He heaved a sigh. "Boy, am I ever blessed."

They stepped outside, and he spun her.

"Watch it, mister!" Jenny laughed. "I'm not sure I trust your twirling ability."

"Oh, come on. I won't drop you. You know you can depend on me."

The evening was cool and crisp, strongly scented with night-blooming jasmine, dewy earth, and the bark of a far-off dog. The smoky trace of a distant campfire and the recollections of their shared moments evoked poignant memories.

He turned. Did he detect a touch of sadness in her eyes? Yearning? Regret?

He wasn't certain.

He set her on the grass and guided her along a tree-lined path.

"Thank you for a delightful time," she expressed with heartfelt gratitude in her eyes.

"Our evening isn't over yet." He stopped near the road's edge and drew her close for a kiss, then steered her to a group of huts scattered among the trees, resembling a charming hamlet.

"You're quite the romantic, aren't you?" she teased.

"I like to think so. I couldn't resist revealing this place to you. Does it strike a chord?" he asked.

Positioned in a secluded corner, the hut sat alone, creating an intimate atmosphere distinct from the others.

"Of course. We used to frequent this place often," she murmured.

"My father's garage and my old house are a mile down the road," Christopher said.

"My house isn't far from there, either."

Recollections of their childhoods flooded his mind, providing a sense of belonging.

"Have you visited your house yet?" she asked.

"Nope. Too many memories."

"Returning to the places you left behind can be challenging, but it's important to cling to the happiness you experienced there."

"I agree," he replied quietly.

She grasped his hand. Her steps slowed, becoming more deliberate as she ventured nearer the hut. "On sweltering days, we were here on countless afternoons."

"Which was every day."

"Right," she said. "The place didn't exactly exude luxury. Any chance of running water yet?"

He smiled. "We're well past that stage."

Her eyebrows rose inquisitively. "Why are we here, Christopher?"

"This is where Sebastian and I first stayed when we arrived. Olive and I took great pride in the transformation."

They stepped inside, to the intoxicating scent of old books and the brackish tang of seawater.

Jenny stopped short. "This can't be the same hut. Everything is brand new."

"I paid particular attention to the updates. It's more elaborate than the other huts."

Polished paneling adorned the walls instead of bare logs or grass. Flamboyant red indoor-outdoor carpet covered much of the floor beneath a queen-sized bed draped with creamy linens. Beside the bed sat a mahogany bureau.

A plush daybed emblazoned in vivid blue rested off to the side, next to a table and chairs crafted from timber. Unfastened wooden shutters allowed a cool breeze to flow through the space.

"How incredible. The furniture is perfect, and I adore the

169

brightness. It's so open." She clapped her hands in enthusiastic applause. "What about that running water?"

"Simple and solved." He directed her to the compact, efficient kitchen, tucked discreetly beside the main living area. A miniature refrigerator was located underneath the counter, besides a two-burner stove and a microwave oven. Above the sink, a window afforded a panorama of the seashore.

"After the fire, I hooked up smoke alarms in all the huts. I'll never forgive myself for overlooking such an important detail." He inhaled deeply, then exhaled. "If I had installed the alarms sooner, I could have prevented the damage to Rusty's hut."

"No one was hurt, and everyone makes mistakes. At least you did it."

He forced a weak smile. "Thanks."

"Is the outhouse still there? Should I have brought a flashlight and a hand sanitizer?" She grinned and glanced out the window.

"A real bathroom is complete with a medicine cabinet and towel racks." He opened a door to display a modern toilet, sink, and bathing area, cleverly separated by a pane of glass. The shower featured a pebble-lined floor, while glazed mosaic tiles in shades of cobalt and lime adorned the walls.

"I'm so impressed." She touched his arm. "Is anyone living here?"

"No one since Sebastian and I moved out." He guided her to the rear entrance, where a wooden veranda jutted out, providing a spectacular view of the ocean.

"I have something special to give you." His hands trembled slightly. His indecision and nervousness showed, and he vacillated. *Was this the right time?*

She twirled a strand of hair around her fingers. "What is it? Should I guess?"

"You can try."

"Are we going on an excursion to the Isle of Palms?"

He wagged his eyebrows. "Too rich for my blood."

"Does the surprise involve a water balloon and a bucket of mud?"

He chuckled. "Excellent guesses, but no." He indicated a chair and asked her to sit. A last, single ray of sunshine shone through the window. "You're an inspiration, Jenny. I wrote something for you the week after you arrived."

"You're still writing? When you were a teenager, there was that article you submitted to the Island Docket Newspaper."

"Two articles. The second was about oyster houses."

"You published both. We were so excited."

"This isn't an article." He broke into a smile and shifted. "I wrote a … poem … for you."

"Me? Really? I can't wait to hear it." Curiosity reflected in her eyes. "I once joked about you being a bona fide Leonardo da Vinci because you sketched floor plans and then would compose a poem."

"Is that so odd?" he asked softly.

"No. Not for you. I remember you telling me your mother wrote poems."

He gnawed on his lower lip. "Maybe that's why I enjoy writing them."

Since it evoked memories of her.

He pondered the untrodden path of his mother's aging, how he mirrored her in certain ways, and the innate desire to forge a bond with her.

How would they have connected on a deeper level? She'd left without a trace, no note or verse to anchor her memory. The writer, his mother, had no words for her own son.

Christopher held back the tears clouding his vision.

He remembered her heart-shaped face, her soft blue eyes,

and her brown hair in loose waves. In her last days on the island, she continuously wore the amulet necklace.

The amulet was supposed to bring peace to the Grant household. How long had peace prevailed? Mere hours? Perhaps days? Regrettably, it had not endured. She was gone soon afterward, leaving him with only unanswered questions and a dull ache in his gut that never went away.

Gullah superstitions had achieved nothing.

He walked to the bureau, eased open the top drawer, and removed a sheet of paper. The paper was slightly damp, having absorbed the humidity in the air.

He sank next to Jenny, breathed in deeply, and presented her with the poem. He prayed she would understand what he was trying to convey. Carefully, he had composed each phrase.

She lifted the paper up to the light. "May I read it out loud?"

"Why not?" His hands fidgeted, and he folded them together to keep them still. He felt more grounded and centered that way.

She cleared her throat and began,

"The waves crash against the shore,
As I stand here once more.
We've come full circle, it seems,
Back to where we first chased our dreams.
I've loved you since we were young,
And as we are here among
The salt and sand and sea,
I realize how much you mean to me.
Now we have a second chance
To rekindle our romance.
I promise to love you every day,
In every single way.
So, take my hand and walk with me,

At the edge of this island, wild and free.
And together, we'll create a love so true,
The ocean will forever sing of me and you."

"CHRISTOPHER." She set down the poem, her eyes bright with unshed tears. "You have a lovely way of expressing yourself. Thank you."

"Do you like it?"

"It's the most thoughtful thing anyone has ever done for me." Her features softened. "But why did you write this?"

"I adore you, Jenny, but I don't have all the answers. We can figure it out together." He uttered the words simply, quietly. "I couldn't determine a more honest way to express my feelings."

She leaned over and kissed him on the cheek. "May I keep this?"

"The poem is yours."

"Thank you." She shrugged the jacket over her shoulders and slid the poem into the pocket.

He steered her outside. A sliver of moonlight beamed down, lighting the clearing. The mighty waves crashed against the shoreline, and the wind whistled. Their world was an endless carpet of stars.

She caressed his cheek and threaded her fingers through his hair. He placed his hand on her back and felt the heat of her skin beneath the fabric of her jumpsuit.

He showered kisses along her neck. "I love you, Jenny. I always have, and I always will."

She withdrew and cast her gaze downward. "Haven't we gone beyond the point of starting over?"

"Our love is genuine." His voice shook, barely above a whisper. "We're home again, and nowhere else on earth matches what we have here."

"I need more time, Christopher. That's the only answer I can give for now."

He reined in his declarations, averted his gaze, and stifled the words begging to be said. "Okay. I don't want to mess this up or lose you again."

He wished he could undo how she had interpreted his rejection when they were teens. He'd wanted what he'd thought was best for her.

"We should start back." A tiny tear made its way down her cheek as she laced her hand with his. "Please be patient with me."

"I have no intention of scaring you away or making you uncomfortable." He struggled to come up with suitable words, suffocated by the power of his feelings. "I won't rush you."

Did he have a choice? He summoned up the bravery to share his poem and express his love, wanting nothing more than her affection.

His heart overflowed with joy and sorrow, hope and fear, all at once.

Would she ever find the courage to trust him again?

CHAPTER 13

Something was wrong.

Dread overwhelmed Jenny the minute they reached the darkened hotel.

Maria perched on a chair in the center of the patio, her silhouette backlit by the lobby lights. Her hands shook as she clutched an empty wineglass.

"Where were you two?" Her eyes blazed with anger. "I phoned you six times, and neither of you picked up. What about your child monitor, Christopher? Wasn't it on you?"

"It was. Yes. Jenny and I played a round of pool after dinner." His posture stiffened. "Then we went for a walk, and I showed her the hut that Sebastian and I used to stay in. There's no cell phone service because it's so remote in the woods."

Maria unleashed a string of inaudible curses. She leaped up, skating her chair back so quickly that her wineglass tipped over. The glass shattered on the tile, spraying them with droplets of red wine. Airborne, the pungent smell of alcohol saturated the floral scent of her perfume.

Jenny's breathing quickened. "What's the matter?"

Ignoring Jenny, Maria twisted to Christopher. "Don't you lock this hotel?"

"Of course. Why?"

"You'll see."

"Where's Sebastian?" His pitch rose with alarm. He scanned the area as if Sebastian were hiding behind a lounge chair or a planter. Soft moonlight filtered through the swaying palm trees. Beyond, a symphony of nocturnal creatures launched their calls and chirps, and glowing fireflies flitted into the night.

"He's fine. I settled him in his bed as soon as we got back, and he fell asleep immediately. Scooby-Doo is in his crate." Maria's knuckles faded to white as she gripped the patio table to steady herself. Then she teetered toward the entrance, beckoning Christopher and Jenny inside with a red-manicured finger. Much of her nail polish had flaked off.

"Come with me." An edict, not a friendly request. "I want to show you something."

"What?" Christopher demanded as they hurried through the lobby.

"The breakroom."

"I've seen it many times." Jenny quickly replied.

"Trust me. Not like this." Maria shoved open the door to the breakroom with her backside.

Jenny stepped inside and put her hand to her mouth to stifle a scream. Her stomach curdled, and bile rose in her throat.

Someone had trashed the room. The furniture was flipped over, the cushions on the couch were slashed, and the expensive espresso maker was missing. All the fresh flowers in the ceramic vase were scattered. The refrigerator door was thrown ajar, and the uncapped water bottles and energy drinks caused liquid to dribble all over the floor. Miraculously, the books on Gullah culture were spared, while the guidebooks were destroyed.

"Fortunately, Sebastian didn't witness any of this," Maria declared, her voice laced with fear. "I only discovered this a short while ago. I can't believe the amount of destruction that was caused."

"Who would do such a thing? The entire area looks like a hurricane hit it." Jenny cast a glance at Christopher, seeking solace in his presence. He was already on his phone, swiftly implementing action to resolve the situation. The urgency in his face mirrored her own sentiments, and she appreciated his quick response.

Within minutes, Francis Grant, Rusty, a half-dozen island volunteers, and Michael Freid, the fire chief, arrived.

The chief ran a hand through his gray hair. "Listen up, folks. This is more serious than I imagined. We'll search and dust for fingerprints."

His words were foreboding, and his arrival signified the gravity of the situation. Someone had planned the vandalism, and the volunteers whispered, worried about the perpetrator.

"We'll all collaborate on this," the fire chief added. "And we'll find this person or persons."

His remarks sparked a discussion. Most had seen instances of petty crimes, often the result of youthful exuberance or frustration.

"Search everywhere and everything," Christopher said. "Notify the chief of any suspicious activity."

Jenny observed the volunteers as Christopher assumed the lead. The immediacy in his manner gave her pause, though she was relieved that he exercised authority.

She scrutinized every inch of the hotel, searching for any clues or signs of hazard risks. "Why would anyone focus on us and this hotel?" she asked the fire chief. "We're on the verge of opening."

"I don't know, but I intend to find out."

Sebastian, in his cartoon robot pajamas and fuzzy bear slippers, stumbled sleepily into the lobby, his steps drowsy and sluggish. His tousled hair stuck out in all directions.

Rubbing his droopy eyes with the back of his hand, he yawned.

"Dad, can I help?" he asked.

Christopher didn't even blink. "No."

Sebastian squared his slim shoulders. "But—"

"Sebastian, get to bed." Christopher's tone was measured and unyielding and allowed no opportunity for discussion.

"I'll bring him back to his room," Jenny offered Sebastian a soothing smile. She gently picked up the child, cradling his head on her shoulder. As she moved down the hallway, she hummed a lullaby, then tucked him in bed. She ducked into the restroom to splash cold water on her face, then reemerged in the lobby.

Maria clutched a replenished glass of red wine, amplifying Jenny's fear that she was drunk.

"Are we safe here tonight?" Jenny questioned Christopher. "There are only the four of us living at the hotel—me, you, Sebastian, and Maria."

"With all these volunteers? We're definitely safe." He offered her a calm and resolute smile. "Francis will stay until morning."

She nodded. "What did the chief imply when he said the situation had gotten more serious than he realized? Is he referring to Rusty's hut? I thought he attributed that incident to mischief."

"He's honestly not sure." Christopher exhaled. His features tightened. "A fire is a scary type of trouble."

"You didn't give your son a chance to finish explaining

himself. You hardly listened when he was only asking to help."

"The last thing I want is for Sebastian to get drawn into all this," Christopher declared. "All the scenarios I play in my mind are far too dangerous."

"I heard that." Maria swung around the corner and drained her wine. "And your final word in that sentence concerns me."

AN HOUR LATER, Jenny seated herself on a loveseat adjacent to the foyer. Maria had retired, and Christopher and the others continued to comb the hotel. Apart from a broken window and the ransacked breakroom, nothing else had been disturbed.

"Your complexion is pale, and you look like you saw a spirit." Francis Grant lumbered over and plopped himself opposite Jenny. His enormous belly protruded over the waistband of his jeans, and the buttons of his shirt stretched over his barrel chest.

She sat back and crossed her legs. "So much is happening, and I'm seeing Christopher in a different light."

Francis retrieved his readers from his pocket and scrutinized her. "Why?"

"He's usually relaxed and joking. Now he's acting so serious."

"He tries to fix everything however he can. He takes action if he believes he'll make a difference. I guess that's just the way he's made."

Jenny greeted the news with a blink. "I admire his dedication, but I worry he attempts to shoulder the responsibilities of the entire planet, overlooking his own well-being."

"He's quite capable," Francis replied.

Jenny's concern stemmed from a profound care for

Christopher and a desire to protect him. She feared his inclination to intervene could lead him into danger or cause unnecessary strain. She had seen glimpses of his vulnerability. His relaxed demeanor was a mask to hide his internal pain.

"He has never gone into any depth about his ex. Was he in the army when he married?"

"To the best of my knowledge." Francis placed his straw hat on the chair next to him. "Difficult predicaments in the military may leave a lasting impression, and he undoubtedly brought some of it home with him. He's shaken off a lot, but it resurfaces when he thinks about protecting and serving. His sense of duty never truly goes away."

She nibbled on a chipped fingernail and reflected.

Her qualms reflected her powerful feelings for Christopher. She vowed to encourage him to find a balance between helping others and looking after himself.

"The importance of self-care," she murmured.

"Hmm?" Francis questioned.

"Oh, sorry. I was thinking about someone." She looked around. "Any idea who could have done this?"

"Most likely, some islanders are stirring up trouble again. It's an unfortunate incident, but we were all young once. Dis happens, but I see it as an opportunity to address the problems in our community. Some juveniles are running amiss."

"You're so sure the vandal is a juvenile?"

"Whenever we've had difficulties before, it was caused by youngsters with too much time on their hands."

"Gullah magic!" A man's raspy shout broke into their conversation.

Startled, Jenny jumped. Rusty had not only walked into the lobby, but he'd actually shouted. Until then, she'd merely gotten grunts and brief head shakes from him. She assumed

180

he was a reserved and brooding man, but his words boomed with conviction.

"There is no such thing as Gullah magic," Christopher called from the hallway.

Rusty kept a hand outstretched, groping his way along the walls and furnishings as he progressed to the piano. He'd combed his hair back from his creased forehead. His blue eyes peered out from behind his eyeglasses, as if he were looking at something unseen.

When he settled on the piano bench, his posture straightened. She hadn't noticed the tremors in his hands before. When had that started?

His head darted from left to right. Then he waited, his fingers resting on the keys. In a sudden burst of energy, he began playing. Jenny recognized the piece—a lush and somber Chopin nocturne.

The music that poured forth was haunting, crammed with the suffering and anguish of a lifetime's worth of loss and struggle.

He skimmed the chords with skill and passion that spoke of years of practice and dedication. All the men, including Christopher, gathered around the piano, and the mood in the lobby shifted.

Jenny glanced up at the second level of the hotel, taken aback by Maria standing near the landing. She peered down at Rusty, leaning slightly forward. Occasionally, she inclined her head to see his face better. Or to catch his gaze, evidently hoping to create a link and bring him into her world. At the last measure, she swayed from side to side, mirroring the beauty of the composition.

Rusty angled his body toward Maria. He seemed attuned to her movements.

Jenny stepped to Christopher, mesmerized by Rusty's finesse and Maria's connection with him.

"Do you think he is aware of Maria watching him?" Jenny asked.

Christopher cocked his head to the side. "Somehow, I think he is, but something profound is happening here. He must've chosen that piece because it holds personal significance for him."

Jenny nodded, her gaze fixed on Rusty's hands as they gracefully moved across the keys. "It's more than his choice of music. That nocturne is speaking to his soul."

Christopher leaned closer to her, his voice barely above a whisper. "His silence, his PTSD, is all locked inside him. He's expressing himself through Chopin's melody. Maybe it's his way of communicating with humanity."

Jenny glanced at Maria, who continued to watch Rusty with unwavering attention. "Perhaps Maria sees her own hunger and hurt in Rusty's performance."

"A silent dialogue between them," Christopher affirmed.

Jenny's gaze shifted back to Rusty, and his eyes focused on Maria. "He's drawn to her because he can sense her empathy. She's offering him a glimmer of understanding."

As the music faded, Christopher and Jenny exchanged a meaningful glance, recognizing the extraordinary moment.

He circled his arm around her and pressed his cheek against hers. "We'll make it through this, Jenny."

"How?" she asked. The question lodged in her airway, still stunned from the intrusion. "Whoever did this violated us in such an aggressive manner. Someone invaded our personal space, and I dread returning to my room tonight."

"I guarantee we'll all be safe. Your room is near Maria's, so you're not by yourself up there."

"I predict that once the sun rises, Maria will hunt high and low for Skipper Andy and book a ferry passage to the mainland." Jenny's mouth went dry at the thought. "After what transpired here, she'll never set foot on this island again."

Christopher smiled. "I highly doubt it. She's enjoying the nice weather and the beach too much. Besides, this place is a pescatarian's delight. We're surrounded by fish."

"Well, I won't fault her if she leaves. I feel as though we're all vulnerable targets. It's just not right that an occurrence like this should happen in a place where I've always felt safe."

"Francis and I will be on watch for what's left of tonight."

Weakly, she reciprocated Christopher's smile, grateful for his support.

"What's more frightening is that the island is small," she said. "We're at a disadvantage because someone is after us, and we don't know who."

"Be brave. We won't be intimidated." He held her tighter. She leaned into him and welcomed his protection. "We have each other."

"You, Christopher Drake, have a caring nature."

"Well, thank you." He gazed down at her. "What brought that on?"

She reflected on her earlier vow and lightly touched his arm. "I want to share something."

He nodded.

"You are truly remarkable—the way you always try to fix things."

He shrugged. "I just want to help."

"I know, and that's what concerns me. You take on a tremendous amount without recognizing the toll it takes on you. Don't neglect yourself. You're only human."

He kissed her cheek. "I appreciate your concern, but what about you? It's okay to prioritize yourself, too."

As she scanned the entrance, she reached into the pocket of Christopher's jacket and fingered his poem. His words were precious to her.

Rusty rose from the piano and ambled to Francis, shifting to a seat beside him. They spoke rapidly, although their conversation was inaudible.

The volunteers organized a meeting in the morning to discuss the incident further and brainstorm solutions. They proposed a neighborhood watch system and emphasized collective safety. Francis suggested a communal program for the youth, involving sports or the arts.

As she listened to the volunteers, the tension in her muscles eased, and she snuggled into Christopher's chest. Their bond of camaraderie and friendship would not be severed.

However, an internal battle waged between trust and fear, between the desire to open her heart fully to him and the lingering scars of the past. A part of her wanted to rely on him completely, while another part was fearful of having her heart broken again.

Their bond had grown stronger these past few weeks. He had shown her kindness, consideration, and encouragement.

He tilted her chin up and swept a feathery kiss over her lips. His heavy-lidded gaze met hers.

"I don't know why it's so important to me that we do this together," she said.

"I do."

"Why?"

He stared at her with so much love in his eyes that her heart expanded.

"Because we're a perfect pair, Jenny," he said. "Fate brought us here together, like two pieces of a puzzle meant to fit perfectly. We'll rise out of this storm stronger than before."

She nodded.

Trust required vulnerability, yet it implied that she'd allow him to see the raw and fragile parts of her soul.

Once more, unease made her hesitate, forming a self-protective barrier that threatened to keep her from showing her love for him.

She rested her head against his chest, listening to the steady rhythm of his heartbeat. "What if we fall?"

"We won't."

"Trust is a choice," she breathed, half to herself.

True intimacy enabled her to be accepted, flaws and all. She needed to take that first step, trusting that he would meet her halfway with understanding and love.

He kissed her temple. "The only way they'll ever defeat us is if we're divided, which will never happen."

CHAPTER 14

he next morning, Christopher dressed in navy blue, loose-fit shorts, and a matching polo shirt, and then strode to the lobby.

He'd assessed the extent of the damage in the breakroom, noting the smashed appliances. Throughout the night, he'd assisted the fire chief and volunteers, removing large debris and broken glass. They'd restored any items that were salvageable, then took an inventory of the disposable cups, plates, and napkins.

Christopher hired a professional carpet cleaning company to address any stains and residue, in addition to the housekeeping staff mopping and vacuuming.

His eyes gravitated toward Jenny.

Earlier, she had attended church service, and was now positioned behind the concierge desk, typing on her computer. Despite the prior night's occurrences leading to dark circles under her eyes, she was lovely. She'd twisted her blond hair into a chignon, though strands stuck out haphazardly.

Her gaze flitted, scanning the surroundings, exposing her heightened sense of nervousness.

He peeked at his watch, which showed past noon, reminding him he hadn't eaten breakfast. So far, nothing else in the hotel seemed out of the ordinary, yet they were a long way from identifying the perpetrator.

Jenny distracted him from surveying the grounds once more. Her floral dress, an intricate print in shades of pink and turquoise, accentuated her slender figure.

She dealt with the morning's messages, telephone conversations, and reservations, even though she was visibly shaken.

He walked to the desk and watched her. "Do you need any help?" he inquired.

"No. I'm stuck in a continuous loop of playing catch-up." She absently picked at the textured print on her dress's sleeve. "I've run out of sources, and we lack a full staff here. I even begged Thomas, the porter from the ferry, to work here."

"What did he say?"

"He's considering it, although he's not thrilled about this hotel. He's a local guy who believes the island should remain unchanged."

"We respect the island, too. Some of us are homegrown." He winked at her. "Thankfully, I have more friends arriving who are ready to work."

"Friends?"

"More of my military buddies."

"Are they reliable?"

"The cream of the crop." He tipped up her chin. "Jenny, how about we set our work aside and venture out for lunch?"

He hoped his invitation might lessen her anxieties from the previous evening.

She kneaded her forehead. "After what happened last

187

night? I try not to think about the break-in, and then I think of little else."

"Food will lift our spirits. I expect the fire chief to arrive soon, and he'll monitor the situation here." Christopher motioned to the patio. "Maria agreed to stay with Sebastian while we're gone, provided we leave our cell phones on."

Maria sat outside on a lounge chair facing the pool and fanned herself with a palm frond. She stretched out her bare legs. Her back was to the hotel. The edges of her hot pink bathing suit peeked beneath the folds of a purple terrycloth robe.

Her usually neat hair was disheveled, like she had been tugging at it in distress.

After a lengthy discussion with Jenny and Christopher, she'd decided to stay. However, she declared that she deserved a day off with pay.

Sebastian sat beside her, hunched over a checkerboard. His laughter escaped through the door, and the cheerful sound brought Christopher happiness. He hoped Sebastian would continue to be excited about the world around him.

"You're quite a planner, Christopher." Jenny hesitated. "But where can we go today? The Drifting Sands is too greasy for my stomach."

"What about giving the crab stand by the marina a chance? We'll analyze our competition—examine what they do well and what they do inadequately."

"Our five-star restaurant and a seafood shack shouldn't compare."

"Fingers crossed, they won't," Christopher said. "Maria requested we bring her back a veggie sandwich. We better hope that the seagulls don't snatch it away on our way back."

"Does such a thing exist? A veggie sandwich?"

He lifted his shoulders. "I suppose so."

She smiled. "Is it similar to a lettuce sandwich?"

"I'm assuming there's more than just lettuce in it; possibly a tomato and an avocado thrown in for good measure. I recommended she include seafood since she's a pescatarian. After considerable debate, she approved. I'll order a sandwich for Sebastian, too."

SHORTLY AFTERWARD, Christopher and Jenny started their walk to the marina. They held hands, navigating a path that snaked through scorching sand dunes and prickly, scrubby vegetation.

The sun radiated overhead, granting a golden sheen to the landscape as the path sloped up.

Jenny paused and picked up a piece of driftwood, then set it down. "Christopher, how familiar are you with the island's history?" she asked.

"You've lived in the Lowcountry longer than I have, so I assume you know more about the Gullah culture than me."

"You were a fancy summer resident," she pointed out.

"I was a summer resident, but certainly not a fancy one." He took her hand, and they resumed walking. A cluster of sea oats swayed in the wind, tickling their legs.

She plucked several and glided her fingers along the fringed edges. "The Yemassee Native Americans once inhabited this area."

Christopher angled his head up to the sky, appreciating the sun's warmth. "And then the Gullah arrived."

"Nope." Jenny paused again, this time to giggle at a pair of pelicans skimming over the water. "They used the land for cotton plantations and later for hunting and fishing. During the Civil War, Union soldiers, who established a base here, occupied it."

"I bet that was a challenging period for the residents."

"Without a doubt," she affirmed. "In spite of this, the

locals held on to their customs and relied heavily on the ocean for their livelihood. Shrimping developed into one of their most important trades."

He nodded. "It still is."

She concurred with a bob of her head and placed the sea oats on the ground. "Once the war ended, the island became a refuge for the Gullah people."

The path rounded a bend, displaying a panoramic view of the coastline. White foam-capped waves sparkled, while to the right, the beach curled in a smooth arc.

Seagulls soared in unison overhead; their wings outstretched as if in a choreographed dance with the air currents. One swooped down and landed on Jenny's shoulder, then plucked at her hair with its beak.

"Yikes!" With a shriek, she shooed the bird away. "This bird is brazen. I always thought they were timid."

"Obviously not these birds." Christopher was poised to jump in if she needed him. Before he shifted, the bird flew off Jenny and alighted on his shoulder.

She chuckled and snatched her cell phone from the pocket of her dress while the seagull fixed Christopher with a sharp, beady-eyed stare.

"Brazen is certainly fitting." Christopher grinned and scratched the crown of the bird's head with his finger, causing it to snap its beak at him.

"This will make a prized photo for the lobby. I might even frame it." Jenny snapped a photo just as the bird glided away. She pocketed her phone and flicked a stray feather from Christopher's shoulder.

"You were more concerned about your photo than my safety," Christopher quipped. "The bird could've pecked me to death."

"How about me?" She smiled up at him through generous black lashes. "You hardly raced to my defense."

"I was right here." He leaned in to kiss her. "You always have everything figured out, Jenny. I assumed you had the situation covered."

She exhaled deeply. "If only that were true."

"Don't second-guess yourself." He studied her pensive expression. "Life is about mistakes and lessons."

"It's hard when trying to achieve something great."

"Take it day-by-day, or sometimes hour-by-hour, if that's easier. Every hiccup is another lesson in disguise, so stay centered on your end goal."

She smiled. "You always encouraged me when we were young."

Tranquility enveloped them—a space for quiet contemplation. Neither uttered a word, each seeking serenity in the silence.

Jenny motioned toward the trees. "We can draw lots of people here if we incorporate more natural elements."

"We're already using a ton of greenery indoors and outside."

"What if we add more flowers to the back entrance and seating area? Hibiscus comes in a range of colors—pink, red, and yellow. And let's not forget about lantana. That has the extra benefit of attracting butterflies and hummingbirds." She gave a small laugh. "Although I don't have a gift for growing plants, I am the daughter of a professional landscaper."

"Decent suggestions, Jenny. Though, remember? We're supposed to be suspending all discussions relating to work."

"Flowers aren't work."

"Sure, they are."

She persisted, disregarding his opinion. "Evan brought personality to the lobby with the seagrass lamp, and we can do the same."

"Ahh, Evan Farrenway, the true genius, who fishes with

191

his bare hands and has the sensitivity of a crab." Christopher gave a patronizing chuckle.

"Why do you continuously make fun of him?"

Did he? Christopher pondered. If so, he couldn't resist. However, noting her frown, he shifted topics swiftly.

"When we were young, I put in loads of time and effort at my father's garage. I was determined to learn his trade, although I'm not the world's most skilled mechanic."

"Your dad was proud of you."

"Perhaps." Christopher deliberated, mulling over his words. "However, my father and I weren't the same. I had no genuine passion for his profession."

"We aren't all alike."

"Our personalities were different, too," Christopher said. "He was impulsive. I've learned to be patient and not rush. An extensive examination typically leads to the best solution."

"Yes, professor." Jenny's lips spread into a smile. "Do you realize your son resembles you in so many ways?"

"How's that?"

"To begin with, he is smart and amazing, and I guarantee he will accomplish remarkable feats in his life. He thinks the world of you."

"I can't take credit for how incredible he is. Nevertheless, I agree." He sighed. "Sometimes, though, I worry I won't live up to his expectations."

"Oh, Christopher, you are also amazing."

"Thank you." He put his arm around her and smiled.

The crab stand came into view, and a flurry of activity surrounded it. Islanders and tourists congregated, adding to the clamor of voices, and the delectable aroma of cooked seafood was everywhere.

Jenny and Christopher joined the queue, ordering two crab sandwiches and a couple of cups of water from an older man with a kind smile. Balancing their plates and drinks, they started for the closest vacant picnic table and settled in. There, Jenny offered a thankful prayer of grace.

"This stand differs significantly from when I previously saw it," Jenny commented after she'd finished her prayer. "When Maria and I arrived in April, there were no customers."

"The island is gearing up for the summer," he said.

His phone vibrated, and he checked the caller ID.

He frowned, a knot forming in his stomach.

"Is everything alright?" Jenny asked. "Is Maria calling about your son?"

"No. It's Michael Freid." Christopher's sense of responsibility kicked in, and he exhaled apologetically. He had to answer the call, though he dreaded what might come next. "Hopefully. there is a breakthrough in the case."

Jenny responded with an affirmative gesture, and he strode off.

He pressed the phone to his ear. "This is Christopher."

The chief on the other line had no updates but had chosen to check in.

Deflated, Christopher thanked him. He then spent a few minutes sifting through voicemails, then hastened back to their table.

Jenny was sitting with Evan Farrenway and was engrossed in an intense discussion. Evan inched closer to Jenny as he spoke, his mouth nearly grazing her ear.

A stab of jealousy pierced Christopher's gut, and he tried lessening the space between them inconspicuously.

"Well, well, look who it is," Christopher greeted the man. "Evan, the charming schoolteacher, spending his afternoon chatting with Jenny."

"Ah, Christopher," Evan said. "Are you here to give me a lesson on the dangers of education and conversation?"

"Absolutely. I ought to remind you that Jenny has a splendid life outside of anything school-related. You're a dedicated educator, so I'm sure you understand."

"No need to get your feathers ruffled." With a relaxed posture and an easy smile, Evan scanned the horizon from his perch on the bench next to Jenny. "How dare I engage in a harmless conversation with a fellow human being?"

Christopher drummed his hands on the table and shifted his weight from one foot to the other. If this guy wanted to exercise a subtle power play, then he was ready. "Just two intellectual minds exchanging profound thoughts on a sunny afternoon, I'm sure."

"You caught us, Christopher," Jenny shot him a tight-lipped smile. "We were discussing the intricacies of quantum physics and the mysteries of the universe."

"Silly me. And here I imagined you were reviewing lesson plans." Christopher threw Evan an icy glare as Evan detailed the history of a Charleston lighthouse with roots dating back to the 1800s. He was completely at ease as he concentrated on Jenny, his demeanor lively and engaging.

Christopher excused himself and bought takeout for Maria and Sebastian, then returned to the table.

"Ready to leave?" he asked Jenny.

Evan stood. "I'm leaving, too. I'm going back to the school to grade final papers. Our school year ends soon."

"I appreciate your fascinating information, Evan." Jenny took a last sip of water. "I assumed I was familiar with every place near here, but evidently I was mistaken."

"My pleasure." Evan fairly beamed with charm. "I'm delighted to offer my expertise, especially to someone as gorgeous as you."

As Jenny and Christopher stepped away, Evan's voice resonated in Christopher's ears.

"That man is like a living encyclopedia, and he quickly found you to share it," he muttered.

Jenny nodded. "Yes, it does seem that way."

His fingers twitched, aching to embrace her, but he restrained himself, uncertain of her reaction.

"Are you falling for him?" His voice trembled slightly, betraying his fear. He searched her face for any sign of confirmation or denial.

"What?" She stopped and glared at him. "I feel like I'm being cross-examined by an expert interrogator."

He chuckled softly, his eyes fixed on her. "And who might that be?"

"You." Her hand hovered in the space between them, and she smiled. "Don't worry. I'm always here to shed light on your imaginary doubts."

"So, your relationship with Evan is all innocent and pure?"

Jenny's delay in responding heightened Christopher's frustration.

"Well?" He glanced at her.

"You're kidding, right? Yes, of course it's innocent, though I'm flattered you're jealous."

"Me? Jealous?"

She attempted to stroke his face, but he withdrew.

He jammed his hands into the pockets of his khaki shorts, the fabric crinkling under the strain. "Then what is it like between you and Evan?"

He tensed, poised for action, ready to fight for her.

"It's not 'like' anything. He's a terrific friend who happens to reside here."

Relief, as if a dam had broken, allowed him to breathe again. But because of the depth of their shared history, doubts clung to him.

"I never imagined you'd lie to me, Jenny," he said.

"What? When? I'm not lying."

"Oh, but you did lie."

Her eyebrows came together. "Considering I try to always be truthful, how can you say that?"

"I recall a certain promise to accompany me to college in Pittsburgh after you graduated from high school."

Her emerald-green eyes flared with anger. This close, he could see the flecks of gold in her pupils. "You're dredging up a conversation that happened over ten years ago."

"Yes, I suppose I am." Christopher set the takeout bags on the ground and paused at an incline overlooking the ocean. He beckoned to a large rock surrounded by flowers. "Shall we sit and talk?"

"Okay."

He took a seat beside her.

With Jenny so near, her velvety skin pressed against him, and he basked in the closeness. If only she shared the same feelings.

"I offered you no promises." She dusted off the sand, partially covering the rock. "And aren't you overlooking two fundamental facts? You didn't end up attending college in Pittsburgh, and I bypassed college altogether."

"Anyika gave me your address, and I wrote you at least fifty letters after you left. You ignored every single one of them." He stole her a glance. The wind tousled her hair.

"Oh, sure, that's believable." She smoothed down her hair. "You're upset because I failed to respond to letters you never sent?"

He kicked at a pinecone on the ground. "I did send them."

"And I never received them. Perhaps my mother hid them from me on purpose, but why would she ever do that? Her intentions were always what was best for me."

"Really?"

"As far as I know."

He searched for an explanation for their differing recollections.

"Or did she believe I was socially unacceptable?" he asked. "She preferred a guy who could provide you with financial stability and a comfortable lifestyle."

"She was never happy here, but this is about me," Jenny said. "She could've been trying to shield me from more disappointment. She knew how devastated I was after our breakup, so maybe she took it upon herself to withhold your letters."

"Face it, Jenny. She intended more for you than winding up with a poverty-stricken guy who lived with a destitute father. There were class differences at play." He grappled for a means to verbalize his frustration. "I knew your mother, and she held certain expectations for your future and social status."

"I can't believe she would betray me." Jenny shook her head. "Do you think she really didn't trust me enough to make my own choices?"

"Apparently not." He hunched over. "When I received no response after I wrote you all those letters, I heard you were doing fine without me. Anyika mentioned that guys were lining up in your new high school because they all wanted to date you."

"I never forgot you, Christopher. You had your promising future all planned out." Jenny leaned back. "I'm at a loss why Anyika would tell you such a lie. After our relationship ended, I was heartbroken, and she knew it."

"Is that why you punched *me*? If anything was shattered, it was my nose."

She gave a quivering laugh. "I'm sorry, but I felt hurt and betrayed. Later, I interpreted your lack of action as not caring enough to fight for us."

"I blundered big time, okay? I believed I was making a

responsible decision by letting you go. When you disappeared, I eventually gave up. I told myself that I was protecting you from hardships by being associated with me and that our split was ultimately for the best."

"Where you saw hardships, I saw potential. I imagined we could have built a life together."

He sighed. "I should've tried harder to reach out to you. I admit, a part of me was afraid."

"Afraid of what?"

"Rejection, I suppose." His eyes never left hers. "I thought we shared an extraordinary bond. Now I'm thinking it was all in my imagination."

"Our bond was so extraordinary that you married and moved to Alaska?"

"After I married, the military sent me on a temporary overseas deployment. They forbade spouses, so my ex stayed behind." He blew out a sigh. "Jenny, if only circumstances between the two of us had been different."

"What do you mean?"

"I wish I'd been there to support you through all your tough times."

"A decade can seem like an eternity, Christopher. It's important to acknowledge that we've both changed."

"I haven't. I've been in love with you since the first day we met."

"No. No more charming declarations. I won't allow myself to fall for it anymore." She shot to her feet, and tears welled in her eyes. "You joined the military, got hitched, and had a baby, while I worked my tail off to set aside enough funds to travel to Europe."

He grabbed the takeout bags and stood with her. "I'm sorry. I don't know what else to say."

"Nothing. Apologies are of no use anymore."

The expanse between them crackled with the heat of

their argument and the memories they both carried. He reached out to touch her, desperate for a connection, but she jerked away as if his hand might burn her.

Defeated, he withdrew. "Fine. I get the message. Farrenway is all yours."

Jenny stared at him, frustration evident in her eyes.

"You're being ridiculous," she snapped. "Besides being an admirable friend, Evan is a noteworthy contact. He's extremely talented and on the road to becoming a top interior designer. He's fielding inquiries from prospective clients from states as far away as California."

Christopher's jaw tightened. "How generous of him to keep you informed of his rise to fame."

Irritation emanated from her, and she drew herself up to her full height. He'd breached a boundary, prompting her to stand behind a shield of defensiveness.

"This isn't only about Evan," she said. "My personal and career interests are important as well. I have dreams and goals, and he's a supportive listener."

Christopher folded his arms tightly over his chest. An emotional retreat, he supposed. Envy and insecurity battled within him and brought a sour taste to his mouth. He struggled to find the appropriate words, torn between his love for Jenny and his own fears.

He was simply being protective; he rationalized and worried about losing her to someone else. Still, he couldn't refrain from asking, "Is there a chance that Farrenway will leave the island for better opportunities?"

Hopefully.

"He'll continue to teach, but his real passion is design," Jenny replied.

He was unconvinced. Farrenway's newfound fame was a threat. Christopher aspired to be a respected man, but his envy reminded him of how little faith he had in himself.

"I'm nearly positive he was flirting with you," he said.

He realized his statement exposed his insecurities. His jealousy was clouding his judgment.

Jenny's eyes widened. "Evan requested I accompany him on a tour this weekend. He discovered some hidden hideouts on the mainland, and he's excited to share them with me."

"How convenient," Christopher murmured.

"There's a ninety-foot-tall lighthouse, a coastal museum, and a famous Civil War landmark."

Christopher's spirits plummeted before she'd finished speaking.

"What did you tell him?" he asked.

Her luminous eyes glinted in the sunlight. "I told him a tour was perfect. He mentioned grabbing a bite to eat at a local seafood restaurant, though it was difficult for him to choose a favorite."

Christopher understood all too well what it implied when a person couldn't decide on just one restaurant. It was an open invitation for another date.

Right, okay, he was being possessive. He thought he'd overcome his childhood self-doubts—a low-income father, a mother who abandoned him—yet deep down they remained. Being incompetent, overshadowed by someone more accomplished, gnawed at him. He couldn't think clearly when a good-looking, successful man like Farrenway showed an interest in Jenny.

Whoa. Rewind.

Jenny wasn't officially his girlfriend, regardless of his poem and their adolescent romance.

The realization descended on him like a storm surge. Did Jenny truly envision a future with him? Was he worthy of her love and affection?

The boundless blue sea stretched before them, a textbook reflection of his emotions. He relived the sultry summers they'd spent together when she'd shown him kindness and understanding. She'd listened to his dreams and encouraged him.

The impact of their argument tugged at his heart, a reminder of the walls he had inadvertently raised between them. He owed her an apology, yet he wasn't positive she'd be willing to forgive him.

"I didn't appreciate the impolite way you spoke to Evan." Jenny's words carried a cool edge, and she pinned Christopher with a steely stare.

"Why? I was being courteous."

"You were rude and dismissive. Evan is an admirable person and deserves to be treated with respect."

"Fine, it was unfair of me." Christopher extended his hand. "But you have to admit, the guy is annoying."

"Oh, Christopher. You are impossible."

She spun around and stormed to the hotel entrance.

Ouch.

Alone, he bore his unworthiness, a burden that increased with each passing day. He longed to be liberated, to cast off the weight that restrained him, but he didn't know how. It appeared to be an insurmountable task, one he couldn't tackle by himself.

He wanted to be a better man and relinquish his fears of being left behind. The gravity of his past mistakes dragged him down like an anchor. For Jenny's sake, as well as his own, he told himself he would try to become a better person.

He stood there, watching her retreating figure. Then he hurried after her, overtaking her right before she opened the door.

"Jenny, wait." He set down the takeout bags and placed a hand on her shoulder, silently pleading for her to face him.

Slowly, she turned.

"You said no more apologies, but I'm sincerely sorry," he

began. "My uncertainties won out, and I shouldn't have taken it out on you and Evan.

Her gaze searched his. "Our disagreement isn't solely about Evan. I can't be with someone who constantly questions my feelings."

He touched her arm, but she pulled away.

"I want more than just words, Christopher."

"I understand, but it's going to take me a while."

Her expression softened, but hurt lingered in her eyes. "I can't wait forever. I need someone who is committed now, not a man who needs some sort of hiatus to figure everything out."

"I get it. I do."

"Perhaps it's best if we have a break from each other. You know, we don't have to be constantly together."

She swiveled, opened the door, and stepped into the hotel.

His hand instinctively stretched out, longing to hold her, but he quickly yanked it back, realizing the pointlessness of his gesture. She was inside now, distancing herself from his grasp, and he had caused their failed relationship.

Again.

He snatched up the takeout bags and headed toward the beach. His unsteady footsteps sank into the warm sand with each stride, leaving imprints quickly erased by the tide. Sunlight glinted on the water's surface, forming a sparkling pathway that gave the impression of leading nowhere. Tiny crabs scurried across the sand, creating miniscule trails.

With each of his steps, the distance between him and Jenny widened. As the minutes dragged on, each stride carried him further away from reconciliation, bringing him to a heartbreaking reality.

Not all love stories had a happy ending.

CHAPTER 15

The calendar showed June 25, and the Grand Michelangelo planned to open its doors in less than seven days, a narrow window of time.

Pandemonium reigned as a recurring theme.

On the patio, Jenny conducted interviews to staff the hotel. Three of the recent hires had quit for an established vacation spot in Georgia. Their reasons were understandable —the popular resort offered better compensation and benefits. This series of developments left her disheartened, as she hadn't expected losing employees so soon after she'd hired them.

The online recruitment ad had been unsuccessful. Jenny had hoped to attract a pool of talented individuals who would be enthusiastic about joining the team, but only a few had shown interest.

Salifu, in his practice role as a bellboy, had attempted to swing open the entrance door to prepare for arriving patrons. The door had jammed and needed two men to help force it open.

An hour later, Jenny stepped into the lobby. Determined

to ignore Christopher, who stood by the elevator, she acted as if she hadn't seen him. The hotel descended into a hush, so motionless that she almost heard the strained sizzle of unease.

"Why is everybody so quiet?" Jenny asked Maria, who sat at a desk, intently studying dinner selections with a pen and paper.

"The talk is you and Christopher had a row." Maria's curiosity intensified with each word.

"Who told you this?"

"Him." Jenny followed Maria's gaze and saw Francis hunched beside Christopher. Nearby sat a scattered assortment of pliers, wrenches, and a drill.

"It was like a game of telephone," Maria said. "He mentioned something to Francis, and Francis informed Fatu, and Fatu told Anyika, and then, you know, things get exaggerated." Maria traced her finger along the stack of menus. "He caught you flirting with Evan Farrenway."

Jenny groaned. To her chagrin, everyone on the island was probably aware of her argument with Christopher. "Evan and I were conversing, not flirting. I was being polite."

"Polite. Is that what they call it nowadays?"

"Please, Maria. It was harmless." Jenny motioned toward Christopher and Francis. "What are they doing? Don't tell me—"

"Yep. The elevator isn't working again. While you interviewed people, they checked the power supply, then inspected the control panel and discovered that a fuse had blown."

"Christopher isn't an electrician."

"True, but he worked with a technician a while back. A pulley was tangled and prevented the elevator from moving. He's requesting volunteers to make the trip up and down."

Maria lifted her hands. "It won't be me. I got trapped the last time, and I'm still recovering."

Jenny powered up her computer and frowned as it tried to boot up. She programmed the hotel's website and clicked to locate a web server that would hold her upcoming ads to seek additional employees. The screen froze. She jiggled the mouse, though it had no effect.

"The Internet is down?" she questioned Maria.

"What else is new?"

"We can't link to the outside world."

"And I can't access my email. I even went to my favorite place to connect, but still zilch." Maria heaved a sigh. "Christopher consulted with a tech expert who is arriving soon. The problem is far more complicated than he expected."

The smell of fresh paint lingered while crewmen painted over minor flaws on a side wall in the breakroom. A crewman had knocked over the seagrass lamp while carrying a ladder, causing the lamp to crash, and Evan Farrenway was slated to bring over a different lamp from a local artisan.

Employees strung Edison lights from a pergola, a recent outdoor addition to the back of the hotel. She expected the lights would add a nighttime glow and hint at a romantic ambiance.

She leaned against the wall and envisioned the hotel once it began operating. Keyboard classics would fill the lobby, accompanied by laughter and the tinkling of glasses.

What a treat to stand at the reception desk, listening to the music. However, Rusty continuously refused to perform.

"I'm not in the mood," he'd grumbled the few times she'd asked him.

The man might have had PTSD, but he was so accomplished. If only he'd agree to share his gift.

A string quartet could be a great idea. Perhaps she should

check, though recruiting four pros to entertain nightly seemed unattainable.

A WHILE LATER, Maria, Jenny, Sebastian, and Christopher all shared lunch. The conversations and clinking mugs were distant to Jenny, hardly penetrating her troubled mind.

Afterwards, Jenny conceded to Maria that lunchtime had been tense, and she was partly to blame. She sensed the undercurrents of distrust radiating from Christopher whenever Evan Farrenway's name was brought up. Studiously, she'd avoided looking at or speaking to him.

As the afternoon progressed, they all waited for the Internet to be turned back on. Jenny fiddled with a pencil, the lead scratching over the paper as she wrote dessert recipes that reminded her of her childhood. Christopher sat nearby, his fingers tapping an impatient beat on the end table. Periodic sighs escaped him, each one heavier than the previous.

Maria stayed silent as Christopher and Jenny competed in a game of avoidance.

"Okay, enough of this! I can't take another minute!" Maria slammed down her glass of iced tea. Since the night of the break-in, she had abstained from drinking. However, she was now irritable most of the time.

Startled, Jenny sat up. "Enough of what?"

"You're shunning each other as if you're both contagious." Maria commanded their attention with a snap of her fingers.

Jenny and Christopher exchanged a sheepish glance.

"There's nothing to say," Jenny began.

"There's plenty, and I'm intervening, so don't play innocent with me." Maria planted both hands on her hips and scowled at Jenny. "What happened when you and Evan Farrenway were chatting at the crab stand?"

Jenny's eyes flicked to the floor. "We had a friendly chat. Nothing scandalous, I assure you."

Maria tapped her chin with her finger. "I leave you two alone for a quick lunch, and today you're at cross purposes. This is not the way to treat each other. You should be able to work through any disagreement without resorting to fisticuffs."

Jenny couldn't help but smile at Maria's use of the word "fisticuffs." Her lighthearted scolding dissipated the tension.

Christopher hesitated before giving Jenny a brief, upraised eyebrow. "Shall we shift this discussion to the breakroom for more privacy?"

"Finally, we're making headway!" Maria addressed the lobby at large.

Francis and Salifu nodded, small grins playing at the edges of their lips.

"You need to have an honest dialogue," Maria instructed Jenny and Christopher. "Be transparent and share both sides of your story. Meanwhile, Francis and Salifu will finish here."

"Wait. What about you?" Jenny inquired.

"I'm wrapping things up for the day." Maria grinned mischievously. "I'm the media figure deprived of Internet access until tomorrow."

"And the restaurant?" Christopher asked. "What's the scoop there?"

"Ready and raring to go," Maria said. "Meanwhile, I'm off to catch some rays and monitor Sebastian. You two make up and go bake some fruit cobblers or something. Life's too short to waste on arguments." She embraced them both in a group hug, added a perceptive smile, then sauntered away.

"I assumed I was a co-owner of this hotel and made the decisions," Christopher muttered. "What was I thinking?"

He extended his hand to Jenny. She refused, but trailed

him into the breakroom. Their footsteps reverberated in the corridor, the soft click-clack punctuating the tension.

He indicated for her to sit and closed the door behind them. The latch snapped shut with finality.

He positioned himself across from her and shifted. "First off, I … I'm sorry I was a jerk. My remarks about Farrenway were way out of line."

A lump formed in Jenny's throat. She took a deep breath and gathered her thoughts. The aroma of freshly brewed coffee wafted from the new coffee maker that had replaced the espresso machine. She longed for a cup, to let its warmth wash away the strain that circled her. Yet she refused to be tempted. This was the opportunity for her and Christopher to confront their issues.

"This isn't merely about what you said," she retorted. "You dismissed Evan and took your jealousy out on me."

"If you hadn't reacted to his supposed charm and behaved like he's all that, we wouldn't have reached this point. Blatantly flirting right under my nose isn't cool."

She felt her cheeks warm. "He's offering inspired concepts to help our hotel stand out, and he's very knowledgeable. But all you do is dismiss him and pretend he doesn't know what he's talking about. You consistently think you're right and won't consider anyone else's ideas."

Christopher's blue eyes flashed. "You never give me a chance. Shutting me down is your favorite pastime."

"That's not true. I respect your opinions."

Their voices overlapped, their phrases blending into a symphony of discontent. She caught her breath, and silence blanketed the room, broken only by their heavy breathing. Her guard crumbled as their gazes collided.

His eyes filled with exhaustion and understanding.

She shook her head, refusing to replay the incident. She owed Christopher an apology, too.

"Look, I gave you the wrong impression," she said. "It was inappropriate of me to encourage Evan, and I should've never put you in such an awkward position. I would've been resentful if the situation were reversed."

Christopher touched her hand. "Really? Would you have been jealous?"

"Maybe. Possibly." Her eyes misted. "I don't want us to be at odds. I consider you a wonderful ally."

"More than an ally, Jenny." His tone grew quiet. "Please understand what an incredible asset you are to this place, to Olive, and especially to me."

"Thank you. Your compliments are so kind."

"And so genuine," he said with a grin. "I truly regret the hurtful statements I made. We've been through a lot together."

She nodded. "I expected you to read my mind, and you expected me to be a mind reader."

They moved closer until their foreheads almost touched.

"I had a knee-jerk reaction when I saw you with another guy," Christopher said.

She glimpsed the vulnerability beneath his rough exterior, hidden away from the world. Not hidden from her, though. She knew him so well.

"Can we leave yesterday in the past?" she asked.

"Definitely. And I'll try harder to understand your point of view." He brought her fingers to his lips and kissed each one, then touched his lips to hers. A tender and loving kiss that spoke volumes, much more than any words could show.

She melted into his embrace, feeling safe and cherished. "And I promise to communicate more clearly and not let my frustrations escalate."

"You're more than the woman I love." He muffled his words in her hair. "You're my confidante, my rock, and a blessing to everyone around you."

Their eyes met, and the intensity of their bond sparked like a bolt of electricity, coupled with relief and contentment.

"Foremost, we're friends and have each other's confidence." He retreated a step. "How about we establish a pact to never fight again?"

She laughed. "As much as I'd love to, it's unrealistic. However, we can commit to finding resolutions to any problems."

"No matter what happens, I'll always be here for you. Never forget that, okay?"

"Okay."

Their hands entwined. Their reconciliation was more than just words—it was a renewed commitment to each other, a promise to strive for greater understanding.

She walked with him out of the breakroom, leaving the awkwardness of their argument behind. Collectively, they'd listened to each other and compromised.

Further difficulties would come, but things would be better if they stayed united.

Nothing else mattered. Nothing held more importance than their unbreakable bond.

CHAPTER 16

*I*n years past, Jenny's mother had coined a term for Jenny's favorite coping mechanism.

Stress baking.

Since the break-in at the hotel, Jenny had resorted more and more to familiar habits. Christopher said he was pleased to see her experiment with Gullah delicacies because he loved desserts. He loved to see her happy, and he loved her. At night, they shared slices of pecan pie or Benne wafers, side by side, under a palm tree, while they watched the sunsets.

Jenny was concerned, as his army comrades had not yet arrived, even though he had mentioned they should be on the island soon.

On the early morning of June 27, a few days before the hotel opening, Jenny proceeded to the restaurant's cooking area, and Anyika joined her an hour later. It had become a routine for them to bake together. Anyika seemed to have a sixth sense and showed up whenever Jenny needed her most.

Lately, they broached the subject of Jenny's realization

211

that her life without long-term connections and dodging love was not ideal.

"I'm happy to listen, honey. One hand can't clap," Anyika wisely proclaimed, meaning it took two or more people to solve a problem.

Today, Anyika brought her grandson, Sorie, affirming that it was alright for him to cut the last day of school. Francis Grant arrived to supervise the boys while they played outside.

Christopher strode in and scanned the kitchen. "Have you seen Sebastian?" he asked.

Jenny removed a bowl of hoppin' John pudding from the oven and placed it on the stove. The aroma of molasses and sugar made her mouth water.

"He's at the beach with Sorie and Francis," she said.

"They're not there," Christopher responded with an anxious scowl.

"Dad, Dad!"

Christopher swerved as Sebastian and Sorie dashed into the kitchen, and his scowl intensified. "Where on earth have you two been?"

"I found some awesome clues." Sebastian waved his magnifying glass. "I'm still trying to figure out who set the beach hut on fire."

"You disobeyed my instructions again." Christopher's voice rose. "I specifically told you to stay away from that hut."

"I'm sorry, Dad. Mr. Grant said the fire chief hasn't solved the case yet." Sebastian stole a glance at Sorie, evidently hoping for his support, though Sorie avoided his gaze.

"We understand you wish to help, but rely on the professionals to do their job," Jenny said.

"What are you thinking by disappearing like that, Sorie?" Anyika ripped off her apron and marched over. "You've only been here a couple of hours, and you're already getting into trouble."

The boy's lips quivered. His brown, saucer-shaped eyes regarded her. "Excuse me, Granny-ma."

She wagged her meaty forefinger at him. "Don't you dare do that again, honey."

Tears trickled down his cheeks, leaving glistening trails on his skin. "I won't. I promise."

Jenny noticed Sorie crossed his fingers and hid them behind his back. She decided not to interfere.

"I'm not blaming you." Christopher patted the crown of Sorie's black curls. "Sebastian and I have discussed this subject many times, and I assumed I had made myself clear."

"Yes, sir."

"Go outdoors." Anyika hugged Sorie, her inflection more sympathetic. She tacked on a magnanimous smile. "Tell Mr. Grant we're leaving in ten minutes."

With his head hung low, the boy scampered off.

"Dad, Dad!" Sebastian bounced up and down on his toes. "I have the coolest story ever."

Christopher arched an eyebrow. "About?"

"Sorie and I saw Jah and Lomboi arguing. We were hiding, and they didn't see us. The way they talked and inspected the ashes makes me think that either or both lit the fire."

"We can't implicate anyone without evidence." Christopher's jaw tightened. "Where was Mr. Grant while you explored?"

"He wasn't that far away from us. Mr. Rusty came over, and they were whispering."

"Where are Mr. Grant and Mr. Rusty now?"

"They're by the ocean with Maria."

Anyika's gaze settled on Christopher, admiration

imprinted on her lined features. "You offered Rusty a different hut, but he refused."

Christopher shrugged. "Rusty is a stubborn guy."

"Francis thinks it's safest if Rusty stays with him and Fatu for a while longer," Anyika said. "Rusty is taking a liking to the kitten."

"They are very generous." Jenny's voice rose and fell, signaling the humor she couldn't contain. "He can't be a picnic to live with."

"Ain't that just a precious way of saying somethin'." Anyika drawled in her rich Gullah accent, arcing her eyebrows so high that they nearly disappeared in her hairline. "Bless his heart. I hope he's not planning to live there forever. No tellin' what sort of mischief he'll cause if he gets too comfortable with them folks."

A loaded silence ensued as they all contemplated Rusty's situation. Jenny worried Rusty's extended stay would affect Francis and Fatu's lives, despite their kindness. She sensed Anyika shared the same concerns.

"Dad, I have some notes." Undeterred, Sebastian held up a sheet of paper with pencil scribblings. "Look what I found!"

"I admire your initiative, son. I really do." Christopher placed a firm hand on the boy's shoulder. "But please pay attention to me. Fire is no joke."

Sebastian's face flushed. "I get it, Dad. But—"

"I want you to be safe. I'm thankful for your offer to assist, but respect my rules." Christopher leaned forward. "Tell you what. I'll finish work early, and we'll investigate the hut together. Agreed?"

"Yay! Yes, Dad."

"Good." Christopher's expression relaxed into a grin. "Don't second-guess the rest of us. Trust the adults and the fire chief to handle the details."

IN THE LATE AFTERNOON, Christopher and Sebastian ventured to Rusty's blackened hut to examine the wreckage. After all, Christopher rationalized that his son was insistent on solving the mystery, and he'd ignored his requests for far too long.

The intensity of the fire had melted the hut's roof, and nothing remained except singed beams. The furniture had become cinders on the ground.

They advanced cautiously, and Christopher pointed to a pile of rubble. He crouched down and motioned for Sebastian to follow. A chubby white candle rested near a shard of shattered glass, and he slid his finger over the jagged edges, noting where it had softened from the scorching blaze.

"The fire may have ignited if someone tossed a lit candle through the window." He stood, pacing, his speech rapid. "Maybe there is some other cause besides the lit cigarette."

"Did Mr. Rusty leave his windows open?"

"I don't know." Christopher flexed his fists, a cloud of suspicion hovering over him. "The window was probably shattered first."

Sebastian tilted his head, seeming to expect more details, but Christopher merely shrugged. "We can't spend all our energy rehashing this crime. Would you like to do something else?"

"Like what?"

Christopher smiled. His son was always eager to explore. "Are you interested in seeing your grandparents' house and where I spent my summers?"

A breeze tousled Sebastian's hair, and the sun cast a golden sheen across his cherubic face.

"Sure thing, Dad!" Sebastian's small hand grasped Christopher's, their fingers interlocking in a gesture of trust.

Christopher paved the way, his stride steady. Sebastian

skipped alongside, admiring the wildflowers and watching the squirrels.

As the sun dipped lower, Christopher indicated a house and garage located amidst a thicket of trees. A pang of nostalgia surged through him as he surveyed his ramshackle, forgotten home. An abandoned tire swing dangled from a branch of a large oak tree, and he remembered his father saying that the tree was over one hundred years old.

Sebastian studied the house. "This is where you grew up? Did you have any adventures?"

Christopher chuckled. "Before I met Miss Jenny, there was a treehouse in the backyard. I'd pretend to be a pirate on the hunt for buried treasures in the woods and build forts."

"Remember in Alaska we hiked Denali Mountain and went dog sledding in the winter with Scooby-Doo? Fishing was fun, too."

"You caught more fish than I did. Those were our Alaska adventures. Now we have a lifetime to explore this island."

"Can we go fishing here?"

"Definitely."

"Is the treehouse still there?"

"Follow me and let's find out."

They wandered into the backyard, stepping over fallen branches and tall grass. As they approached a towering oak, Christopher sighted his old tree house.

"This is a secret hideout!" Sebastian said. "I can use it as my base camp!"

Christopher grinned, reflecting on his own youthful memories. "I wrote many stories up there while I watched the world below me. But you're not going up into that treehouse until I verify it's solid."

"Today?"

"No. Some other day." Christopher stood still, taking it all in, the memories of his past, while his son scoured the over-grown garden.

"Dad!" Sebastian crouched and burrowed a hole beside a rock. "You'll never guess what this is."

Intrigued, Christopher hurried over.

Hidden beside the rock and buried by sand was a plain tin box with a simple latch to keep it closed. Inside, a soft lining protected a folded note. Christopher pulled out the note—addressed to him in his mother's unmistakably scribbled handwriting.

"What does it say?" Sebastian's face lifted, all shiny eyes and full lips.

Christopher scanned the paper. "It's a poem."

Slowly, he read the words to himself. He broke into a sweat as tears welled up.

MY DARLING SON, take note it's true,
   my love for you is endless, too.
   But life's been tough, and I must go,
   to seek some peace and let it flow.
   But someday I'll return to show you how,
   To thrive and live with all your might,
   And transform each day into a precious light.
   So don't be sad, my beloved one,
   I'll forever be your loving mom.

SEBASTIAN HOPPED from foot to foot. "Who wrote the poem, Dad?"

"Your … your grandmother." Christopher's breath stalled in his throat. Language was a task he could no longer manage.

Patchy remembrances swam up and resurfaced as if it

were yesterday. Sometimes his mother would recite her poems to him at night or when he'd been bedridden with an asthma attack.

Afterward, she'd flutter away like a butterfly after messing up his hair when he tried to hug her, leaving him with a bittersweet longing to keep her near.

"Will you read it out loud to me?" Sebastian asked.

"Someday." He swallowed. "Just not today."

What more could he say? A part of him was glad his mother had written something to him. This was much better than believing she'd simply wandered off.

She hadn't forgotten him.

After Christopher reread the poem, he placed it in his pocket. Then he stood and brushed the dirt from his knees. At some point, he'd return and settle things, he decided, beginning with mowing the lawn and clearing out the weeds.

He had heard that someone had boarded up Jenny's cottage as well. It would be helpful for them both to make peace with their pasts.

Sebastian sprinted off, and Christopher strained to see where he went. A door slammed, followed by a faint rattling.

"Dad," Sebastian shouted. "Come inside. I'm in the bedroom."

Christopher strode to the back and entered the rear entrance. A clock on the wall was stuck at five o'clock, the time his father usually quit work for the day.

Damp and oppressive air closed in on him. Shutters masked the windows, shrouding the cottage in near darkness, save for the slivers of light and a creeping vine filtering through gaps in the wood. The atmosphere was impenetrable, with odors of mildew and dirt particles collected over the years.

The rattling floor planks, reminiscent of an ancient ship, squeaked as he advanced towards the bedroom. Soundless and far-off memories returned, bringing back the countless times he had sprinted across this same floor in his childhood.

The lace curtains his mother once favored hung in tatters, most likely nibbled at by mice. Floral wallpaper peeled in large sections, revealing crumbling plaster. He traced a line of dust over an antique mahogany bureau as he passed.

He spotted Sebastian. He was squatting by Christopher's parents' bed.

The scene was unexpected, and for a split second, he froze.

"Here, Dad! Look!"

Christopher bent to reach the hidden prize. Concealed beneath the bed was a cloth sack stuffed with an object, and he recognized the glint of beads and seashells.

"What's this?" Sebastian asked.

Carefully, Christopher clutched the bag, gauging the weight of something substantial yet delicate.

He peered inside, and his pulse quickened.

Of all things.

His mother's beloved amulet.

He'd almost forgotten about it, though here it was, glistening in the afternoon sunlight as if expecting him.

He inhaled and drew the amulet from the bag. With wetness blurring the edges of his vision, he mapped the curves of its design. The seashells were stunning, their unique shapes and textures transporting him to the ocean. Images of his mother wearing it invaded his mind, and his heart pained with anguish. She believed it would protect her from any peril.

He shook his head, fully aware of how wrong she'd been. The amulet, for all its supposed fortune and protection, could not shield her from her inner despair. Ultimately, it whisked her away, leaving only a hollow void.

He stowed the amulet in his pocket for safekeeping, a

persistent reminder of what he'd lost. A priceless memento, and one he would safeguard, for it was all he had left of her.

"Dad. Look." Sebastian edged further under the bed and pulled out a black-and-white photograph encased in plastic and discolored with age. He peeked at the photo, then handed it to Christopher. "Is this Grandma and Grandpa?"

All the muscles in Christopher's body tightened as he gripped the photo and studied it. There, captured in the photograph, was his mother—her features illuminated with a radiance he'd never seen before.

She'd twisted her hair in a bun, and curls kissed her cheeks in gentle wisps. She looked young, carefree, and utterly captivated, her smile directed at a man whose wavy blond hair cascaded effortlessly about his face.

The man grinned down at her.

But the man was not Christopher's father.

A jolt of disbelief coursed through Christopher's veins. His grip tightened on the photograph, as if holding onto it would anchor him to reality. Questions flooded his mind, each one more bewildering than the last.

He turned it over, hoping for a clue, a hint that might provide answers. The reverse side held no details. A blank canvas, withholding the secrets of its origin.

The unfamiliar background only fueled Christopher's growing unease. Did his mother travel somewhere to meet this man? Had she been involved in an affair? If so, this acknowledgement unraveled the very foundation of his understanding. She had violated the trust he and his father had invested in her.

Even if this weren't the case, why was this photo kept private?

Had she remarried?

Did she have another family and more children?

Was it possible to reconcile his anger with his love for her?

He couldn't speculate any further while his son stared up at him.

He stashed the photo in his pocket, not uttering a word. He'd distance himself to process his reactions. He refused to permit one photo to tarnish his memories, though as the acknowledgement of her infidelity rested upon him, the thought cast shadows on the woman he held so dear.

In the stifling stillness of the cramped bedroom, a sudden tremor shook Sebastian's fragile form. It was as if a lightning bolt had struck him, leaving him panting for precious air. His tiny chest heaved and sank in quick, shallow gasps, each breath a herculean task. Despite a valiant effort to stand, he crumpled in a heap.

His widened eyes betrayed his unmistakable terror. His complexion reddened to a deep shade, and he clutched at his middle to revive his failing lungs.

Fear clenched its icy grip around Christopher's chest, intensifying with every rasping wheeze that tore through the room.

"Sebastian!" Christopher sank to his knees, his hands shaking. Frantically, he retrieved Sebastian's inhaler, his fingers struggling with the familiar device. With a gentle touch, he guided Sebastian into an upright position, offering a stabilizing presence. He shook the inhaler, the metallic rattle serving as a beacon of hope.

He placed the mouthpiece on Sebastian's lips and rubbed circles on his back in reassurance.

Another breath, slow and deliberate, reached Sebastian's vulnerable lungs. The tension in his body eased, and his breathing recognized a regular rhythm.

Christopher's heart swelled with relief, and tears threatened to spill over. He held Sebastian, providing a safeguard against the harsh realities of a world that could turn against them in an instant.

Then he helped Sebastian to his feet, their connection unbroken.

A small, grateful smile graced Sebastian's lips, a flicker of resilience in the face of adversity. Christopher kept his gaze, his eyes mirroring the love that coursed through him.

With his arm hugging his son's waist, Christopher steered him from the bedroom.

Once, long ago, the cottage had been a cozy haven. Now it was merely a shell of its former self.

Everywhere he stepped, he scattered a trail of dirt, reminding him of quicksand, and his legs wobbled as if he were walking on stilts.

This was a turning point, a reminder of the fragility of life and the depths of love for his son.

Christopher navigated the narrow, weather-beaten steps that led them outside. The tired wooden planks groaned beneath his weight, mimicking the gravity of his terror and subsequent relief. He scanned the porch, pleased to see a familiar, broken-down rocking chair that sat in a corner. Bright-yellow paint had faded to a muted shade, worn by years of exposure to the sun.

Christopher collapsed into the chair before his legs gave out completely. He cradled Sebastian close to his chest as they rocked, the rhythmic creaking a gentle lullaby that whispered comfort and security.

In solitude, he replayed the events leading up to this moment, his own private battlefield for self-condemnation. The vision of Sebastian crumpling to the floor, gasping for air, haunted him.

The experience served as a reminder of how far his own health had come and the strength he now possessed.

However, things weren't the same for his son. How could he forget for even one minute?

He'd decided on an impulse to rediscover his childhood home, and he alone was to blame for ignoring the risk—a risk that had cost Sebastian dearly.

All his fault. All his fault.

He couldn't escape his thoughts. He had to protect Sebastian, guide him, and keep him safe. And yet, his reckless, selfish behavior had brought about his son's suffering.

His choices had consequences, and now he had to face the repercussions. Sebastian deserved nothing less than his love and protection.

CHAPTER 17

$\mathscr{A}$ couple of days later, Evan Farrenway entered the hotel carrying a hand-crafted seagrass lamp to replace the one that had shattered. The lamp featured a base constructed from gnarled driftwood. Atop the base, the lamp boasted a shade made from dried sea grass, in muted hues of tender green and sandy beige.

"It's exquisite." Jenny admired the dainty lattice where the grass was woven together. "That type of craftsmanship requires considerable patience."

"I work with only the best people," Evan said. "This artisan works in the Charleston area. She specializes in natural materials, and this piece is unique."

Evan dressed in his usual elegant style; a pristine ivory linen shirt complemented by sleek chino shorts. But what truly caught the eye was his silk tie, a bold geometric pattern in shades of emerald green that brought an aura of sophistication to his clothes.

"I'm sorry this replacement took longer than I expected." He positioned the lamp on an end table. "I've been busy responding to calls from both coasts."

"The hotel hasn't opened its doors yet, so you're fine. This is such an exciting season for you." Jenny turned to fasten a sixteen-by-twenty-inch canvas photo behind her computer station. She'd taken the photo on her cell phone during Christopher's encounter with the seagull. She'd shown it to him beforehand, and he'd chuckled and consented when she asked if she could display it.

The print's background showed a spectacular landscape, with the sky a luminous turquoise. Christopher stood in the foreground. His eyes and mouth were wide open, and he'd angled his head slightly towards his shoulder, where the seagull had perched.

She'd caught the gray and white seagull in flight, its kaleidoscope-patterned wings spread, its eyes searching the sky. The bird's white color contrasted with Christopher's navy-blue shirt and was a dramatic sight.

The photo provided a dose of whimsy. If nothing else, it was a source of discussion for guests and a lighthearted memory preserved in time.

Evan retreated a step. "This has a slightly comical vibe, as if Christopher and the seagull are both characters in a quirky cartoon."

"I found the situation amusing," she said. "I hope it brings a smile to anyone who sees it. And I appreciate you bringing by the sea grass lamp." She started toward the breakroom to snag a protein bar, but Evan intercepted her.

"Do you have a few minutes to discuss something important?" he asked.

She offered a half-hearted shrug. "If it's about our weekend excursion, I'm afraid it isn't possible. This hotel opening has me completely swamped."

"I understand. Wild times. The hotel is coming together, though."

"Thank you. We're thrilled and incredibly proud."

Nodding, she glanced around the lobby. The architecture and décor captured the essence of the seaside. They had included driftwood accents, sea grass weavings, and an ocean mural painted by the aspiring painter who worked in housekeeping.

Evan adjusted his eyeglasses. "Mind if we find a private place to chat?"

"Sure." She glanced at Christopher and Sebastian, seated together in a secluded nook. They were working on Sebastian's final school project for the year, which was scheduled to be emailed to the homeschool office by the end of the day.

Eyeing Evan, Christopher advanced, possessing a natural grace and ease. How did he consistently convey such an easy balance of masculinity and refinement?

His wavy brown hair fell over his forehead, adding to his boyish charm. A T-shirt touting the hotel logo fit him perfectly, accentuating his toned physique and sun-bronzed skin. His eyes, the shade of the sea on a cloudless day, held a wealth of depth and emotion. Often, the shade varied with the light. Today, Jenny read fortitude and an unshakable spirit in his gaze.

Since his excursion to Rusty's ruined hut, Christopher had been quiet and contemplative. He confessed it wasn't the hut itself, but what had happened afterward. He'd brought Sebastian to his childhood cottage, and Sebastian had suffered a severe asthma attack there. In addition, Christopher had discovered a poem that his mother had written to him.

Jenny hadn't had the chance to discuss anything further with him since they'd devoted all their hours to eleventh-hour hotel preparations.

"Hi, Evan." Christopher greeted the man and extended his hand for a shake. "Happy to reconnect with you."

Jenny squinted. Christopher's upbeat greeting was almost certainly not genuine, though she said nothing.

He folded his arms. "So, what brings you here?"

Evan indicated the lamp, and Christopher inclined his head. He seemed to push away any negative reactions he'd previously harbored. Both he and Jenny had concluded that they needed Evan to bolster the hotel's image, a tactic to entice more guests. After all, Evan was on his way to becoming a celebrated decorator.

"Well, it's a pleasure." Christopher stepped back and nodded toward Sebastian. "My son plans on attending the school here in the fall. Will you continue to teach?"

"I'm uncertain." Evan held his head high, resembling a peacock that had just received a promotion. "The fate of the universe rests upon the sheer number of decorating proposals I receive."

"Huh? Oh, right." Christopher kept his response brief. "Well, I'd best help my son finish. Sebastian is writing multiple paragraphs about his favorite animal—what the animal eats, where it lives, and what makes it special."

"Which animal did he choose?" Jenny peeked at Sebastian and gave him a quizzical smile.

Christopher beamed. "A dog."

"No shock there."

"So, Jenny?" Evan prompted, as Christopher returned to Sebastian. "I'd appreciate a tour, and then we can talk?"

"Certainly." She guided him through the lobby to the back, showing the latest updates—a tiled patio and inviting seating area under the pergola.

"Sebastian made this wind chime." She gestured at the seashells and beads, painted in lime green and powder blue, hanging from the rafters of the pergola on a string. Grinning, she recalled when the little boy, bursting with pride, proudly showed it to her.

Evan flashed a smug smile. "You people sure adore quaintness."

"What's wrong with quaintness?"

"Nothing. It's just not my thing. I prefer more extravagant embellishments."

"You can't value the beauty of a child's creativity?"

"Hey, I'm not saying it isn't pretty. I'm merely implying that I wouldn't hang it in any of my hotels."

When they retraced their steps to the front entrance, Maria was lazing in the sun on the beach, flipping through a glossy magazine. She'd insisted that sunbathing was the most reliable method for her to look relaxed and well-rested for when their guests arrived.

She flicked up her bangs and sent a friendly wave in Jenny's direction before returning to her magazine. Her red bikini halter top highlighted her bust, while the bottom emphasized her hips.

She stationed a tall beverage on a table beside her, which Jenny prayed was water and not gin.

When Jenny and Evan reached the edge of the patio, they decided not to venture any further so as not to damage their shoes on the sand.

Jenny sported her preferred outfit, a skirt in a rich orchid. The rayon fabric cascaded in graceful folds to her ankles. Her T-shirt in vibrant magenta displayed the hotel's logo. The shirt hugged her silhouette and framed her arms, while the neckline was conservative and flattering.

Evan ushered her to a chair and sat opposite her.

"I have a serious proposition to discuss with you." He steepled his hands in front of him. "A business proposal."

She straightened in her seat and observed him—a once humble schoolteacher was swiftly becoming a hotshot decorator. "Please go on."

"Recently, I've invested in several hotels, and I own a share of one in particular."

"Congratulations."

He coughed and adjusted his tie, a subtle display of nervousness beneath his confident exterior. "The resort is in Los Angeles. It's called the Luxe Haven."

"I've heard of it." Jenny perked up at the name. "I remember reading an article about it in a travel magazine. The resort is top-notch."

He bobbed his head, acknowledging the reputation. "The accommodations are modern and include an excellent restaurant, spa, and fitness center with a personal trainer."

"Congrats. But what does this have to do with me?"

"We need a different manager, and I have faith that you're the ideal candidate for the job."

"You're suggesting I uproot my life here?" She cocked her head to the side and emitted a brief, disbelieving chuckle. "Why on earth would I consider moving to California?"

"A change of scenery is stimulating, and the Luxe Haven is on a considerably larger stage than the Grand Michelangelo." Evan lowered his voice to a conspiratorial whisper. "Also, the salary is significantly higher than what you're currently earning. Plus, the Luxe has established itself. Let's face it. Who can predict if this hotel will survive even a single season?"

She leaned back in her chair, chewed on her lower lip, and contemplated.

Living in a modern city near the Pacific Ocean and bordered by mountains appealed to her wanderlust. Then there was the renowned entertainment sector. She'd often dreamed of shopping at the luxury boutiques and flagship stores on Rodeo Drive.

"I'll handle the logistics," he continued. Sensing her hesitation, his tone became more persuasive. "If it helps, I'm planning to move there eventually, too. Malibu Beach is gorgeous. You'll be able to see many marine animals, and possibly dolphins and seals."

"I'm grateful for the privilege, but I need space to mull it over." Her chair legs scraped against the tiles as she pushed back her chair and stood. "Even so, I certainly wouldn't leave this position before this hotel opens."

"Jenny, I admire your integrity, and you have my utmost admiration." He rose and offered a firm handshake. "Take your time. Nonetheless, the sooner we wrap this up, the more advantageous it will be for you."

Jenny granted him a small smile, already evaluating her options. The appeal of an unexplored, glamorous city sparked excitement. But at what cost? Did she truly want to leave Christopher and Pink Coral Island behind?

"WHAT WAS THAT ABOUT?" A while later, Maria questioned Jenny. Inquisitiveness fairly dripped from her.

Jenny tweaked her chair and switched on her laptop. "Evan is a partial owner of the Luxe Haven in Los Angeles and extended the position of manager to me."

"The Luxe Haven?" Maria's face lit up like a Christmas tree. "You're considering it?"

Jenny stared at the computer screen and the blinking void before her. "The offer is appealing, but how ..."

Bidding farewell to Pink Coral Island meant farewell to all those she had ever loved, from Christopher to Sebastian and all her beloved friends. The idea stirred grief in her heart, though she realized that in order to pursue her ambitions, she might have to make a hard decision.

"I understand why you're uncertain." Maria smiled sadly. "But would you really take off and forget about me? And

Christopher? I thought you two were an item. After being apart for almost an eternity, you're finally reunited." Through the open patio doors, Jenny glanced at Christopher, where he chatted with Francis and Rusty, who had come by to visit.

"Plus, what about Sebastian?" Maria asked.

"Yes, that's what makes this decision even more difficult." Jenny met Christopher's stare, and the bewilderment in his expression caused her to tense.

She buried her face in her hands. Each person on this island had become her family.

Maria stood and hugged her. "Look, this is hard, but we'll always be here. At least Christopher and his son will. I'm still undecided if this place is my wheelhouse."

Jenny rubbed away tears with her knuckles, unable to speak. Memories of the past few months surged over her, similar to a tidal wave, threatening to drag her under. She closed her eyes, envisioning the sound of laughter and the unconditional love that encircled her. Each day was more precious and irreplaceable than the last.

She lifted her head and encountered Maria's unwavering stare.

"Wherever you go, you'll have our support," Maria said. "You know that, right?"

"Yes, I know. Thanks for the pep talk," Jenny replied. "No matter where I end up, this island will always be a part of me."

As NIGHTFALL DREW NEAR, Jenny remained seated on the oceanfront patio. She divided her attention between her computer screen and the subtle changes unfolding around her. The once bustling lobby had grown quiet, and the atmosphere exuded an unusual tension. The reception desk stood empty, its polished surface reflecting a subdued glow from the dimmed chandelier lights.

Despite not being able to identify it exactly, it seemed as if an impending storm, both metaphorical and literal, loomed close by, ready to alter the course of events.

Christopher stepped over to her, his eyebrows furrowed. He expertly balanced two glasses of iced tea, a bowl of strawberries, and an array of utensils. He set them down with a flourish. The scent of sunbaked sand, wildflowers, and an afternoon rainstorm surrounded them.

"May I join you?" he inquired, his voice formal.

"Certainly." She saluted him. "I'm finishing my tasks for the day, boss."

He raised a hand in a gesture that silenced any jokes. "Please. I'm not in the mood, okay?"

Her gaze connected with his. "Is anything wrong?" she asked.

He slid an iced tea glass toward her. "You tell me."

"I'm fine." She powered down her computer and forked a plump strawberry, the flavor tart on her tongue. A reminder of the basic pleasures of the island. "These are delicious. I appreciate your thoughtfulness."

He stretched out his legs. His blue eyes burned with fierce intensity, as if he searched for an unspoken truth.

"How is Sebastian?" With each bite of strawberry, she waited for him to tell her more about his recent experience at his cottage. "His asthma flare-up must've been scary for him and for you."

"Dust does not agree with an asthmatic." Christopher clasped his hands together. "I knew that, and it's usually never far from my mind. I should've weighed the potential dangers before allowing him to go inside. I obviously wasn't thinking."

"The main thing is that he is okay." Jenny studied Christopher's expression. "You didn't have trouble breathing, too, did you?"

"No."

She wrapped her fingers around the cool glass. "You mentioned you found a poem your mother wrote for you."

His gaze grew distant. "I'll read it to you sometime."

"I'd love to hear it." She forked another strawberry and chewed slowly, biding her time. "What else did you uncover when you were at the cottage? You hinted at more."

He dipped into his pocket, retrieving a necklace that glistened with seashells, capturing the colorful streaks of the sunset. "Such as finding this, for instance."

Jenny's skin tingled, a creeping unease, a fleeting sensation of a spiderweb.

Aware of the significance of the amulet and the legend of the Gullah woman who had created it, she examined each seashell. "This is like traveling back in time. A secret that was hidden for a generation."

A snicker escaped Christopher's lips, and she ignored him and went on. "This necklace brings prosperity and good fortune." She gingerly glided her fingers over the design. "It's a sign of the power of connection."

"You're not serious, are you? Surely, you don't honestly believe that nonsense."

She met his sharp gaze, registering his skepticism. The amulet was merely a piece of jewelry to him, devoid of cultural importance.

"Regardless of your opinion, keep the necklace somewhere safe," she said.

He shrugged dismissively. "What did you expect me to do with it, exactly? Throw it into the ocean?"

A chill raced through her at his lack of belief.

She hugged her arms. Despite the warmness of June, the evening temperature was cooling. "There is no need to resort to such drastic measures. I'm merely offering some cautionary advice. Is there something else I should know?"

Christopher sighed, a heaviness in his breathing. "Two more things. First, I came across an old photo of my mother when she was young."

"Where did you find it?"

"In the cottage," he replied. "She was with a man I had never seen before. They gave the impression of being very much in love. Quite honestly, it upset me."

"I'm so sorry, Christopher." She reached out and touched his hand. "That's a lot to process, but remember, pictures are often deceiving."

He placed the necklace on the table and stared out at the horizon. The last remnants of daylight lingered, and the sky was transitioning to a deep indigo. Stars timidly emerged.

"I know," he replied. "It just left me confused."

"Do you have the photo on you?"

"It's in my suite." His fingers tapped the armrest of his chair. "Speaking of deception, there is another matter. Since Farrenway took off this afternoon, I've heard rumors regarding his generosity in offering employment."

Jenny's muscles tensed, her gaze darting briefly to the lobby. "He brought a beautifully crafted seagrass lamp."

"How princely of him."

"Spell it out, Christopher. Coyness doesn't suit you. Is something bothering you?"

"Maria told Rusty that Farrenway offered you a promising job in California. Speculation has resulted in nonstop gossip."

Jenny slumped her shoulders. "Tales certainly travel fast here."

"The rumor got bigger and bigger," Christopher continued. "Think of a snowball rolling down a hill. Rusty told Francis, and Francis told Fatu, and so on. It's an entire hierarchy here. People may have revised the facts, though, and the gossip might not be reliable."

She sighed. "Facts stayed the same, and the gossip is correct."

Her heart sank as the conversation took an unexpected turn. The mention of the job offer stirred clashing emotions. She was considering the opportunity, seduced by the enchantment of exciting horizons and personal growth. Yet, as Christopher revealed the extent of the rumors and its impact on the island, more doubts crept in.

"From Rusty's perspective, informing Francis seemed like the right call, and everyone is getting the message," he said.

"What message is that?"

"That you can't wait to leave."

She detected a trace of vulnerability in his tone.

Despite this, defiance colored her response. "I haven't come to any conclusions or accepted any positions yet."

"I realize you have higher aspirations than this place, and I want you to go after your dreams. I really do. But what of us? Our history ... our connection. Have you thought about what leaving might mean for us?"

She had. In fact, that was all she had thought about.

"It's not just about us," she said. "Is it such a crime to pursue success?"

"Well, here's your chance." He paused, seeming to consider her question. "I guess it depends on your definition of success."

He rose quickly and swiveled.

His disappearing form left her stunned. She struggled between the thrill of new opportunities and sadness at leaving the bonds she had formed.

And most of all, living a life without Christopher and Sebastian in it.

CHAPTER 18

Christopher convinced himself he was indifferent. Jenny could do whatever she wanted. She could accept the hotel manager's job in California and relocate with Farrenway, and Christopher wouldn't make a fuss about it. Maybe Jenny and his ex would meet there.

Talk about an ironic twist of fate.

In any event, he was content with his life and didn't need Jenny in it for him to be happy.

The next afternoon in the breakroom, as he poured himself an energy drink, she approached with favorable news. It was June 28, two days before the opening, and the hotel was fully booked.

"I'm not sure how to phrase this." Her voice trailed off. "But I have some other news, too."

He put aside his glass. "Good or bad?"

"Not necessarily either, but I wanted to tell you before the entire island heard about it. My ex, Dominick, texted me."

The announcement hit Christopher like a wave of ice-cold water, and he flinched. This was hard to accept.

Too many men were interested in Jenny, but he was the

236

man who should hold sway over her affections. After all, his claim was the most valid. They had been friends since childhood and shared so much history.

He opened his mouth, the syllables tripping over his tongue. "And then what?" he asked.

"Dominick apologized for the way he left things and asked me to return to Italy. He's touring the Amalfi Coast and wants me to accompany him. He's paying for my flight, too."

His forehead tightened, though he tried to mask his reaction.

"Dominick is a fool." He peered deep into her almond-shaped eyes. Normally a vivid emerald, today they took on a subdued shade of sage green.

"Why?"

"Because he let you go."

"Oh, well, I know another man who also did that."

Her jab hit him like a blow to the chest. Yes, he had, and was he ever sorry.

"So, your stint here will end with all these other opportunities pouring in," he said. "You have your choice of wherever you want to go—Italy, California, anywhere."

"You are serious?"

"Completely."

"You want me to go?"

"I didn't say that."

All he wanted to do was hold her, but he was determined to keep his pride intact and held back.

Please stay, Jenny.

No. He wouldn't beg.

Her magnificent eyes glistened. A single tear rolled down her delicate cheeks, and his chest shattered in two. He was tempted to wipe the tear away, but he knew she would reject him.

She had flipped his entire world upside down, and it was too late to retract his remarks.

He struggled to steady his tone. "I'm sorry. I didn't mean it. It came out wrong."

"I … I should head out." She snatched her purse and turned, ready to inflict more emptiness into his life. History was repeating itself. His mother and his ex-wife had both left him alone and hurting.

The forceful slam of the door returned him to the reality of the present.

He focused on the empty space, tracing the outline of where she had stood. He'd been adamant about being indifferent but had just been fooling himself.

Panic and fear of losing her controlled his words, his actions, and now he was paying the price.

He paced back and forth. When did the breakroom become so cramped?

Once, he'd viewed the room as a pleasant oasis, a place to take a breather after the hustle and bustle of the long workday. Today, it was frigid and unwelcoming. The vibrant orange and teal blue walls were drab and colorless. The aroma of freshly brewed coffee was gone. It its place was the stale odor of old popcorn.

He collapsed on the sofa like a pile of wet rags.

The plush throws and pillows were neatly arranged on a chair, as though they sought to separate themselves from the emotional turmoil.

Mocking him, the room recalled the pain he had inflicted.

LATER THAT SAME AFTERNOON, outside on the patio, Christopher typed furiously on his computer. He detailed emergency procedures to authorities and insurers for guest protection.

A laughing gull roamed near a tidal flat and provided a cheery background noise with its distinctive call.

"Ha-ha-ha."

Christopher's hands hovered over the keys as Jenny approached, her steps slow and hesitant. Her long blond hair cascaded over her shoulders, catching the afternoon sun's rays and shining as if it were pure gold. Her light sundress was simple yet colorful, and billowed in the breeze, creating a soft fluttering sound.

As she presented him with a neatly folded note, her fingers quivered. Her green eyes glittered like jewels, casting a radiant sparkle.

His hand tightened around the note, the creases digging into his skin. Should he open it? He stalled, afraid of what he might discover.

"What is this?" he asked.

"My resignation letter."

A chill crawled through his stomach and traveled down to his toes. His mind raced, striving for an explanation. Why? Their previous exchange had been strained, and his jealousy, yet again, had gotten the better of him.

"Ah, you can't wait to go to Italy? The land of pizza and pasta." He forced a humorless grin.

She frowned. His effort at light-hearted banter had fallen flat.

She tucked a strand of hair behind her ear. "No. I won't be traveling to Italy anytime soon."

The chill in his stomach strengthened, an unsettling combination of disappointment, confusion, and longing.

With a weary sigh, he powered down his computer and observed her, taking in every detail of her lovely face. He caught a whiff of her fragrance. Lavender and lemon, a blend of calmness and freshness—a tranquil garden on a sunny day.

"Will Dominick be showing up here instead?" he asked.

"Not likely." Hands clasped, her posture translated into a single word. Strong-minded. "Dominick loves Italy."

"You've set your sights on California, then? I heard the avocado toast is life-changing."

Did she not recognize the hurt in his voice? Did she not understand the depth of his emotions?

Her shoulders rose. A defense mechanism, perhaps. "What more could a woman want than a slice of avocado toast?"

"Nothing that I can think of." He unfolded her note and scanned it, then folded it back up and handed it to her. "Unfortunately, Jenny, you'll have to wait to resign from this job."

The mere thought of her exit sent his thoughts reeling. He couldn't lose her. He needed her.

Because he loved her.

"Wait for what?" she asked.

"Olive, because I can't accept your resignation."

"Why not?"

"Because I didn't hire you." He prided himself on thinking so quickly. "Contact Olive. However, he's gone on a fishing trip. He neglected to bring his cellphone, but told me he is traveling to Pink Coral Island for the hotel opening."

"Oliver is coming here? I'll meet him in person?"

"Yes." Christopher replied.

His conscience niggled. True, Olive was fly fishing somewhere along the Irish Sea, but he stayed accessible because of his reliable staff. He could always be reached.

"Is there anything I might do to change your mind in the meantime?" Christopher stood, restless.

"No. My decision is final."

"Then, for my part as a co-owner, I accept your resignation."

His declarations were quiet, a tacit acknowledgement of their evolving circumstances.

After talking more, Jenny agreed to stay for the hotel's unveiling and then submit her two-week notice, showing her commitment to the project. It was a minor intermission, but a chance to savor their last days together as colleagues. He would cherish their conversations and any shared moments of unity.

As they concluded, he thanked her for her time and service. He extended his hand, a gesture of finality and presumably closure. Their palms briefly touched, a fleeting connection that contained a multitude of unsaid words.

She turned, her silhouette receding. The fitted bodice of her dress hugged her curves, accentuating every contour of her figure. Slim straps crisscrossed her back, revealing an enticing glimpse of sun-kissed skin. She was a vision of understated elegance, radiating a serene confidence that would forever enchant him.

He gained consolation by telling himself he was blessed to have known her, even if only for a few chapters in their intertwined stories.

AS DAYLIGHT SUBSIDED, Christopher found Jenny sitting at a picnic table near the marina with Maria, Sebastian, and Scooby-Doo. They were finishing a feast of crab cakes, shrimp, and French fries smothered in molten cheese from the crab stand. Clams and mussels were steamed to perfection, and he inhaled a whiff of smoking grilled fish.

All day, he'd worn a linen shirt with rolled-up sleeves, khaki shorts, and comfortable loafers.

He glanced down. He hadn't bothered to change his wrinkled shirt and shorts. Jenny's sudden resignation had left him frazzled.

"Who is minding the hotel tonight?" Maria inquired as he neared.

Both Maria and Jenny wore sunglasses, their hair fastened in loose ponytails. They sported casual beachwear like pros: Jenny in her flowing maxi dress, while Maria wore a white tank top with snug denim leggings.

"Nobody's at the hotel right now," he answered Maria. "But you can all rest easy. I've secured the hotel with tight locks and security cameras."

"Maria let me drive the golf cart, Dad." Sebastian's chin was spattered with ketchup, and his eyes shone. His bright yellow T-shirt touted the hotel's logo, and his Bermudas were impeccably neat compared to his disheveled brown curls.

"Blisters are forming on my feet from all this walking." Maria extended a broad smile to Christopher. "So, we drove the golf cart and are now off to Francis and Fatu's house."

"Is Rusty there?" Christopher wondered aloud.

"Oh, he's there. Wanna come with us?"

"I'm not going." Jenny's eyes flickered to the golf cart, a wistful expression on her face. "I'm heading back to the hotel. I have some last-minute work."

"Well, that's a shame." Maria, ever the independent spirit, expanded her smile. "I'm up-to-date and ready for some fun."

"I'll drive!" Sebastian volunteered.

"Okay," Maria said. "But hey, don't crash it like you did coming over here."

The boy stared at her blankly. "I didn't—"

"Remember, you accidentally backed it into a tree?" She winked amiably at Christopher's scowl. "Kidding, kidding."

"Spare me your attempt at humor, Maria." Christopher caught Jenny's gaze. "May I join you on your walk back to the hotel?"

"You just got here."

"I was lonely and wondered where everyone had gone." He held out his hand as Maria and Sebastian stepped away. "Shall we make amends?"

She paused before relenting with a brief nod, though she refused his hand. "Alright."

The night was strangely silent. The air was cool, in sharp contrast to their heated argument. They had hardly spoken since the breakroom.

He well remembered his sarcastic remarks but didn't dare speak for fear of breaking their fragile truce.

As they walked, Christopher noticed gray tendrils of smoke curling up into the darkened sky.

Panic gripped his chest as the deafening blare of a fire alarm resonated across the beach, signaling danger.

Jenny stopped and stared at the sky. "The smoke is coming from the hotel."

"Maybe not," he said, trying to reassure her.

"Yes, it is." She inhaled sharply and grasped his fingers, standing rigid as a mannequin. Then her knees buckled, her body folded, and she crumpled to the ground.

He knelt beside her, taking her hands and encouraging her to stand. She resembled a lifeless doll, her form limp.

"Tell me it isn't true." She gasped, her voice barely audible.

"We know nothing for sure yet, Jenny. Please, we must keep going."

Urgency gave him strength, and he helped her to her feet. He guided her onward, quickly, their progress hindered by jutting pieces of driftwood. His lungs burned with exertion, each step a struggle against the burden of his apprehension. Smoke billowed above them, blackening the sky as if it were a menacing giant.

When they reached the hotel, Christopher's worst fears were confirmed.

Vivid flames licked at the heavens, illuminated by an angry orange glow. Incessant crackling assaulted his ears.

A sea of sparks overcame the back entrance. The fire quickly consumed the picturesque pergola, reducing it to smoldering ashes. Burning wood and haze choked the air, mingling with the sickly, sweet stench of melted plastic and metal.

Stunned, Christopher remained motionless, his body numb as he viewed the devastation. It seemed impossible, as if the blaze was playing a cruel trick on his senses.

A familiar figure materialized from the smoke.

Michael Freid called out, his shouts cutting through the chaos. "Déjà vu?"

With a labored exhale, Christopher acknowledged him.

The hotel's debut was overshadowed by a destructive force that consumed all their hopes.

The volunteers extinguished the fire, and the crowd dispersed, leaving Christopher, Jenny, and Michael to confront the aftermath.

"The front of the hotel was relatively untouched." Michael clasped his hands behind him. "All the same, the back needs a total renovation. Weren't you opening in a couple of days?"

Tears had swollen Jenny's eyes and streaked her cheeks, giving her a dazed appearance. She nodded in unison with Christopher.

Christopher's gaze fastened onto Michael's. "How did this happen?" he demanded.

"Faulty wiring might have triggered a short circuit near the loading dock. And I spotted paint thinner in the storage shed, which could've kindled." He rested his chin on his chest. "Or—"

"Or …?" Christopher took a step forward; his fingers tightly interlaced.

"Or it could've been arson. A person or some people set the fire intentionally. It's a hunch, though. Only a hunch."

Jenny's face went pale. "You believe somebody did this on purpose?"

"Hunches are often baseless. When it's safe to investigate further, we'll know more." As always, Michael's assessment was pragmatic. "For tonight, let's salvage what we can. The back area will need a complete refurbishment. The damage is fairly extensive."

Christopher shook his head, unable to fathom the maliciousness.

Why? Why? Why?

Possibly the motive was driven by financial gain, revenge, or a competitor aiming to eliminate competition. A deliberate act to cause harm or hinder the hotel's success.

"All our endless work," Jenny breathed. "Everything is gone."

Christopher wiped her tears and tentatively embraced her, trying to console her. "We'll rise above this and rebuild."

"You really believe that? It will take months, and the summer will be over."

"We have each other. We'll tackle this setback, one step at a time."

It was more than a setback, but she didn't question him. Their quarrel from the previous day seemed minor compared to this.

They stayed close, their eyes fixed on the remnants of their aspirations. Their future, once filled with expectations, now lay in ruins.

Christopher gained comfort in her presence and their combined strength. The path ahead might be challenging, but he held onto the belief that their bond would guide them through the bleakest of times.

He prayed it would also set the foundation for a new beginning.

CHAPTER 19

Two days later, Christopher found himself on the beach in front of the hotel. The sun was setting over the horizon, casting long shadows over the sand.

Despite the forty-eight hours that had elapsed since the fire, an eerie silence persisted. The ghostly stillness was a haunting reminder of the chaos and destruction.

He'd inspected the skeletal framework of the pergola multiple times. Where the beautiful structure once stood, now there were twisted and blackened timbers.

Christopher still saw the scorched wooden posts planted in the ground, and he easily remembered Sebastian's art project. The unusual wind chime, made from seashells and beads, produced a pleasant clinking sound and reminded him of his son's imaginative nature.

Gone were the vibrant hanging plants that had once adorned the pergola, their lush foliage and colorful blooms reduced to a memory. Burnt remnants of leaves and vines clung desperately to the ruined posts.

A testament, he supposed, to the life that had once thrived there.

Without a computer to distract him, Christopher dwelled on the past—the Internet was down but was promised to be reconnected soon. In spite of his best efforts, the persistent "what if" thoughts persisted. To take his mind off the rebuild, he reflected on his plans once they restored the hotel.

Jenny consumed much of his thoughts, leaving little room for anything else. She hadn't spoken about her departure, and he refrained from asking. He hoped she had reconsidered and opted to stay.

Michael Freid's predictions had proved accurate, with the fire completely consuming the back storage area, leaving only a shell of charred debris in its wake. The flames had wiped out vital equipment and valuable inventory. The once-active loading docks lay empty.

The smoke had saturated the sofas and carpets inside the hotel, and the staff helped them air out and wash their clothes.

Fortunately, the fire had spared Christopher's suite as well as Jenny's and Maria's rooms.

However, no one could live at the hotel until they completed repairs. Maria refused to use the elevator again, no matter the reassurance.

She cited two reasons for her refusal: Heat exposure to electrical wiring components and the fact that the structure of the building could impact the elevator's stability.

Jenny and Maria currently shared a beach hut, while Christopher and Sebastian occupied another nearby. Maria's family in Connecticut had rallied together and were reportedly journeying to the island to offer their help.

Christopher's gaze drifted to the tranquil expanse of the ocean. A ferry boat was slowly gliding toward the pier, a speck on the horizon. The waters were calm and inviting, reflecting a pale sapphire. Waves slapped the shore, and a sea turtle bobbed, throwing a shadow on the soft sand.

As the ferry drew closer, it gradually revealed its size, its white hull catching the golden light of the sun. The sun's rays bounced off the water, creating a spectrum of colors across the sky.

A breeze kicked up the tree branches, rattling them and seeming to whisper, "Never give up."

He spun, but not a soul was there.

As he scanned the wet sand and sun-soaked rocks, he couldn't help feeling that something inexplicable was at play. Perhaps it was only the wind, but it was capable of stirring up secrets and untold stories.

Perhaps there was more to the message.

He'd retrieved his mother's poem, still intact, in a lockbox in his suite. Her verses were a bridge to his ancestry and a symbol of his purpose, and he'd been grateful the poem hadn't been destroyed.

Jenny stood by the patio, and he hailed her over. She wore a bright-yellow V-neck sundress; her skin had tanned from lengthy days in the Carolina sun. Farrenway hadn't visited, but Christopher suspected that he and Jenny had been in contact by phone.

In the meantime, Christopher and Jenny had been preoccupied with canceling hotel reservations. They hadn't discussed personal issues—whether they were getting back together or even remaining friends.

He watched her face as she turned. The creases of concern on her features had eased, leading to a solemn expression that left him curious.

Was she lost in contemplation or taking in the island's beauty?

He wanted her to be happy; seeing her come alive as she baked with Anyika was one of his greatest pleasures since she'd arrived months earlier.

He stood tall, locking eyes with her as she met him by the shore.

"How is today going?" he asked.

"It's long and difficult."

"Another storm, but we'll weather it."

"Will we? Storm after storm." She twirled a strand of her golden hair around her fingers. "And you lost your savings."

"Thankfully, the hotel has insurance. Property, business interruption, liability, worker's compensation, you name it."

"Then you'll be alright?"

"I should be. And ..." He cleared his throat and draped a casual arm over her shoulders, trusting it was a friendly enough touch that she wouldn't shake him off. "And I hope you'll stay, Jenny. Please. You're the backbone of this."

She surveyed the hotel, once the epitome of luxury and promise, now only an illusion of its former glory.

"I'm not sure," she murmured.

Boisterous shouting and laughter erupted from the beach, drawing Christopher's attention. As he peered toward the commotion, he identified the distinct voices of five familiar men from his prior military career. They marched in unison as they called out raucous greetings to him.

The sand shifted beneath their boots with each confident stride as they approached, duffel bags slung over their shoulders. Bold tattoos peeked out from under the sleeves of their shirts, American flags and symbols reflecting their patriotism.

Jenny squinted at the group of men. "Who in the world are they?"

"My army buddies." Christopher grinned. "I developed a lot of close friendships when I served." As they drew closer, he embraced each of them, laughing and clowning as if years hadn't passed since they'd last seen each other.

As the men walked away to examine the damage, Jenny

said, "They really showed up. For a while there, I didn't know if you had simply imagined them."

"You gotta have faith, Jenny. I knew they wouldn't disappoint. Once you've stood shoulder to shoulder in combat, those ties last a lifetime. We went through some scary times, and these guys are like family to me."

"Are any of them married? Don't they have families?"

"They might. We'll find out soon enough."

"How long are they here for?" she asked.

"We're not going anywhere, buddy." Benjamin, one guy, clapped a massive hand on Christopher's shoulder as he strode over to him. He was a towering figure, built like a professional football player. "Give us a month, and the Grand Michelangelo will be up and running again. I'm not a fan of hot summers, so I'll be gone by the end of July."

"Thank you. I knew I could rely on you guys," Christopher said. "Is Olive coming?"

"He's supposed to fly into Hilton Head tomorrow, though who knows where he'll end up? Las Vegas might tempt him to take a detour and try his luck at the blackjack tables instead." Benjamin chuckled, then gestured to Jenny. His hazel eyes gleamed roguishly. "And who is this lovely lady?"

Christopher smiled and wrapped his arm more firmly around her, proud to introduce her. "She is the love of my life. Jenny Ormani."

Benjamin's expression lit with recognition, and he extended a large hand for a hearty shake. "Ah, it's great finally to meet you in person. We've heard all about you."

"Likewise," she answered with a smile. "So, I've been the subject of discussion. What are they saying?"

"The word is you're a breath of fresh air." Benjamin stole a glance at Christopher. "Olive couldn't stand listening to Christopher prattle on about you all the time, so he hired you here just to shut him up."

"No way." Christopher's skepticism was obvious in his tone. "Olive? Romantic? He doesn't have a romantic bone in his body."

"Trust me. He does, and there's no stopping him once he gets an idea in his head."

"I'll have to phone and thank him for bringing us together." Christopher kissed Jenny's cheek. She flushed and leaned in closer as he directed his attention back to the men. "We have several vacant beach huts you can stay in. They're not all luxurious, but they serve the purpose. Jenny and her friend Maria are in one, and my son and I are living in another. A few of the islanders who work at the hotel are also staying there."

As if hearing her name, Maria sauntered over, carrying a large cup. She was dressed in frayed cargo shorts, the white threads dangling off her shapely legs as if unraveling ribbons. She cast a slow, deliberate look at all the men, particularly the tall and good-looking Benjamin.

"I just adore handsome surprises." Her laughter filled with mischief. "I'm the media person and in charge of food and drinks. Who wants a refreshing coconut and rum concoction?" She raised her cup.

Christopher's eyebrows shot up as he eyed Maria's cup. "I thought you were abstaining from alcohol."

"After that horrific fire? Come on, I can't just meditate my way through all this." She swatted at the air with her free hand. "I needed something to calm my nerves, and coconut is my trusty go-to."

"I'm not sure that's exactly how it works."

Jenny peered over at Maria's drink. "Is that rum?"

"What? No, no, no."

"You said it was."

"Did I? My bad. Actually, it's coconut water. You know

me, the master mixologist." Maria took a gulp and smacked her lips. "Want some?"

Jenny shook her head. "No, thanks. I'm good."

As Christopher and Jenny walked away, Christopher whispered, "You realize that's not coconut water, right?"

Jenny sighed. "Of course. Maria's idea of a drink is anything but water. I should've seen this coming when she applied for the food and beverage job."

"At least she's taking her responsibilities seriously."

"I hope so, though I'm concerned about her."

She turned as deafening music sounded and Salifu appeared. He rattled portable speakers and set them on the sand, turning up the volume so loudly that Christopher felt the vibrations.

Unbridled in his enthusiasm, Salifu gyrated to a Gullah call and response. His motions were a blur of twisting circles.

Francis and Fatu pulled up in their golf cart with Rusty, and Francis immediately led Fatu in an intricate dance. She laughed, her feet moving in small steps while her hips swayed with the beat.

Meanwhile, Maria waltzed away from Benjamin and looped her way toward Rusty, who then awkwardly steered her in a clumsy shuffle.

Sorie and Anyika arrived in a flurry of dust, and Sebastian ran to them with Scooby-Doo at his heels. Sebastian seized hold of Sorie's hands, pulling him into a dizzying spin.

The tunes drew people from every corner of the island. The steel drum and thumping bass blended seamlessly, and the addition of scraps of metal created a raw, tribal rhythm.

Christopher and Jenny stood side by side and observed the scene unfolding before them. Undeniably, it was a surreal moment, enhanced even more by the arrival of Christopher's comrades.

Francis emerged from an outdoor storage shed with

several portable grills. The air buzzed with the scents of locally caught shrimp, marinated with zesty garlic, tart lemon juice, and fragrant spices. The barbecue sizzled with plump, juicy corn on the cob.

An ocean breeze mingled with the fragrance of sand, wildflowers, and oleander flowers. The salty air added to the scents as Christopher and Jenny chuckled and conversed with the islanders.

Fatu greeted them with a welcoming smile and handed them each a frosty soda from the improvised bar. The crisp, effervescent bubbles tingled on Christopher's tongue.

"C'mon, man!" Salifu shouted at Christopher. "You may be an old-timer, but are you still able to dance?"

"Yeah, why?"

"You're not dancing!"

"I can move like I did when I was twenty." Grinning, Christopher set down his soda, and Jenny did the same. He snatched her hand, spun her around, and then guided her to a secluded patch of grass. "Shall we show them how it's done?" he whispered.

"Sure." Jenny laughed, her voice velvety and inviting. "He's not lying," she called out to Salifu. "He's really pretty good."

Christopher held her in his arms, and a smile spread across her face.

"Sometimes, I wish time could stand still," she said.

"Is this one of those times?"

"It is. It truly is."

He kissed her. "I doubt the real world would it appreciate if time stopped."

She laughed and whirled, her blond hair flying in the wind. "Who needs the real world when we have this island?"

He smiled. This was a moment of pure bliss, and he was determined to stretch it out as long as possible.

A pelican soared past, its wingtips inches from the sea. Skinny-legged herons hunted for minnows. Oyster beds clustered around the rocks, and crushed shells covered the shore.

Salifu, shirtless and drenched in sweat, glided over to them, his hips swaying to the beat of the music. "Hey, love-birds. Wanna return to the party? The shrimp are calling your name, and I have an amazing challenge planned."

"What kind of challenge?" Christopher quirked an eyebrow.

"I'm challenging everyone to a limbo competition."

"Limbo? Is that a way to distract us from the hotel repairs?"

Jenny's expression relaxed. "It may seem counterintuitive, but this is more than a party for the islanders. It's uniting and supporting each other through hardships."

"Jenny is right, man. Don't you understand the Gullah community by now?" Salifu wiped his forehead and grinned. "Even in the toughest seasons, we set aside our worries."

Jenny looked up at Christopher. "Consider tonight a necessary break."

He stepped back. "I can't believe that you, of all people, are actually saying that. You, the workaholic."

She beamed. "Believe it."

"Can you handle it?" Salifu asked Christopher. "Are you ready to limbo?"

"Challenge accepted," Christopher replied.

"I'm totally down," Jenny said. "Count me in. But beware, I've been practicing my backbends."

"Speak for yourself," Christopher muttered.

"Ah, it would be wise for you to stretch those muscles and do some calisthenics, my friend," Salifu said. "We don't want you throwing out your back trying to keep up with the rest of us."

Christopher turned to Jenny. "Can we slip away for a few more minutes? I wanted to spend more time alone with you."

Salifu chuckled. "Sorry to disappoint you, but Jenny has a more refined taste. Besides, you're not the only person who wants to be in her company."

She gave Salifu a playful shove. "Stop it. You know I only have eyes for Christopher."

"That's what I like to hear." Christopher grinned, his disappointment dissipating. He squeezed her hand, feeling the smoothness of her satiny skin. "Seriously?"

She leaned in and whispered, "Seriously and always."

As they strolled back to the barbecue, Christopher spotted Sebastian. His son had clamped his teeth around an ear of corn, a smudge of butter on his chin. He and Sorie were giggling at Fatu and Francis as they danced.

This, Christopher thought, was what summers on the island were all about.

The ever-resourceful Salifu fashioned a limbo bar out of discarded materials. One by one, the guests lined up to take their turns, with hoots and applause ringing out each time someone successfully crossed under the bar.

"I'm actually pretty good at it," Christopher told Jenny. "I didn't think I had it in me."

"You don't," Francis, who stood beside him, replied. "I've seen toddlers with better skills than you."

"I didn't fall on my face like you did."

"Hey, it's not my fault the sand was uneven."

"Right, blame it on the sand." Christopher smirked. "You just can't handle the pressure."

As each person bent and twisted under the makeshift limbo bar, gleeful cheers greeted their movements. In the end, Maria emerged as the undisputed champion.

Christopher offered her his hand for a congratulatory high-five. "Nice job, Maria."

Maria struck a humorous pose, exuding confidence and theatrical flair. "Behold, the queen in all her glory. My moves are so slick, I could probably limbo under a limbo stick on a unicycle without breaking a sweat."

"You may be getting a little ahead of yourself there, Maria," Jenny quipped. "I wouldn't call the Guinness World Records quite yet."

Maria huffed. "Fine, but mark my words. Someday you'll see me in the limbo Olympics."

Christopher winked at Jenny and drew her away from the crowd. "You'll always be a queen in my eyes. You've won my heart a thousand times over."

Her gaze shimmered with warmth and affection. "You captured my heart as well, on that very first day we met, all those years ago."

"Then I've won the greatest prize." He graced her lips with a sweet, tender kiss. "Your love is my genuine victory."

CHAPTER 20

The month of July sped by in a dizzying whirl, marking a haze of activity.

Jenny stood at her usual station, behind the counter in the lobby of the Grand Michelangelo Hotel. They'd decorated tastefully, with more driftwood and seashells. Sebastian had been especially proud of a perfectly spiraled seashell he'd found on the beach.

A touch of rustic elegance, she mused, as she peered out the wide front windows that seamlessly connected to the hotel and the ocean beyond.

Christopher's military friends had quickly attended to the final touches of the repairs and renovations.

However, parts of the back section remained enveloped in a cloud of dust, as the team had not yet pulled down the tarps and protective coverings. Crewmen scurried hence and forth, their movements resembling ants at a picnic. A saw echoed through the halls, accompanied by the muffled grunts of men as they shifted heavy furniture.

Olive had backed out of his trip to the island at the last minute, claiming a pressing matter with a London hotel investment. Christopher assured Jenny that Olive would attend the grand reopening, but she couldn't shake the feeling that he might never come. There were moments when she questioned whether Olive was even a real person.

And the elusive Evelyn Ekard?

Jenny had her suspicions. A single female had booked a suite for Labor Day weekend. She hadn't scheduled room service, but that was an option she could easily do upon arrival.

Labor Day. The beginning of September. Would Jenny still be living on Pink Coral Island?

She wasn't sure.

The hotel's air conditioning kicked on with a low, recognizable rumble, filling the lobby with a cool breeze.

She couldn't deny her pride at the efficient work accomplished by the entire team. The wait was almost over, and the hotel was on the verge of a spectacular comeback, leaving behind its troubled past.

Maria and Benjamin sat near each other on a sumptuous sofa and conversed. Jenny overheard Maria ask him, "Hey, have you ever experienced the thrill of paddle boarding?"

"Thrill?" Benjamin gave a slight shake of his head. "No, because I'm not aiming to die, nor am I a big fan of drowning."

She giggled and stroked his arm. "Where's your sense of adventure? I'll be there to save you if anything goes wrong."

"Promise?"

She threw a cream-colored velvet pillow at him. "Promise."

"Fine. But if I end up with a mouthful of salt water, it's on you."

Jenny grinned as they discussed where they could rent paddleboards and hit the waves before they walked away.

With a towel, washcloth, and rubber band fastened

around her wrist, she stepped to Sebastian, who sat in the breakroom.

She surveyed the vibrant orange and teal-blue walls. Christopher had once said that the colors revitalized the spirit, and she agreed with him.

Sebastian perched on a chair near the table. He'd poured himself a glass of water infused with cucumber and mint. She did the same.

Before she asked, Sebastian said, "Can you make me a bunny towel today, Miss Jenny?"

Jenny knew children needed safe objects to help them feel secure during difficult times. She didn't expect him to be a serious, responsible adult.

Children were just that—children. Her towel animals provided him with normalcy, allowing him to focus on positive thoughts.

"My pleasure." She laid the towel flat, folded it lengthwise, then rolled up one end to create a long, thin cylinder. With a rubber band, she secured the bunny ears in place. Then she formed a small towel into a ball and attached it to the cylinder using the second rubber band.

"Ta-dah! It's all yours. Now draw some whiskers, eyes, and a nose on it with markers," she said.

"Yay! Thank you." He grabbed the markers from a drawer, then carefully drew the bunny's face on the towel. When he finished, he glanced up at her with an earnest expression. "Miss Jenny, do you have any idea who caused these fires?"

"I'm uncertain, sweetheart," she replied gently. "But don't worry. The fire chief is doing everything in his power to find out. He'll make sure that he holds whoever did this accountable."

"Why would someone do something that terrible? Am I able to help?"

"Oh, Sebastian, I agree with your father. I have faith that

the chief will get to the bottom of all this. In the meantime, you could still pretend to be Shaggy Rogers."

"I told Sorie that he's better at being Shaggy Rogers."

"Well, you can keep wearing your detective hat," Jenny suggested.

Christopher peeked into the room. "Hey, I can picture it now, Sebastian. Who needs Shaggy when you have brains and style? Incidentally, Jenny, you are a strategic mastermind."

"You realize I merely made a towel animal, right?"

"Well, you take the art of towel-making to a whole new level."

She chuckled. "Thanks, I guess."

"I'm grateful for you devoting so much attention to Sebastian."

"Truly, it's my pleasure."

Christopher extended his hand. "Will you come with me? Maria and Benjamin agreed to stay with Sebastian for an hour or so. I have my cell phone with me in case there are any problems."

She hesitated before slinging her tote bag on her shoulder, then set her water glass in the sink. "Sure."

They stepped outside, greeted by the briny scent of the sea. She inhaled deeply, taking in the breeze that always cleansed her lungs and cleared her mind.

As they walked to the back of the hotel, she sighed. "I'm still concerned about who is causing all this vandalism."

"I'm frustrated too," Christopher replied. "I've implemented greater security measures, expecting it will prevent this from ever happening again."

"You added so much new equipment already."

"I've added more surveillance cameras and intrusion sensors on all the doors and windows. I'm constantly in touch with Michael, and that's all we can do for now."

"We can worry. We can do that."

"No more worries. It's too nice out." Christopher grinned down at her. "By the way, did I compliment you today?"

"You might've missed a day," she quipped, returning his grin.

"Well, let me rectify that." He cleared his throat. "The pink color of your dress flatters your skin."

"Wow, you're getting fancy."

"I'm a poet, remember?"

She smiled, smoothed down her maxi dress, and faced him. "Where are we going?"

"Two places." He steered her down a winding path that led to Sun-Kissed Treats. They walked past a pond filled with a chorus of frogs, and tall oaks provided pockets of shade.

As they drew nearer to the bakery, the once-colorful storefront looked completely different. The sign above the entrance creaked, its rusted hinges protesting as it swung in the wind. The owners had boarded up the windows, giving the impression that the place had already been forgotten. How sad to see such an important part of Gullah history fade into obscurity.

She couldn't resist the urge to peek inside, peering through the crack in the boards until her pupils adjusted to the dim light. She detected the silhouette of baking equipment, abandoned, and left to gather dust.

A large stainless-steel oven stood against the far wall; its lustrous surface blemished by a fine layer of grime. Next to it was a commercial mixer with a bowl big enough to knead dough for dozens of loaves of bread.

Near the cooktop sat a collection of baking tools. A rolling pin still had bits of flour clinging to it, as did a pastry scraper with a worn handle and a set of cookie cutters in various shapes and sizes. At the rear rested a massive refrigerator and freezer, towering like two sentinels.

"Can you imagine the treats that were stored here through the years?" she asked. "It's as if the baking tools themselves are holding onto the memories."

The bakery had once been a hub of activity, a beehive where the community convened to share coffee, Gullah baked goods, and stories.

"This business is begging for a new tenant, and I know the perfect person to take it over," Christopher said.

"Who?"

"You."

She denied the idea with a shake of her head. "I'm not good enough. I don't have the experience or expertise."

"Anyika is an excellent cook and would be thrilled to share her family's recipes."

"But what if I fail?" She doubted her skills and her knowledge. The prospect of being judged and criticized was a powerful deterrent.

"You're a perfectionist. No need to be great at everything from the start."

"But what if—"

"Stop second-guessing yourself." He stepped closer, and she turned. He tilted her chin to meet his gaze. "This island needs a bakery. This island needs you, and so do I."

Genuine love shone in his eyes, along with an unwavering belief in her dreams.

The potential for the bakery's revival sent a thrill through her. Could she restore the magic of this revered place?

"There's something else," Christopher said.

"Can't we stay a few more minutes?" She turned back to the window. "I want to look around."

"Without a key, we'll have to wait anyway. We'll track down the previous owners' contact information and the asking price when we get back to the hotel."

"I hope I can afford it."

"You can rent for a while if they're open to the option."

Wherever she put up a wall of doubt, Christopher was there to tear it down and encourage her.

He tucked her fingers in his hand. "Remember, I wanted to show you two places?"

"Where's the other place?"

"It's the hut Sebastian and I share."

"I've seen it many times."

"I want to show it to you again."

They strolled along the shoreline, the ground damp from the rise and fall of the tide. Occasionally, he caught sight of elusive creatures—a shy turtle basked on a sun-drenched log, quickly slipping into the water as they approached. A racoon peeked out from behind a thicket, its masked face observing their every move before disappearing into the underbrush.

Christopher bent down to pluck a smooth seashell from the cool, gritty sand.

"Look, Dad, here's a beautiful seashell. Mr. Grant said it's a symbol of good luck."

His heart missed a beat. He well remembered when his son had skipped along the beach with Francis and called out to him.

As he and Jenny continued to walk, colorful songbirds flitted from branch to branch. In the distance, a graceful deer grazed peacefully, its form blending with the natural surroundings.

Soon the hut emerged, snuggled among the trees.

When they entered the living room, his palms broke out in a sweat. He had planned this moment for days, wanting everything to be perfect. He'd carefully chosen a dozen roses from a florist on the mainland. The petals unfolded in shades of pink, their distinctive scent mingling with the anticipation in the air.

"These are for you, Jenny." His voice trembled as he

gestured to the bouquet on the small wooden table. He plucked a single rose and handed it to her, their fingers brushing.

"Thank you." She sunk her nose into the velvety flower and inhaled.

"Azaleas aren't in bloom. I ... I know they're your favorite. But I hope these are okay. The pink complements your dress."

"You're apparently into pink today."

He smiled. "Apparently, I am."

The roses overshadowed the absence of her beloved azaleas. Perhaps each blossom hid secrets that were only whispered to hearts that dared to listen. He kept the thoughts to himself and pulled her close.

"One more thing." He removed a small black velvet box from his pocket, his pulse racing as he presented it to her.

His eyes never left hers.

She clasped the box for several seconds before she opened it, revealing the gold ring, the solitary diamond.

She inhaled a quick breath.

"Jenny, will you marry me?" He searched her gaze, hoping to see the answer he longed for.

She hesitated. "A million thoughts are swirling through my brain."

He'd hurt her before, and he wanted nothing more than to erase her doubts. "Will you stay on this island with me?" He stretched out his hand to her, then paused. He waited, the seconds marching on, and he made no further move to touch her.

At last, she tilted her head upward, her sparkling green eyes locking onto his. "Would you kindly?" she whispered. "Kiss me?"

He pushed out a breath. Without hesitation, he caught her

in his arms and hugged her tightly. She twined her hands around his neck and leaned into him.

His mouth met hers, and she returned his kisses.

The sheer joy of embracing her, savoring the softness of her lips, consumed him. The fear of losing her, like a fragile illusion, made it difficult to release her.

Retreating slightly, he posed the question once more. "Will you marry me?"

She hesitated, then nodded. Words seemed to escape her.

His embrace tightened. "Good," he murmured. "Because I'll never let you go again." He kissed her with intensity and tenderness, his mouth moving against hers with all the affection he felt for her.

He eventually broke the kiss, still embracing her, and ran his fingers through the soft strands of her hair, admiring its beauty.

"Why did you hesitate?" he inquired.

"Why did it take you so long to ask me? I've waited for ten years."

He grinned, unable to resist her unique sense of humor. "You're the only woman in existence who would bring up a decade-long misunderstanding at a moment like this."

Her face took on a serious expression, although an impish glimmer danced in her eyes.

"I need to confess something," she said.

His body tensed, thoughts immediately drifting to Farrenway. "And what might that be?" he asked cautiously.

"I didn't tell you the full truth about my pool-playing skills. I really started shooting pool when I was twelve, not fourteen."

He drew her close with a relieved chuckle. "Do you think you can outfish me?" he teased.

"Only if I use my bare hands."

"If that's what it takes, then I suppose I'll have to guide

you along." He stayed silent for a moment, absorbing her every nuance, every smile. "Perhaps we should start by addressing your previous response, when I wrote you a poem and told you I loved you. You said you needed more time."

"I asked you to be patient with me." She placed her fingers over his chest. His heartbeat raced. "If you're willing to give it another try, I'll show you that I have a better reply."

He tipped up her chin and gazed deeply into her eyes. Tears pooled at the corners of her lashes.

"Jenny Ormani, I love you," he said.

"I love you, too. I love you, and I love your son."

"That's quite an improvement." He smiled as he slipped the ring onto the fourth finger of her left hand. Cradling her face, he stared at her. "Why the tears?"

Her quivering fingers delicately brushed the hint of a stubble on his jaw. "Because, until this moment, I wasn't sure that you'd ever ask me to marry you."

A knock on the cottage door made them both turn, and Maria stepped inside. She flashed a wicked grin, prompting Christopher to wrap his arm tighter around Jenny.

"Excuse me, but you two have been gone far longer than an hour, and cell phone service is non-existent," Maria began. "So there goes your theory about carrying your cell."

Christopher frowned at her. "How did you find us?"

"Where else would you be? I peeked into your cottage this morning and saw the flowers. I suspected something was brewing."

"Where's Sebastian?" Christopher asked.

"He's outside. Benjamin brought along a beach ball, and they're tossing it back and forth on the sand."

"I should get back." Jenny sighed and pulled out of Christopher's arms.

Christopher grabbed her hand. "You, my love, are not setting one foot into that hotel to work."

"Benjamin will take care of anything you haven't completed," Maria piped up. "He's been waiting to step in."

"I assumed you both were going paddle boarding today," Jenny said.

"We were, after we finished watching Sebastian." Maria surveyed them both with an exasperated look that gradually dwindled into a smile. "However, paddle boarding isn't his thing. He'd rather work behind the Grand Michelangelo hotel desk, taking phone reservations."

Christopher arched an eyebrow. "He would? Benjamin, the outdoorsman?"

"He was a manager of a hotel somewhere in the northeast," Maria replied. "He has experience in daily operations and overseeing staff."

"Benjamin wants to stay here on the island?" Christopher laughed disbelievingly. "I thought he wasn't a fan of hot weather."

"He said it's because I'm here."

"Women make us men do irrational things, don't they?" As he gazed at Jenny's face, the smile faded from Christopher's expression, replaced by a gaze so intense that Maria left them alone.

AN HOUR LATER, Christopher and Jenny sat outside his cottage on a loveseat on the back veranda. The sun descended gracefully, and the distant silhouettes of sailboats smoothly glided by.

"I sincerely wish Benjamin the best," Jenny said. "That leaves a question, though. What am I going to do now?"

"Be my wife."

"Besides that." She good-naturedly nudged him. "I'd like another career."

"Sun-Kissed Treats is ready, willing, and waiting for you."

"I've worked so hard to manage a hotel." She pushed out a sigh. "What will people think of me when I change professions?"

"You deserve a job that makes you happy. It doesn't matter as long as your choices are honest. The locals will applaud your courage to pursue your passion. Who knows, you may inspire others to do the same."

He clasped her tightly. The consistent rhythm of her heart resonated against his chest. As he breathed in the scent of her hair, thoughts surged, leading him to the first day he'd set foot on this beach.

They shared a childhood, with the summer sun reflecting off their faces and the surf splashing their feet. Now they were standing in the same hut they'd stood in as children, and he was proposing a new life for them.

Her breath caressed his neck. "We were meant to be together. You know that, don't you?"

"I do." They gazed out at the vast expanse of blue. A pod of sleek gray dolphins emerged from the frothy crests of the waves, leaping and frolicking.

"Christopher!" She pointed at the sea. "The dolphins are a sign of success and prosperity!"

He shook his head. "I love you, Jenny, but I refuse to buy into superstitious beliefs."

"Whether you believe it, I also have a surprise." She drew a weathered, leather-bound journal from her tote bag.

He eyed the journal. It looked familiar. "What is it?"

"I took it upon myself to go to your childhood cottage, and I found this in a bureau. I apologize for prying without your knowledge, but my inquisitiveness got the best of me." She handed the journal to him. "Here, this is for you."

He ran his fingertips over the cover, recognizing his mother's messy handwriting.

"Your mother's poems," Jenny murmured. "Look at the last one."

He flipped through the pages, each filled with his mother's musings and reflections. He landed on the final poem, and the words leaped off the sheet, speaking of love, loss, and hope.

His speech faltered as he recited:

"THROUGH THE STORMS that life may bring,
We hold fast to the power of the sea,
For in its depths, we find our strength,
And rise again, resilient, and free.

WITH EVERY CRASHING wave that breaks,
We face the trials that come our way,
And though the winds may howl and shake,
We stand firm, unyielding, and brave.

FOR WE ARE creatures of the deep,
Born of the ocean's endless might,
And when our hearts fill with grief,
We turn to the sea for solace and light."

HIS WORDS STUMBLED as he extended the journal to Jenny. He swallowed, trying to clear the emotion from his throat. "Please finish reading. I … I can't."

Jenny read the final stanza.

. . .

"So let us confront each tempest with courage,
   And let our spirits soar and sing,
   For though the storms may test our faith,
   We know we'll triumph in the end."

Jenny's tear-stained face looked up at him. "Your mother's words are so beautiful, and it's like she knew. She was so right."

He couldn't deny it. He'd been angry at her for leaving him too soon, but he was beginning to understand the pain she must have been in.

Forgiveness was the key.

After he closed the journal, he gazed at Jenny. She'd been the woman who had brought this precious gift to him, and he would always be grateful. He grazed a thumb along her fingers, thanking her for helping him find a road to healing.

"Life has a funny way of surprising us," she breathed. "Perhaps this is one of those times."

Perhaps it was.

Their lips met in a deep and passionate kiss, a demonstration of their commitment to each other. Their resolve would help them rebuild their lives, no matter the obstacles.

"I'd like a Gullah-inspired wedding," she murmured.

He smiled. "How long will that take to plan?"

"Not long. The Gullah hold the weddings outside, and the officiant is usually a respected member of the community. Anyika is ideal. Of course, you and I would wear appropriate clothes that pay tribute to their traditions."

"Gullah-inspired clothes?" He repeated her words, his gaze fixed on her mischievous grin. "Please, go on."

Her eyes sparkled with enthusiasm. "I'd wear a boldly printed gown and a beautiful head wrap, you know, resembling a twisted turban. I've seen the dress Anyika's daughter wore at her wedding—puffed sleeves, a fitted bodice, and a full skirt to the floor. I'll add beading and embroidery. And as for you …"

He chuckled, his finger delicately tracing the graceful contour of her neck and jawline. "Let me guess. An African-inspired suit and a striking headpiece?"

"How did you know?"

"I had a conversation with Anyika already. I thought a Gullah wedding was the perfect fit for us."

Apparently satisfied, Jenny shifted gears and returned to wedding planning. "Some women spend well over a year arranging their weddings." She highlighted the extensive effort some couples dedicated to their special day.

"No way. Not a chance," he replied firmly, dismissing the idea without hesitation. "We've already waited ten years."

"Five months then?" she suggested.

"Four."

"Four months," she conceded, a hint of wistfulness in her voice. "It sounds quick, yet it will seem like an eternity."

"Four weeks," Christopher corrected. "We'll put our entire hotel staff on wedding planning duty, and I'll ensure you have plenty of hours to plan."

She regarded him hesitantly, but eventually a smile broke across her face, and she agreed.

Content, he returned her smile and shifted his gaze back to the ocean.

The splendor of Pink Coral Island was something he'd never been able to put into words. It was more than the crystal-blue waters and sandy beaches. More than the exotic palm trees and breathtaking sunsets.

Maybe it was the rugged beauty. The rocks jutting out from the turquoise water, the coral reefs teeming with life. Maybe it was the landscape that was both wild and serene, or the way the island hummed with vitality.

It was a place where nature was in control, where the elements were both brutal and breathtaking.

But it was more than the island's natural wonders. It was the people who called it home, the close-knit Gullah community. The powerful pull of the island was a physical attraction.

Though it was also a spiritual one, a connection to something both ancient and timeless.

His arm encircled Jenny's shoulders. They shared stories, reminiscing about that fateful day on the beach when they'd first met as children.

A few minutes later, he detected a gradual increase in weight against his side, and to his next teasing remark, she remained unresponsive.

Casting a quick glance downward, he noticed her long eyelashes gently resting on her cheeks. She was sound asleep.

"What an incredibly tiring day for you, love," he whispered as she stirred and snuggled nearer to his chest.

He coaxed her closer and kissed her temple.

Life was full of twists and turns, but he was ready to welcome them all with the woman he cherished most.

Jenny. The only woman he had ever loved.

THE END

A NOTE FROM JOSIE

Dear Reader,

I've always been fascinated by second-chance love stories. Not the tidy kind where two people pick up where they left off, but the messy, honest kind where they have to reckon with who they were, who they've become, and whether any of it still fits.

That's Jenny and Christopher.

They were sweethearts once. Then life happened, the way it tends to, and a decade passed. When they find themselves back on Pink Coral Island trying to restore a crumbling hotel they both care about, neither one is prepared for what resurfaces along with it.

And if that weren't complicated enough, someone is sabotaging everything they're working toward. Vandalism. Fires. I'll let you draw your own conclusions about who, and why.

What pulled me deepest into this story was the island itself. Pink Coral Island is steeped in Gullah culture and superstition, and that atmosphere shaped Jenny and Christopher's story in ways I didn't expect when I started writing. There's a richness to that setting that I loved exploring.

Christopher's seven-year-old son also has a lot to say about the situation. He is not subtle about it.

I hope this story stays with you a little after you've turned the last page. That's all any writer really hopes for.

If you loved this story as much as I loved writing it, please help other people find it by posting your review.

Pink Coral Island is available in ebook, paperback, Large Print paperback, audiobook, and Hardcover.

I'd love to meet you in person someday, but in the meantime, all I can offer is a sincere and grateful thank you. Without your support, my books would not be possible.

As I write my next sweet or inspirational romance, remember this: Have you ever tried something you were afraid to try because it mattered so much to you? I did, when I started writing. Take the chance, and just do something you love.

With sincere appreciation,

Josie Riviera

Love music?

My Spotify Playlist for Pink Coral Island is Here.

P.S. Pink Coral Island is fictional, but was inspired by an island off the coast of South Carolina, Daufuskie Island. I've had the privilege of visiting, and the island is truly captivating.

INSTRUCTIONS FOR
MAKING A TOWEL ANIMAL:

Materials: One large bath towel

Instructions:

1. Lay the towel flat on a clean surface.
2. Fold the towel in half lengthwise.
3. Starting at the folded edge, roll the towel tightly towards the unfolded edge.
4. Fold the rolled towel in half to create a loop, with the rolled edges facing outward.
5. Take one end of the rolled towel and fold it down, creating a triangular shape.

6. Fold the other end of the rolled towel down to create another triangular shape, with the point meeting the first triangular shape.

7. Tuck the two folded ends of the towel into the loop of the rolled towel, creating the head of the animal.

8. To create the ears, pinch and fold the top corners of the head down towards the center of the head.

9. To create the body, fold the remaining towel in half lengthwise and place it underneath the head, making sure that the head is centered on the folded towel.

10. Roll the two ends of the folded towel toward the center, creating two tube-like shapes.

11. Bend the tubes to create legs, and adjust the shape of the body and head as needed to give your towel animal its final form.

Congratulations! You've made a towel animal. With a bit of practice, you can experiment with different shapes and styles to create a variety of towel animals.

BONUS SNEAK PEEK:
ALOHA TO LOVE

CHAPTER ONE

Angelina Conte stood along the railing of the *Bird of Paradise* cruise ship as the achingly familiar Los Angeles, California, skyline disappeared from view. The ship's horn blew, and people waved madly from the shore.

In the deepening dusk of a glorious December day, the intimate ship began cruising the sparkling Pacific Ocean waters, leaving San Pedro Bay far behind.

Sipping her refreshing glass of iced tea, she turned and gazed through the glass doors of the grand atrium, the center of the ship. A sweeping spiral staircase, bedecked with brilliant red poinsettias, commanded attention, and the bubble elevators eased passengers up and down to the various decks with amazing efficiency.

Every detail of the cruise shouted "Happy Holidays" and high living, and she would have loved to savor the experience. There was a catch, though, and a big one. Unexpected script changes for her screenplay, *Aloha to Love*, had to be fixed by January first. And all these fixes were because of one man, the eminent volcanologist, Dr. Caleb Sloane.

Partridge Production Studios had paid for her cruise under the stipulation she attend Dr. Sloane's lectures on board the ship. The studio had hired him after she'd handed in her screenplay, and he had problems that the studio insisted she discuss face-to-face with him.

"Dr. Sloane insists that correct details are equally as important as your story," her boss, Devon, had quoted. "Working with him directly will give you a better grasp of the destructive nature of volcanoes."

"I know, I know," she murmured, although it was difficult to abandon her view of the stunning scenery to go below deck and plug away.

She scanned the red-and-green flowered garland strung along the deck railings. A gigantic gingerbread display had been set up in the main lobby, and each guest had received a celebratory tote bag upon boarding. On Christmas Eve day, church services would be held. The most important part of

Christmas, she mused, was what one of her favorite pastors had once said, a quote she'd seen many times: "The child of Christmas is God."

She set her iced tea on a side table as a woman who appeared to be in her forties rounded the corner. Her head and face covered by an impossibly broad fedora straw hat, she had graying red hair, wore a flowing sun-flowered caftan, and was noticeably pregnant.

"Hi. I'm Rachel Olson. Or rather, aloha." The woman took a bite of the chocolate ice cream cone she held in one hand while extending the other for a handshake. She apparently had come from one of the numerous ice cream bars. "The cabin steward described you to me when I dropped off my luggage, so I presume I'm your roommate for the next few days. Did you know that most people think that *aloha* means both hello and goodbye in Hawaiian?"

"I didn't, but now I do," Angelina said with a smile.

"Although people use the term for both greetings," Rachel licked her ice cream, then finger-quoted, "Aloha really means 'something that genuinely comes from the heart.'"

Angelina's smile was now largely from relief. Because the studio had had to book her berth at the last minute, she had to share her cabin with a complete stranger. Fortunately, she immediately liked Rachel Olson.

She shook Rachel's free hand. "I'm Angelina Conte."

"Is this cruise a last-minute decision?" Rachel asked.

Before Angelina could answer, a voice came over the loudspeaker and Captain Jorgen Berg extended a welcome greeting. An acquaintance of Angelina's had taken this cruise before and had told Angelina that the wild-haired, thick-browed captain was known for his humor. She wasn't surprised when he ended his message with a joke.

"Now if I can find the manual on how to steer this ship, we'll get underway."

With a hearty laugh, Rachel turned back to Angelina. "Most people book their cruises months ahead of time," she said. "From the small size and low deck location of our cabin, apparently not you?"

"My boss reserved this cruise for me a couple days ago." Angelina kept from glancing at the woman's pregnant belly by focusing on the people queuing up for the departure buffet in the Hibiscus Star, one of the main dining rooms. "At least we have a porthole window."

"True."

"Are you alone?" Angelina asked.

"My husband and I are moving to Hawaii. He has family there. I was supposed to travel with him but last-minute details kept me at my office longer than I expected. Rather than fly, he insisted I enjoy a little luxury and cruise to Hawaii." The words tumbled from Rachel's lips in an unending rush. "He arrived in Honolulu a few days ago. Hilo is our first port on December 25 and Honolulu is our second port on December 26. Happily, Fred and I will celebrate Christmas together when the ship docks, although I'll be a day late."

Christmas. Happy celebrations. Once upon a time.

Memories flooded to the surface of Angelina's mind. A tiny evergreen tree set up in an equally tiny living room in the first apartment she and Jake, her late husband, ever shared. The burned turkey she'd served on Christmas Day— and the good-natured ribbing that followed.

How long had it been since she celebrated Christmas? Certainly not since Jake had died.

Rachel went on. "I'm officially retired from my demanding job to assume my new role as a stay-at-home mom. Thus, I'm eating for two." She lifted her ice cream cone for a last bite. "Fred and I have been married ten years and are finally expecting our first child."

Angelina picked up her glass to toast the expectant mother. "Congratulations."

"Thanks. I'm proof that miracles can happen at any age."

This was the part where Angelina should say something about experiencing her own miracles, or at least smile politely or murmur agreement. But a miracle had never happened to her.

A Christmas marvel, during God's most joyful season of the year.

Fanciful hopes. Fanciful dreams.

Rachel gestured toward the sunset—cotton-candy pinks and oranges canvassing the sky. "Nothing is as enchanting as a Los Angeles sunset. Especially when you're saying good riddance."

Angelina blinked. "I'm sorry?"

"Don't be sorry. I'm certainly not."

"I take it you don't like California?"

"I'm tired of all the noise and traffic. It's not good for me or the baby." Protectively, Rachel patted her stomach. "Are you a California native?"

"Yes." Angelina again put her glass aside. "I live near Hollywood."

"Lucky you." Rachel made no attempt to hide the sarcasm in her voice.

"It's not bad. I'm used to the buzz and in-a-hurry lifestyle." Angelina propped her elbows on the railing and took in a breath of fresh sea air. "Both my parents were involved in the acting business, so I'm used to it."

"I've always been enamored by Hollywood. Can I tell you a secret?"

"Let me guess. You wanted to be an actress and ended up bartending instead? That's the story I hear most often."

Rachel laughed. "No, I'm an accountant."

"So, what's your secret?"

"This was all Fred's idea."

Angelina snapped her head around. "The baby was Fred's idea?"

"Not the baby." Rachel's green eyes twinkled with mirth. "We're thrilled about the baby. I meant moving to Hawaii, although now I'm glad he talked me into it—a thrilling new adventure." She pulled her cellphone from her caftan pocket and scrolled to a picture of an older man sporting a gray mustache. "This is Fred."

"He's …"

"Older than me. Yes. He's twenty years my senior. He was my professor in grad school and ever since we met we've been madly in love." She batted her eyelashes in playful coquetry, then sobered. "Fred's grandmother lives in Honolulu." Rachel inclined her head toward the miles and miles of ocean. "You mentioned your boss booked this cruise. I assume you're traveling on business?"

"I'm a screenwriter, and got a coveted assignment from a colleague to write a romantic comedy about Hawaii."

"Lucky you. Screenwriting must be very interesting—rubbing shoulders with all those famous actors and actresses."

"I've never met any of them." Angelina gave a helpless laugh. "Although screenwriting is my passion."

When she wasn't punching a clock with Mr. Stick-in-the-Mud Volcanologist.

"While you're on board, make time for fun. Cruising is so romantic." Rachel flashed a wicked grin. "Where's your flower, by the way?"

"What flower?"

"I don't see a flower tucked behind your left or right ear."

Enjoying Rachel's teasing and personable humor, Angelina teased right back. "I don't see a flower tucked behind your ear, either. And I confess I don't know the difference."

"If a woman is taken she wears a flower behind her left ear. If she's not, she wears a flower behind her right ear. It's part of the Hawaiian culture. When I get off the ship to meet Fred in Honolulu, I'll wear a flower." Rachel sighed dreamily. "Please forgive me for prying, I'm a hopeless romantic. There's no special man in your life?"

Somehow, Angelina knew Rachel didn't want to be forgiven as long as she received an answer. "I'm not convinced I need romance," Angelina said. "I was married … once."

Rachel was quiet, studying her. "And now you're divorced?" she finally asked.

"And now I'm a widow." Angelina choked back a sorrow that never went away. All the heartbreak returned in a rush— the familiar pressing ache in her chest, a soreness in her lungs that never ceased.

"I'm sorry for your loss," Rachel said. "You must have been devastated."

"I was." Angelina swallowed. "We were only married a short time."

Gently, Rachel touched Angelina's hand. "I don't know what to say."

"Thank you. It happened a long time ago."

"With your good looks you're probably fighting off hordes of men."

"I'm not interested in dating." Self-consciously, Angelina moved away. "I'm focused on establishing my career. Screenwriting is highly competitive."

Lately, though, she questioned whether perfecting a screenplay about Hawaii hadn't been done a hundred times before. Devon had insisted she explore ways her story could have a greater effect on her audience when it was put on film. A different pitch, he insisted, to add a hook to her romance.

Rachel tucked a silvery-red strand of hair behind her ear. "Screenwriting is an enjoyable and lucrative field?"

"Enjoyable, yes. Lucrative? Well, hopefully. The movie is just about ready to shoot and we'll see how it's received by audiences when finished."

"And you didn't have any family wanting to come along for the cruise?"

*** End of Excerpt *Aloha to Love* by Josie Riviera ***

ABOUT THE AUTHOR

Josie Riviera is a *USA TODAY* bestselling author of contemporary, inspirational, and historical sweet romances that read like Hallmark movies. She lives in the Charlotte, NC, area with her wonderfully supportive husband. They share their home with an adorable shih tzu, who constantly needs grooming, and live in an old house forever needing renovations.

To receive my Newsletter and your free sweet romance novella ebook as a thank you gift, sign up Here.

Become a member of my Read and Review VIP Facebook group for exclusive giveaways and ARCs.

PRAISE AND AWARDS

USA TODAY bestselling author

5 STAR READER REVIEWS

"Josie Riviera gives us a taste of traditional Gullah culture in this sweet romance. Is it possible for long ago feelings to be rekindled when Jenny returns to *Pink Coral Island* and finds that Christopher, a special friend from her youth, has also come back and that she will be working with him as part of her new job?

The road to their future is uneven and there are moments when I wondered how they would work out their problems.

The main characters are well developed and I enjoyed getting to know them. The setting is beautifully described for the reader – I felt like I "knew" the island. The story certainly held my interest and kept me on my toes to see what would happen next.

Travel to Pink Coral Island to enjoy this beautiful tale." - Mary F.

"A beautiful story of coming home, finding your first true love and a purpose for your life. Jenny and Christopher and his son are lovely characters." - Gina J.

"Second chance romance is a favorite trope of mine. I love when the hero and heroine have a history together, as Jenny and Christopher do, having been childhood sweethearts on the island. As Christopher went off to college, they both left the island and a misunderstanding kept them apart. Now ten years later Christopher returns to renovate the hotel and Jenny takes the job to manage it without knowing he's the new co-owner. He has always loved her and sees this as their second chance, but Jenny is not going to make that easy on him. A sweet romance with some conflicts and a heroine that wasn't ready to trust again." - Catherine B.

ACKNOWLEDGMENTS

An appreciative thank you to my patient husband, Dave, and our three wonderful children.

ALSO BY JOSIE RIVIERA

Valentine Hearts Boxed Set

1-800-CUPID

1-800-CHRISTMAS

1-800-IRELAND

1-800-SUMMER

1-800-NEW YEAR

The 1-800-Series Sweet Contemporary Romance Bundle

Irish Hearts Sweet Romance Bundle

Holly's Gift

A Chocolate-Box Valentine

A Chocolate-Box Christmas

A Chocolate-Box New Years

A Chocolate-Box Summer Breeze

A Chocolate-Box Christmas Wish

A Chocolate-Box Irish Wedding

Chocolate-Box Hearts

Chocolate-Box Hearts Volume Two

Chocolate-Box Double Hearts

Recipes from the Heart

Leading Hearts

New Year Hearts

SENIOR HEARTS

A Summer To Cherish

Summer Hearts

Romance Stories To Cherish Volume Two

Cherished Hearts

Christmas in the Air

A Very Christian Christmas

The 1-800-Series Volume Two

Christmas Tails of the Heart

Cocoa's Christmas Love

Pawfect Christmas Hearts

Pink Coral Island

Whispers of Love in Sweetwater Springs

Whispers of Maple Memories in Sweetwater Springs

Whispers of Holiday Magic in Sweetwater Springs

Whispers of Sweetwater Springs

A Harvest of Miracles

A Winter Promise

A Season Out of Time

Hearts and Horseshoes

Wishes and Wildflowers

1-800-CUPIDON (French Edition)

1-800-CUPIDO (Spanish Edition)

1-800-AMOR (German Edition)

Most books are available in ebook, audiobook, paperback, Large Print paperback and Hardcover.

Many are FREE on Kindle Unlimited!

A GIFT FOR YOU

To keep up on newly released ebooks, paperbacks, Large Print Paperbacks, audiobooks, as well as exclusive sales, sign up for Josie's Newsletter today.

As a thank you, I'll send you a Free PDF ... The Beauty Of ...

Josie's Newsletter

Did you know that according to a Yale University study, people who read books live longer?

www.ingramcontent.com/pod-product-compliance
Lightning Source LLC
Chambersburg PA
CBHW010824250626
47169CB00010B/2952